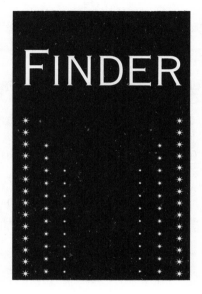

# FINDER

## Other books by Emma Bull

*War for the Oaks*
*Falcon*
*Bone Dance*

## Other novels and anthologies of the Borderlands

*Borderland* (edited by Terri Windling and
Mark Alan Arnold)
*Bordertown* (edited by Terri Windling and
Mark Alan Arnold)
*Life on the Border* (edited by Terri Windling)
*Elsewhere* (by Will Shetterly)
*Nevernever* (by Will Shetterly)

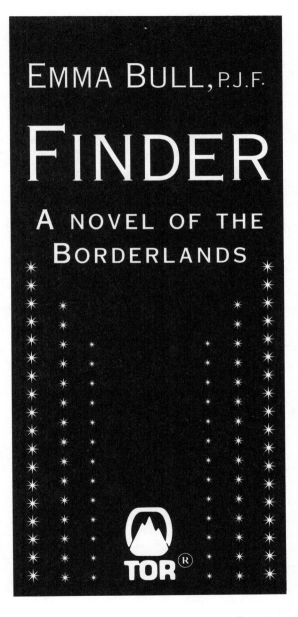

EMMA BULL, P.J.F.

# FINDER

A NOVEL OF THE
BORDERLANDS

TOR ®

A TOM DOHERTY ASSOCIATES BOOK
NEW YORK

FINDER: A NOVEL OF THE BORDERLANDS

Copyright © 1994 by Emma Bull and Terri Windling

Bordertown and the Borderlands were created by Terri Windling, with creative input from Mark Alan Arnold; from Will Shetterly, author of the novels *Elsewhere* and *Nevernever*; and from the authors of the stories in the anthologies *Borderland, Bordertown,* and *Life On the Border*: Bellamy Bach, Steven R. Boyett, Emma Bull, Kara Dalkey, Charles de Lint, Craig Shaw Gardner, Michael Korolenko, Ellen Kushner, Will Shetterly, and Midori Snyder. Borderland is used by permission of Terri Windling, The Endicott Studio.

"Genesis Hall" copyright © 1969 by Richard Thompson. Lyrics printed courtesy of Warlock Music Ltd.

Edited by Terri Windling

This book is printed on acid-free paper.

A Tor Book
Published by Tom Doherty Associates, Inc.
175 Fifth Avenue
New York, N.Y. 10010

Tor® is a registered trademark of Tom Doherty Associates, Inc.

*Design by Lynn Newmark*

Library of Congress Cataloging-in-Publication Data

Bull, Emma
    Finder / Emma Bull.
      p.   cm.
    "A Tom Doherty Associates book."
    ISBN 0-312-85418-8
    1. City and town life—Ficiton.  I. Title.
    PS3552.U423F56  1994
    813'.54—dc20                           93-43230
                                                            CIP

First edition: February 1994

Printed in the United States of America

0 9 8 7 6 5 4 3 2 1

To Lynda,
who was the first to meet the people in this book.

# ACKNOWLEDGMENTS

Many thanks to Terri Windling, for letting me mess around in her town; to Patrick Nielsen Hayden, for telling me it would be All Right; to Fred Levy Haskell, for answering the question I was supposed to ask, instead of the one I did; to the Scribblies (Steven Brust, Kara Dalkey, Pamela Dean, and Will Shetterly) for reading duties above and beyond the call; to Sunnyvale Syntactic and IssaQuery Ink (Gordon Garb and Jon Singer, respectively) for reading the next draft; to all the Borderlands writers for drawing the circle and calling the quarters; and to Will, especially, for everything.

My father he rides with your sheriffs
And I know he would never mean harm . . .

—Richard Thompson, "Genesis Hall"

# CONTENTS

# FALLING OUT OF PARADISE

I REMEMBER WHERE I was and what I was doing when Bonnie Prince Charlie was killed. Not that I knew it at the time, of course. But while Charlie was travelling the distance from the Pigeon Cloisters belfry to High Street with all the dispatch that gravity can muster, I was sunbathing.

If the weather had held, I'd have been on the roof of my building the next day, too, spread out like a drying sweater. But it promised rain. (If the forecast had been different, would the past be, too? Would a lot of people still be here? This town is strange and has weather to match, but I never imagined it was a matter of life and death.)

So when Tick-Tick pounded on the frame of my open front door, I was in and washing dishes. She poked her head in and shouted, "I am the queen's daughter, I come from Twelfth and Flynn, in search of Young Orient, pray God I find him!"

I lifted my hands dripping from the suds, took the herbal cigarette out of the corner of my mouth, and said, "Ex*cuse* me?"

"Well, in a manner of speaking," said the Ticker placidly. She stalked in, the picture of elven self-possession, and picked a saucer out of the dishpan with thumb and forefinger. "Mab's grace. So low as you've fallen, my precious boy."

"I'm out of cups. Nothing else would have driven me to it." The water had killed my cigarette. I sighed and flicked it out the window.

She dropped into my upholstered chair and swung her long legs over the arm. Her concession to summer's heat, I noticed, was to tear the sleeves off her favorite pair of gray mechanic's coveralls and roll the legs up to mid-calf. And still she did look rather like a queen's daughter; but the elves usually look like royalty. When they're trying not to, they only look like royalty in a cheap plastic disguise. Tick-Tick had a face like the bust of Nefertiti, only more daunting, and her eyes were huge and long and the gray of January ice.

"Is it still overcast?" I asked.

"Oh, yes. Nice summer thunderstorm tonight. Ah, of course, my condolences. Your tan isn't finished."

"You don't exactly finish a tan."

"I wouldn't know. But I'm *trying* to share your sentiments on the thing, really."

The skin on her face, her arms, her ankles, was smooth and almost buttermilk-colored. As far as I know, elves don't sunburn, either.

"So have you come to help me wash dishes?"

"Earth defend me. No, I've come to take you away from all this. I've work for you to do."

I raised my head like a cat hearing a can opener.

"Road trip?" Tick-Tick and I had a pleasant and profit-able line of work established, guiding foragers, explorers, merchants, and whoever through the less-charted areas of the Borderlands, the Nevernever. There the magic boiling out of the Elflands makes Alice's looking-glass garden, where you have to walk away from your destina-tion to get there, seem like a trivial navigation problem.

"No, sorry. Not work for us, just for you. It's probably only the work of fifteen minutes, but I'll pay you in din-ner. And it's an excuse to stop what you're doing."

"You're my partner, you ass. You don't have to pay for it."

"All right." She grinned, and commanded, "You may find my torque wrench *and* do me the favor of joining me for dinner."

I laughed as the last glass slid from my fingers back into the water. Then—"Ah," I said. "That was quick."

I can't explain it well. I've lived with the phenome-non for eight years, and still it defies proper description. Somewhere in me, in my mind or my bones or my nerve endings or none of these, there was a pulling sensation, a highly directional drag at my attention. It was both less and more uncomfortable than I make it sound. I knew that, if I ignored it, it would go away in a few hours, but that they would be an unpleasant few hours. Not painful; just unpleasant. I told you I couldn't explain it well.

The very asking of the question does it. "Where is . . . ?" and fill in the blank with the non-abstract noun of your choice. But it has to be something that either the client or I know exists. Your left shoe; your grand-mother's diamond ring (even if you've never seen it, if you know it exists, and it hasn't been pitched in a vol-cano, I can find it); a jar of mustard (a specific one, or just the nearest available for sale—you have to tell me which). And once the question's been asked, I can't just tell you "Under your bed," or "At the Marvel Mart at the corner of Ho and Peppergrass." I have to follow the pull; I have to track it down myself, as if I were a dowsing rod. It's not a perfect system. But at one time or another, everybody loses something, and my rates are reasonable.

Now the Ticker raised her eyebrows hopefully, and I said, "Thataway," and pointed.

"Bless you, my child. Get your hat, then. We'll go straight from Thataway to dinner."

I got my sunglasses instead.

I admit to a certain bias, but in my opinion Tick-Tick had some of the best wheels in Bordertown. Harley-Davidson made most of the rig in about 1962, but the Ticker rebuilt and modified the engine and installed the spellbox that operated the bike in the pockets of the Borderlands where the sensible mechanisms of real-world physics turn tail and run. She put on six coats of midnight-blue lacquer and bought a spell that protects it from flying gravel. Best of all, she found the sidecar. Riding in it, I felt like an oil sheik with my bodyguard.

I pointed out the turns to her, playing hot-cold-hot from block to block to find my way around buildings. Horn Dance passed us on their way to a show: twelve assorted bikes, their riders' jackets trailing a wake of flying ribbons, more ribbons snapping from the antlers mounted behind the headlights, engines not quite drowning out the ringing of morris dance bells.

We crossed Ho Street at Danceland's corner, and I saw that the club's black-painted doors stood open to catch a little breeze. It was too early for a band, too early for the most determined would-be audience; Dancer must have set the staff to cleaning the place.

Snappin' Wizard's Surplus across the street was open,

and the tempera-paint sign on the front window glass read, "Chase Lights! Curse Limiters! LEDs! Pre-owned Spellboxes! Big Big SALE!" Tick-Tick slowed down for just a moment; she could never completely resist the siren call of Snappin' Wizard's. But she must have remembered that it was her wrench we were after, because it was only a moment.

Outside the Free Clinic near Fare-You-Well Park I thought I saw somebody wave. But I was in pursuit of a feeling with a torque wrench at the end of it, and we couldn't pause to talk.

We were well south of Ho in a neighborhood full of what had probably been warehouses and light manufacturing back before the Border appeared, with the Elflands on the other side of it, to make Bordertown what it is today. I flagged Tick-Tick to a stop outside a squat brick building with no windows, and she killed the engine.

She tugged her helmet off and smoothed her already precise cap of chrome-yellow hair, fluffing the single long lock that fell, fine as mist, over one eye. She was smiling. "That's interesting," she said. "Walt Felkin's place."

"I don't suppose you lent him the wrench and forgot."

"Good. I'm glad you don't. Are you in a wagering mood?"

"Um. Depends."

"I'll wager you five dollars that he'll deny ever having seen my wrench until he finds out who you are."

I snorted. "I might as well just buy my own dinner."

"Quite right. Never mind." She was whistling something under her breath as she picked her way through the stacks of old tires at the curb. It sounded suspiciously like Camper Van Beethoven's "When I Win the Lottery." There was a broken piece of tailpipe lying against the side of the building; she snagged it up and swung it like an umbrella as she walked to the door.

She used the tailpipe to knock. It didn't make a friendly sound. After a minute's wait we heard locks being unlocked. The door opened a crack; Tick-Tick jammed the tailpipe in to hold it open. A wide, watery blue eye appeared in the space.

"Hallo, Walt," said the Ticker. "I believe you've borrowed something of mine."

"I got nothin' of yours."

"Oh, Walt. It's a torque wrench. I find I have need of it. Do pass it out like a good fellow, and I'll let you get back to your dirty magazines, or whatever it is you do to pass the afternoon."

"Get gone, Ticker, or I'll pass you a couple inches of this." In the opening, something metallic flashed.

The Ticker slammed the tailpipe upward. There was a curse from Walt, and a clatter; the knife fell half-in, half-out of the door. Tick-Tick kicked it out onto the sidewalk with her foot and used her assault weapon to lever the door open. It must have banged into Walt's nose, because he was clutching it when the door finally swung all the way open. He was wearing grease-stained jeans and no shirt. He didn't have a tan.

"Walt," said Tick-Tick, smiling, "you know Orient, don't you?"

His face went blank and white as restaurant china.

"Hi," I said. "Sorry to barge in on you like this."

"The wrench?" Tick-Tick reminded him.

A patch of pink appeared on the skin under each of his eyes. "Uh. Oh, has it got, um, blue paint on the end of the grip?"

"Yes," said the Ticker, smiling. "Exactly the color of my bike, in fact."

"Oh. Hey, I thought that was Chillie Billie's wrench, Tick-Tick. Honest. I'll, uh . . ." He'd already backed his way out of the door; the rest of the sentence was lost somewhere inside the building as he disappeared. Then he reappeared with a torque wrench and another "Honest," even more desperate than the last.

As soon as Tick-Tick laid hands on the wrench, the nudging, pulling feeling in me stopped. A little tension went out of my shoulders that I hadn't known was there.

"Thank you, Walt. I *do* hope it works as well as it used to."

Walt nodded as if the back of his head wasn't very firmly attached and he had to be careful. Then he shut the door.

As I climbed into the sidecar, I said, "Weren't you a little hard on him? The knife aside, I mean."

"I don't like thieves."

"Wasn't being caught at it enough humiliation?"

She turned to me, surprised. "You don't know about Walt Felkin, then?"

I shook my head.

"He's an under-lieutenant in the Pack. He's admitted to that spot of arson at the Dancing Ferret, and bragged about beating up shopkeepers in Dragontown. No one can be brought to make a claim against him, though. The Bloods have sworn to make fiddle strings of his guts at the first opportunity. He's an oily little Nazi."

The Ticker sounded very much unlike herself, and it was a few minutes and several blocks before I said, "But he caved in as soon as he knew I was with you. And you knew he would. You could have told him I was there as soon as he opened the door."

We travelled even more blocks. Her helmet kept me from seeing her expression, but her jaw was stiff. We were growling down Ho Street (the technology was on, just then) when she finally said, "You're right. I wanted to frighten him. I think I rather hoped for an opportunity to hit him. That was inexcusable."

"It's not as if you make a habit of it."

She lifted her head. "It's easier," she said, slowly, "to be angry on someone else's behalf than on my own. And yet I find I have a well of anger in me, that I have been filling for years from my own hurts. If I spill it out in defense of another, I can deny that it's mine." She swung the bike up to the curb outside the Hard Luck Café and killed the engine. "Does that make sense, or is it a purely fey madness?"

"Oh, no," I answered. "It makes a lot of sense."

She smiled with half her mouth, the little wry twist that has as much sadness in it as anything. "Silly question. Of course you understand."

I swung my legs over the lip of the sidecar and slithered out onto the pavement. "Hah. If we're so single-minded, why don't you understand about my tan?"

"But I do, my rambling boy! With my head, if not my heart."

Elves are given to quicksilver slides from mood to mood, but when you know one of them well, you can tell the difference between that and genuine gratitude for a change of subject. I held the door for her, and we swaggered into the Hard Luck like the pair of reigning outlaws we pretended to be.

It was warm inside in spite of the fans, and busy, and noisy, and remarkably like a combination of farmhouse kitchen, private club, and arts salon. Anyone who makes trouble at the Hard Luck Café is considered an incurable misfit, even within the loose social contract of Bordertown, and is not welcome anywhere, to anything. Consequently, the Hard Luck's habitués include humans, elves, and halfies, people from Dragontown and slummers from up on the Tooth, painters and gang leaders. It's such a desirable place to simply *be* that it's almost too much to hope that the food is good.

The food is good.

I peered at the back wall and the blackboard that serves as menu. The Hard Luck is a cooperative, and the people working the kitchen cook whatever they feel like that day. Certain things are almost always available—burgers for the philistines, for instance—but if the staff decides they want to do Chinese that day, that's what's for dinner. If you don't like it, that's—all together now—Your Hard Luck. That day it looked like mixed down-home: fish chowder, lentil and spinach casserole, stuffed peppers, Brunswick stew.

"Bother," Tick-Tick said at my shoulder, "no booths—wait, other side in the middle."

We nodded to people as we crossed the room. An elf, identified as a member of the Bloods by the red leather headband and a cut-off, shredded red tank top, glared at me for an instant; then his face cleared and he nodded back. I'd found his kid sister's stolen cycle a month ago. A muscular man, mahogany brown, with a blackwork tattoo over half his face and down his neck, looked up from a copy of *Dubious Truth* and a cup of tea and smiled vaguely. He was a sculptor; he'd come to me about a copy of a book on Calder's mobiles. I read it before I passed it on. Life ought to be one long education.

County Hell Fairgrounds was on the sound system, and the window glass quaked audibly with every extra-low note. We claimed the booth just as the bass player grabbed a fistful of strings and climbed the alphabet with them.

"How does he make his hands do that?" I asked.

"Too much Fairport Convention in his youth," suggested Tick-Tick. "Shall I make the A-sign at Peach?"

I thought about the alternative. "Yeah. It's too hot for stout. Ale sounds right."

The Ticker sat up very straight, caught Peach's eye across the room, and made a pyramid with her hands. Then she held up two fingers.

The front door opened again and produced a partial pocket of silence. Well, no, it wasn't the door, but the person who'd pushed it open. He moved smoothly on long, supple muscles that made him seem taller than he was. He grinned at the reaction in the room, which produced more of it, because the grin was full of large, white, pointed teeth in a long jaw, and the face and body were covered with smooth red-brown fur.

Tick-Tick made a scratch-that gesture to Peach and held up three fingers. The same hand turned into a waving white flag to summon Wolfboy.

"Ay, Lobito," I said when he came up. "You'll just have to sit with the scaff 'n' raff if you want a booth." Wolfboy raised his hands palm-up and rolled his eyes to heaven in a perfect "Why me?" Tick-Tick slid over to make room for him.

"How's Sparks?" the Ticker asked.

Wolfboy dragged a notebook and pen out of his back jeans pocket before he sat; then he flipped to a new page, wrote quickly (it must be hard to write quickly and well with claws on the ends of your fingers, but I suppose anything comes with practice), and showed it to us. *Way good. She's minding the store,* it read. Wolfboy and his girlfriend Sparks ran the best used bookstore in town. It made me feel almost old; the Ticker and I had known him since before any of us did anything useful with our time.

He slid the notebook back to his side of the table and wrote, *Heard a great new Camphire-ism today.* Camphire was a Ho Street mural painter, and by either human or fey definition, odd. If there's an elven equivalent for LSD, she might have done too much of it when she was about six. He added to the page, *"You have to break an omelette to make eggs."*

I stared at the sentence. "Oh. That almost makes sense."

"You're right," said Tick-Tick, and shook her head. "It must be the apocalypse."

Wolfboy raised one shoulder and both eyebrow equivalents, and wrote, *Or Camphire's a secret Sufi master . . . nah.*

Peach set our bottles of ale in front of us, dug out her pad and looked hopeful. She was too shy to actually ask for an order. The Ticker opted for the casserole, Wolfboy for the Brunswick stew, and I decided on the fish chowder. Peach smiled at me as if she'd been waiting all night for someone to do that.

"You're sure? I'm buying, remember," Tick-Tick said.

"You've never had Lucy's chowder, I can tell. Are there mussels in it today, Peach?"

She blushed like her namesake. "Lots. Um. And Bill just brought a cheesecake in."

"See?" I said to the Ticker. "I'm having dessert."

Peach smiled, blushed harder, ducked her head, and bolted for the kitchen.

Wolfboy wrote, *What did the Human Compass do to rate dinner?*

"Hisss," I said. "I drink your blood, Dog Nose."

"No killing," Tick-Tick said, "or Peach won't bring my order. He found my stolen wrench." She told the story with, I thought, less relish than she might once have. I couldn't decide if I felt bad about that or not. Partway through Wolfboy shot me an odd sideways look, as if to suggest that he'd ask for the rest later, from me.

Peach ducked past again. "I set a piece of cheesecake aside for you," she told me, about as fast as the human mouth can move without stuttering, and darted away.

The Ticker propped her chin in her palm and regarded me with bland approbation. "She thinks you're cute," she said. Wolfboy giggled, a terrible thing to hear from a guy covered with fur.

I grimaced.

"Come now," Tick-Tick said. "What's wrong with Peach?"

"Nothing. She's a sweet kid." Wolfboy's cider-gold eyes fastened on me. "Guess I just like wild women."

"You like women who use men like you for tooth-picks," the Ticker said, and now *she* had me pinned in her sights. Elf-silver and wolf-gold—or maybe wolves don't have gold eyes.

"Ahem," I said, looking at Tick-Tick. "Since I promised not to mention your last boyfriend in your hearing ever again, I'm at a little disadvantage here."

She grinned. "He was a double-dyed, thoroughgoing, ratfink louse. But he was the only thoroughgoing ratfink louse in my romantic history, which suggests that, unlike *some* people, I do not repeat my mistakes."

"Not yet, anyway."

Wolfboy sniggered and covered his eyes with one hand.

She ignored us both. "You realize, don't you, that your love life has a certain nightmarish quality? That where other people have affairs, you have imbroglios?"

I held my beer bottle in front of me like a crucifix. "Down, girl. No more about my love life before dinner."

"Okay. Let's try your social life instead." It was a new voice, and familiar. I turned quickly.

Anyplace with laws ends up having something like police eventually. Bordertown had some laws. Sunny Rico was something like a cop.

In a town where everyone dyed their hair, hers was uncompromisingly natural: light brown and showing a little silver over the ears, short on top and around her face and curving over her collar in back. Her tan was better than mine. I didn't know the color of her eyes, and couldn't see them now; silver Night Peepers wrapped across them. Her loose trousers and looser jacket were tweedy gray linen with a fleck of red. Very nice, and only a little conservative for the neighborhood's catholic tastes. She had a red Eldritch Steel T-shirt underneath. Both her hands were in her pants pockets.

"Detective Rico," Tick-Tick said, in the tone she uses when several drunk Pack members are blocking her way to the bar.

"Tick-Tick," Rico nodded in greeting. "Lobo. Orient. How do. Mind if I sit?"

I kept my face empty. "We have no minds."

"That's what Dancer tells me." She hooked a chair with her foot and pulled it up to the end of the booth.

Tricky, to remind us that she was a friend of Dancer's. They'd run in a B-town gang together once, before Dancer grew up and opened a nightclub and Sunny Rico grew up to fight crime. And there you have a yardstick for maturity in Bordertown, I suppose. I asked, "What brings you south of civilization?" She wanted a favor, of course; that was what the reminder about her and Dancer had been for.

She studied us. "Social life. You know Bonnie Prince Charlie?"

Wolfboy nodded, and the Ticker said, "Somewhat."
Rico looked back to me.

"Yeah."

"He died yesterday."

It held us frozen for a moment, like the glare of a camera flash. "Violently, I suppose?" Tick-Tick said. Rico nodded, and her eyes came back once more to me.

I was damned if I knew why. Yes, I'd known Charlie. He came into Bordertown cocky, desperate to be a desperado. He told us his name was Charles Bonney, and to anyone who didn't recognize it, he pointed out that Bonney was Billy the Kid's name. It was Scully, lounging at a back table in the Ferret, who finally drawled, "So you're Bonnie Prince Charlie? Welcome hame to the ane true Prin." The name couldn't help but stick.

Charlie didn't usually keep the company I did, or if he did, it was out at the brittle edge. Charlie worked questionable jobs for unpleasant people, ran errands in the service of projects I didn't want to know about. I didn't like him, I didn't dislike him. If he was dead, I probably didn't want to know why.

You can't always get what you want. "He fell out of the belfry up on High Street yesterday," Rico said. "The tattle is that he was playing a little turnabout on his employer. Got laid off in a big way."

"Why are you telling us?" I asked, because somebody had to.

"Because I'd like to find his employer."

Wolfboy spread his hands: Don't look at us.

I felt the same way. Then I heard, really heard, the infinitive verb in Rico's sentence.

"No," I said.

Wolfboy and the Ticker looked politely confused; they hadn't picked up the clue yet. Rico went on, quickly, as if she had to convince them before they caught on. As if she had to convince anyone but me. "Charlie was running for somebody doing business in a particular kind of designer drop. Looks like he ran the wrong way with something."

Tick-Tick leaned across the table. "Are you *choosing* not to speak English?"

Rico slid the Peepers down her nose and gave her a stare over them. Brown eyes. "He was taking illicit substances to people who wanted to purchase them, exchanging them for money, and possibly failing to take the money back to the place where the illicit substances came from. Better?"

Tick-Tick nodded, her whole face working to stifle a grin.

"Come on," I said, and I heard the way my voice cut across the civilized mood. "Charlie was a little thug. A little *Soho* thug. Thirty of 'em could be mowed down in an afternoon and the Silver Suits wouldn't look up from their paperwork."

"Not quite true," Rico assured me, her expression mildly wounded. "But you're right. I don't really give a damn about Charlie. So why am I here?"

We exchanged an uncertain glance—or at least, Tick-Tick and Wolfboy did, and tried to include me.

It was Tick-Tick who picked up Rico's question, cool and academic and dauntingly elven. "It's not the drug problem. Capital D, capital P. The Mad River itself is a dangerous drug for humans, after all, and I've never seen the police concern themselves with what Soho's children choose to intoxicate themselves with."

Rico nodded. "Victimless crime. We don't care who they sleep with, either, or whether they charge 'em for it. Though if they ask, we'll tell 'em it's a bad idea."

"Are you having fun?" I asked. "Tell us a story, Detective."

Rico took off the Peepers and folded them, set them on the table. She studied me before she spoke, as if she were seeing something or someone who wasn't me. "Humans can't get into the Elflands; maybe the Wall recognizes them. But what if someone gave you a vial of blue stuff to shoot and said it'd change you, make you just enough like an elf that you could step over the Border into Faerie?"

Wolfboy watched Rico, narrow-eyed. His lip twitched on one side, not quite a snarl, but maybe the possibility of one. He was a little ahead of the Ticker and me, I think, in following the idea to its consequences; he usually is. Tick-Tick frowned at Rico. "It wouldn't be possible," she said at last, but warily.

"Isn't it? There are plenty of substances that shuffle chromosomes. They use 'em out in the World for bioengineering."

"Leaving aside that the Elflands are overrated," the Ticker said, "I'd guess a great deal of money could be made with a product like that. If it has any effect."

"Oh, it has an effect. It brings on hallucinations and euphoria. At first, that's all it does. With repeated use, it cranks up or damps down certain glands. You have a growth spurt, you lose weight. It seems to break down melanin; skin color fades. Hallucinations become increasingly intense." She picked up the Peepers and sighted down the earpieces. "And then it kills you."

If that was what Wolfboy had guessed ahead to, I understood the snarl. I thought of the runaways in Soho who wanted to see the Elflands—which was all of them. Or the less-than-halfbreeds who felt the pull of their elven heritage. Or dumb Jewish boys who'd arrived in

Bordertown willing to do anything to stop being what they were, how they were. A shiver ran down my arms.

"I've hit the wall on this," Rico said. "Charlie was a mule for the person or people behind the stuff. I found out that much, and we were on him like polish on a shoe for maybe twenty-four hours. Twenty-four God-damned hours later, he's dead, with nothing to connect him to his bosses. Whoever it is I'm after might as well be an illusion."

She paused to toy with her Night Peepers again, as if her next line didn't come easily. Tick-Tick made a noncommittal sympathetic noise, and Wolfboy grunted, which was probably the same thing.

Rico raised her head and stared at me. "Then I remembered how you tracked down the killer in the Danceland murder."

I remembered it, too. Normal people can take only so much of that. That's what people like Rico are there for. I wanted to look around the table, at my friends, to see whether they'd known that was coming, whether they'd seen what Rico had meant to do. Oh, lord, I should have understood. She wanted me, but she'd been careful to explain herself to them, to do this in front of them, to put my friends on her side.

"I am not a public utility," I said.

Rico raised her eyebrows. "I'll pay the going rate."

"Then you can make me mayor and the King of Elfland. I wouldn't do it for less."

"Why not?"

I drank off the last of my beer with a ferocious snap. Then I rose and leaned over her, so I could look into her face, and said, "Because I tracked down the Danceland killer."

I straightened up, smiling like a plastic mask. "I'm gonna get another. Anybody else?"

"Me," said Tick-Tick. She understood: Have another beer, business as usual, because the matter is closed. Wolfboy shook his head. Rico sat where she was, like a woman prepared to wait.

I picked up the empties and turned. I was two good strides away before Rico raised her voice and said it, like the answer to a question.

"Richard Paul Weineman."

I took another step. One of the beer bottles slipped out of my fingers and shattered on the floor. I turned around and said, my voice unstrung, "I beg your pardon?" but it was too little, too late.

Rico was leaning back in her chair and staring at the ceiling. The Ticker was alarmed, by my face, I think. Wolfboy looked at me and turned to Rico, lips pulled back in a full-fledged snarl. He didn't know how it had been done, but someone had just hit a friend of his, and he was ready to fight back.

Rico had even pronounced all three syllables of the last name.

She gestured me back to the booth with a jerk of her head. I came as if on a leash. The sound of breaking glass had stopped the conversations around us; now they started back up. I wondered if anyone but us had caught that name. When I was seated again Rico said, "The Suits have had a file on him for a few years. He'd be, oh, twenty-ish now."

I watched her lips move. Mine felt like glaciers—cold, slow, and inclined to break around the edges.

Rico went on, "Five-foot-ten—maybe about six feet by now. Black hair, dark blue eyes. Good-looking kid. A lot like you. You okay? You're a little green."

My fingers were tight around the remaining bottle. I let go of it and laid my hands flat on the table instead.

"Charged with grand theft auto, back in the World," Rico concluded. She folded the Peepers with a click. "And murder."

I thought the Ticker's shoulders moved. I was afraid to look at Wolfboy.

"If I found him," Rico said, eyeing the wall above the booth, "I'd have to extradite him. If B-town got in the habit of harboring fugitives, we'd never be able to keep the damn real cops—the ones from the World, I mean—out of here. Nobody wants that."

I scrabbled up enough self-control to speak. "What do you want me to do?"

"Help me find Charlie's boss."

"It's not that easy. One of us needs to know who I'm looking for."

"I've got to try." For an instant, Rico looked hunted and hungry. That's right, she'd been on the street. She'd imagine her friends falling to this. She put the Peepers on again. "Can you start now?"

"He doesn't want to." Tick-Tick, in her fine, measured voice, like a reciting poet or a courtroom lawyer. "Nor does he have to. He's committed no crime—" I saw the stop in her thoughts mirrored in her eyes, when she wondered if I *had* committed a crime. "And if he has, arrest him. Where is it written that mere authority allows you these liberties with another person's life?"

The smooth silver curve of the Night Peepers was opaque; all I could see there was the room, my face, the Ticker's, and Wolfboy's unreadable one over his clenched, black-clawed fingers.

I pried my hands loose from the table and stood up. "Isn't that what authority is?"

Rico had the grace to flinch.

I smiled stiffly at Tick-Tick. "Tell Peach to eat my chowder and think of me."

"Heartbreaker," she said, as if it hurt her. Wolfboy made a quick, impatient gesture, then seemed to stop himself. I wondered what he would have said, if he could.

I led the way out of the Hard Luck, for the sake of my self-respect. Rico, for whatever reason, let me do it.

## ✳ 2 ✳

# CHANCE OF A GHOST

To HATE A part of yourself is to hate *yourself,* and I know no blacker feeling. The Ticker had helped me come to terms with my talent—we were business people, she always said. We made our living in B-town from the things that made our old lives hell. We were proud to take payment for what we did: fixing things, in her case; finding stuff in mine. You can live in Bordertown without actually supporting yourself. You can scavenge or bum or steal—but that's a hard life, harder every year you live it. Tick-Tick showed me that, with the ability I hated and feared, I could do better.

I hadn't hated my talent like this for years.

Rico had a car. They're not common in Bordertown, because a motorcycle is so much easier to spell-power, and rarer still in Soho because they're expensive. This one was close to the ground, shaped in needle points and glossy curves. It looked as if it ate road surface for break-fast. I got in the passenger side.

"Triumph Spitfire," Rico said, pride in her voice. "Older than I am—hell, way older. When anything breaks, I have to find somebody to build the part. Belt up."

I was sitting in a nest of nylon webbing that I finally realized was a racing harness: lap belt and straps over both shoulders, fastened by one quick-release. Then I realized that the arc of metal over the top of the car was a roll bar, and I shot a look at Rico. "Do I need a fire suit?"

"I drive like an idiot," she said, embarrassed.

She did, too. It made me feel better, the summer night thick with coming rain yanking at my hair and shirt, the rubber smell and screech from the tires, the staccato of intermittent streetlights flashing over me. Loud music would have made it perfect. Loud music and different company and a whole new set of reasons for being there.

She was called Sunny, I knew from that night at Danceland. "What's your real first name?" I asked.

"Why?"

"Curious." I chose not to say anything about making us even.

She shot me a glance. "Alexandra," she said finally.

I leaned back in the seat. "Feminine form of Alexander. Means 'helper of men.' "

The glance was longer this time. "You just happen to know that?"

"I was in a private treatment center." It was called that; I've always thought of it as a reform school with pretensions. "The only book in the place that wasn't a tract for behavior modification was about the meanings of first names. I memorized it." I stared at the buildings going by until I was dizzy.

"Murder," I said finally.

"Mmm."

"Pretty steep."

It was a moment before she said, "Investigating officer's report makes the scene sound a little ambiguous. It might have been reduced to manslaughter, if there'd been a hearing. And the suspect was a juvenile, of course, which still counts for something. But since they can't find the guy . . ."

I had my elbow propped on the door, my chin in my fist. A parody of a relaxed pose. "Darn shame," I said across my knuckles.

"What can you tell me about Richard Weineman?"

"He's dead."

"That has a nice melodramatic ring." She stopped the car at a four-way and said, "Why don't you just tell me what happened that night?"

Air came and went in my lungs. My hand was lightly curled and resting against my lips; I could feel my thumbnail digging into the lower one. I kept my eyes on the scenery, though it was no longer moving. "Because it's none of your business."

Her hand shot out, grabbed my wrist; she pulled my hand away from my mouth, my arm down across my body, and held it there. "I think my business is exactly what it is. I'm a cop."

We were twisted mirror images of each other: both breathing a little too loud, staring into each other's eyes. Our hands met at the mirror plane.

"You're not asking because you're a cop," I said, my voice weightless. "You're asking because you know I have to tell you. Because you're a cop."

Something happened in her face, something that was both harder and softer, and neither. She let go of my wrist and turned, eventually, back to the wheel. The car eased forward again.

"Maybe I'm asking to find out if I've got a psychopath in the passenger seat."

"I think you're safe," I said. "And so do you."

Neither of us spoke again until we stopped.

Juvenile Detention, on Water Street, was the whole of my experience with copshops in B-town, and that only from the visitor's side. This wasn't J.D. Something about the architecture suggested an old library, the comforting municipal sort that must have had columns stipulated in the endowment. Rico saw me looking and said, "Chrystoble Street Station. Sometimes known as Scotland Backyard. Come on, you'll be a nice addition to the ambience."

I followed her up the steps, through the heavy double doors, and into a surprisingly civilized room. The walls were wainscotted halfway up in oak; above that they were painted the green of a honeydew melon. The long windows wore louvered wooden shutters, the louvers open now to encourage the hot, heavy air to circulate.

The furniture was various and battered, but well-made. There were three big dark wood tables sidled up against a wall, one of them in use—at it, a woman uniformed in silver was reading the top sheet of a pile of yellow paper. Two rows of cushioned side chairs occupied the middle of the floor, none of them matching; I thought of a dozen dining rooms like my mother's, all of them missing a chair. A little table stood between two of them, holding a chess board with an unfinished game. A map of Bordertown covered most of one of the room's walls, and another offered quite a nice painting of the Chrystoble Bridge and the riverbank.

As we entered, an elf came out of a door at the other side of the room. He was very tall; I thought the dip of his head as he went under the lintel wasn't required by instinct alone. Age is a subtle thing in elves, but he seemed older than Tick-Tick. His long white hair was drawn tightly back and braided, which added to the length and angularity of his face, and focused attention on his eyes, warm gray and large. On him, the silver uniform jacket seemed like formal wear. He smiled at Rico, and she returned it with a nod.

"Captain Hawthorn," she said. "What brings you to this end of town?"

"Work, Detective. Speaking of which, aren't you here a little late?"

He had a lovely broadcaster's voice without a hint of Elflands accent. I wondered if he'd been born in B-town. He seemed like the wrong generation for it, but again, I couldn't be sure of that.

"Some. Do you know if my partner's here?"

"Yes, he said if I saw you to tell you he was waiting. Nice running into you, Detective. Don't burn it at both ends, hear?" With that fatherly admonition, he went out into the night.

"Gracious," I said, looking after him. "Does he always sound as if he's auditioning for 'My Three Sons'?"

"Hawthorn's all right; he gets it from his co-workers. The Suits up on the Tooth don't exactly trust the Soho cops. Probably afraid we'll go native under stress."

She got to the door Hawthorn had come in by and stopped. "What I did, in the car," she said suddenly. "That was wrong. I'm sorry. I'll try not to yank your chain again."

"The choice of words there is unnervingly apt."

"I know. I'm sorry about that, too. But I have to have your help."

I wasn't sure what she was waiting for, but I said finally, "Here I am." It seemed to be enough to get us through the door.

We turned corners more times than I could keep track of. At last we stopped in front of a heavy-looking door with a little window in it, and Rico knocked. Chill air hit me when it swung open.

"Hold it," I said. I had figured out where we were. "Why do we—"

"It's the only thing I have. Scared?" She sounded pleased.

Detective Linn greeted me gravely, and might even have remembered me from the Danceland business. I remembered him. Rico's partner was sort of a cross between the King of Elfland and Mr. Spock, but he dressed better than either of them. He was sublimely out of place in the cold little room, tall and white, his almost luminous white hair freshly cropped and showing the tops of his pointed ears. He wore a dark maroon suit with an agate pin in his cravat.

"How do you get this place so damn cold?" I asked.

"Magic," he said, and didn't seem to think it was funny. "You are good to help us."

I decided I didn't have to answer that.

Linn stood by a sturdy marble-topped table that, now that I think about it, probably started work in a commercial bakery. The thing on it was covered with a white sheet. Rico put a firm hand between my shoulder blades and got me beside the table, and Linn drew the sheet back.

After a moment I stepped away and leaned against a wall. "Long walk off a short pier," I said, when I could talk.

"And somebody drained the ocean," Rico replied. She shook two herbal cigs out of a pack, tapped them down, and handed me one. "Can you use him to find whoever killed him?" She lit for me.

"No." I rubbed a cold hand over my face. "And if I could, I'd just have a fix on another legman."

"Jesus Christ on the Tree, do you think I'd mind having a fix on a legman? I wouldn't mind having a fix on the legman's goddamn *laundromat*. Don't you understand? I don't have *anything* right now. Will you just try it?"

I looked up. Rico wore that hungry face again.

"All right. But for God's sake, cover him up."

Linn did, except for one bare, discolored arm. I stood over Charlie's unlovely corpse, empty of anything. Outside, people were drinking, dancing, fighting, making love. Outside was a foreign land, and there were no flights to it from here. *Who killed you, Charlie, and where is he now?* Nothing answered me. I reached two fingers out—from sheer horrified fascination, I think—and touched dead skin.

Rico had her hands under my armpits, holding me up. My legs were folded under me. Rico's face, looking down into mine, was ashy under her tan. "What happened?" I said.

"Just what I was going to ask. You touched the body and dropped like a brick."

"Death trauma," Linn said above me, his silver eyebrows drawn down in alarm. "In Faerie, if death comes in manner sudden or suspect, one summons an adept, who by such contact with the corpse, reads the final moments of the life that's gone. If it was violent death, the mage may take the trauma on himself, and be much harmed."

I stared at him. "Why the hell don't you call somebody in and do that now?"

He looked sad. "No human corpse will give its secrets up, that we have found. And even fey flesh, in the Borderlands, is sometimes mute, or muted. Here it is not a tool that pays its use."

"Offhand, I'd guess that in Faerie you don't go to your grandmother's funeral and give her a last kiss in the coffin."

"Indeed not, if one's grandmother died by murder or mischance." He sounded as if he thought this was an inappropriate subject to discuss in a morgue. "Had illness or her great age sent her hence, one could bestow such strange salutes as that, and fear no consequence."

To tell the truth, I didn't think much of kissing dead people at funerals, either. I hung in Rico's arms, shaking, sucking down air.

"Do you remember anything?" Rico asked.

"No. If I hadn't been sitting on the floor, I wouldn't have believed it happened." She looked sour. "Sorry," I added, as she helped me to stand. My cigarette was scorching the floor a few feet away. I started to pick it up, then decided I didn't want to put it in my mouth. I stepped on it instead.

"What about his effects?" Rico said to Linn.

"It won't help," I told them.

Linn turned to a tall chest of little handleless drawers against one wall. He spoke softly in the language of the Elflands, and one drawer slid out. This he carried to Rico.

"It won't," I repeated. "Now if you wanted me to *find* his effects, maybe I'd put you on a show. But I can't—"

Rico cut me off with one of her looks. "We're going now. You wanna come, or are you sleeping in here tonight?"

I made a shoot-myself-in-the-head gesture and followed them.

We stopped in a tiny office. The walls were pale aqua at the bottom, shading slowly to turquoise at the top and across the high ceiling studded with wisps of painted cloud. The free-standing coatrack, I now noticed, was painted on the wall. So was the window with its blinds drawn, and a four-drawer file cabinet, and the pile of books on it. I wished I was close enough to see the titles. The way Rico stepped through the clutter to the desk chair told me the office was hers.

Linn moved a file box of papers, a huge leather-bound book that looked like a photo album, and a wrinkled, flattened silver jacket from a chair. He motioned me into it. For himself, he pushed the mess on the desk toward the center and perched on the cleared edge. Rico caught a box that fell off the other side.

"Bad cop," she said, with a glare at Linn. "No donut. Is this your way of telling me we should go to your office?"

"Not at all. Comfort and convenience dull the sharpest mind."

They sounded like the Ticker and me. How long had they been partners? I felt a moment of jealousy. She had her best friend to back her up. Why couldn't I have mine?

Rico dropped the drawer on top of the clutter. It was full of the things people wear or keep in their pockets: keys, some jewelry, an impression ball, a tooled leather coin purse. No buttons torn from a murderer's coat. No matchbook with an address pencilled inside. Wolfboy'd taken me to too many movies. "No clothes?" I asked Rico.

She grinned. "You wouldn't have liked 'em."

"Oh." I picked up the impression ball first. The song it played, started by contact with my palm, was the Pit

Bulls' "Jump Me Now." "That's Charlie all over," I muttered.

Rico and Linn began to laugh hysterically.

"Shit," I said, torn between laughter and anger.

"Sorry," Rico gasped. "Cop humor."

I swapped the ball for a ring, dull silver metal and a big piece of red glass. I pushed it around my palm, wondering what to do with it. A glance showed me Rico watching, sober-faced now and with that look in her eyes again. I sighed.

Finding things. I had the thing already. What was to find? What it had done? Where it had been? All over Bordertown, knowing Charlie.

No, not where it had been. Where it *belonged*. Could I do that? I'd never done it before, but that didn't mean I couldn't. I asked the question in whatever way I do, called for the answer in whatever language my talent understands.

And I felt the tugging. It was faint, but enough to give me a direction. I stood up and began to walk as much toward it as I could, given the hallways. The pull was so weak that I concentrated only on it, not on where I was. So finding myself at the door to the morgue was a nasty shock.

Behind me, Rico said, "It works."

The jewelry all belonged on the corpse, but faintly, as if the pieces forgot their owner even as I held them. The coins belonged anywhere—money's like that. Their formless, omnidirectional pull made my head ache. The impression ball gave back nothing but lousy music. Maybe my hand was where it belonged; an i-ball is meant to be held, after all. Or perhaps the magic in it crossed wires with my talent. If I understood how my talent worked, maybe I'd know. But the keys . . .

The keys were the jackpot, as I might have expected if I'd thought about it. There were three of them, and each one pulled me, strong and steady, in a different direction. I held them up and jingled them, feeling abstractly pleased.

"Keys," Rico said, "belong in locks."

"Uh huh. Doors, cabinets, ignitions. These could be to his front door, his wheels, and his mom's house."

Rico stood swiftly. "Let's go find out."


The first two stops were Charlie's bike, abandoned on High Street and impounded in the copshop garage, and Charlie's squat on Hell's Gate. The third was a boarded-up rowhouse near Fare-You-Well Park.

"If his mom lives here," Rico said—eyeing the rusted fence fallen into the basement entry, the trash on the steps, the wound in the wall where someone had yanked out the intercom system—"then I know where that boy got his sense of style." Her Night Peepers were back on her nose, and I wondered for the first time just how much better she could see in the dark than I could. "Do the honors, will you?" she added, and offered me a flashlight.

I unlocked the front door and turned to find Rico close behind me, with a gun in her hand. "Those things make me nervous," I said.

"Shh, you'll wake Mom."

We went quietly into the front hall. It stank of damp plaster dust and decaying wood, and nothing else. The building was uncompromisingly silent. I phrased a question Wolfboy-style: with eyebrows and tilt of head. She nodded toward a piece of wall next to one of the hallway doors. I stood against it.

Rico moved to the other side, back flat to the wall, and turned the knob slowly. Then she slammed the door open and snapped back out of the way. It was as good as a movie. Absolutely nothing happened. She edged out to look around the doorframe. Nothing happened then, either. She prowled the room like a tiger trained in Tai Chi, gun ready; then she made another textbook entrance into the next room in the suite. The whole suite was empty, except for little piles of wallpaper that had fallen off the walls from damp. Swaths of the ceiling paper drooped loose over our heads, and half-loosened strips dangled from the walls like lolling paper tongues.

There were four doors on the first floor, each with a suite of rooms behind it, and we treated all of them equally. I'd expected to relax as we continued to find nothing. Instead, I felt as if I were vibrating all over. If I'd had a gun, too, I'd have opened fire on the first cockroach that moved.

We found a door to the basement. It was locked, and the key didn't open it. Rico looked at me, shrugged, and headed for the stairs.

The second floor had the same floor plan. I took my place beside the first door, and pretended I had no desire to scream.

The first suite was empty. The second was empty. The third seemed empty at first.

The first room certainly was. But the windows were covered over with plywood and tar paper, and loose wallpaper had been pulled down and consolidated in a musty heap in one corner, as if it had been in the way of something, or someone. Rico angled her head toward it, and I nodded. She couldn't have been more careful at the door to the inside room than she'd been before, but she certainly wasn't any less.

Nobody waited for us in the inside room. The windows were sealed up here, too. The room contained nothing but another heap of fallen wallpaper near the door, a rickety card table in the middle of the floor, and on it, a sheet of paper.

Rico gestured for me to hold the light on it. It was thick paper, smooth-finished, expensive, and there was a line of writing on it. In dense black ink, in the perfectly formed, soulless hand of penmanship texts, we read: *Set down your burden of clay, and enter happily into paradise.*

The flashlight faded and died. I toggled the switch again and again, without result. By the door, there was a rustling of paper.

A pale shape rose in the corner by the door. It had started, I thought, as the heap of fallen wallpaper, but something was happening to it; something was sprouting from the paper in faint, bluish light. The shape was humanoid, tall, thin, wild-haired. I thought I heard a little tittering sound from it, like the laughter of demented mice.

I didn't move. There was no place to move to. I wasn't sure where Rico was in the dark room, and I was afraid to look for fear I'd find I was alone. Then I heard a small, sharp *clack* beside me, and Rico's shaky whispered curse. "If it comes toward us," she murmured, "go left. If we split up, we might make the door."

A flash of spitting light from the ceiling, and a resonating *whump*. Then a near-human groan above us: the voice of wood and plaster straining.

Rico screamed, "Down, down, *down!*" Something slammed into me from behind and sent me lunging toward the apparition in the corner.

Then the sky fell.

I had something heavy on my back, and my face was

pressed uncomfortably against the floor. Or something like the floor. I was coughing.

The thing on my back shifted and coughed, too.

"Rico?" I asked between spasms.

"Yeah. I don't suppose you managed to hang onto the flashlight?"

"Here."

"Here *where?*"

At that, I had the sense to thumb the button, and a cone of dust-filled light appeared at the corner of my vision.

"Ah. My hero." Her hand closed over mine and took the light. "Do you hurt anywhere?"

"Besides everywhere?"

"Yeah. Here, roll over. Easy, now."

The flashlight illuminated a heap of architectural carnage. "What happened?" I said, and started coughing again.

"An embarrassing trap, that's what," Rico said sourly. "I want Linn to look the place over, but I'll bet the trigger for everything was the light from the damn flashlight."

"Trigger?"

She stood up, cautiously. "Careful—a lot of the third floor has already fallen on us, and I'd just as soon the rest didn't. Yeah, you've just seen a demonstration of the Rube Goldberg school of spellcasting. Light on the paper triggers the illusion that pops up out of the trash pile. While that keeps us in the middle of the room, it also sets off whatever cracked the ceiling beams. And boom. If I hadn't decided on the lesser of two evils and gotten us up against the outside wall, we'd be hamburger."

She was right. There were three lengths of foot-square wooden beam collapsed into the center of the room, along with antique gas piping, an upstairs radiator, old wiring, shattered studs, and an incalculable amount of plaster and lath.

"What I want to know about," Rico continued, "was the technology outage."

"Huh?" I said wisely.

Even in the half-illumination of the flashlight, I could make out her look of martyred patience. "Did you think the batteries had died?"

I remembered the flashlight going out. I said nothing.

"My pistol wouldn't fire, either. Not that it would have helped. If we're after someone who can turn the laws of physics off at will, we're in deep, deep shit."

"You'll have to learn to fence," I said. It was her turn not to respond.

I followed the light as it moved through the fog of plaster dust. The strange landscape of empty rooms was stranger still. The front room was three-walled now, no division between it and the one we'd brought down on us. The air was opaque with dust. In the hall, another piece of ceiling had fallen, and a bearing wall, and the rotten roof. The sky hung heavy and starless above us.

The air was hot and weighted down to motionless with the threat of rain. We went carefully but quickly down the stairs, always listening for more building preparing to give way. I thought Rico was listening for something else, too, and remembered all her careful entrances into rooms. Of course—she was still waiting for the ambush.

It didn't happen. We made it to her car in perfect safety.

Rico let her guard down at last; she stood by the car with her arms folded over the roll bar, her head resting on them. I sat on the curb.

"You'll never get your nice suit clean," I said. "And all for nothing, too."

"Shut up," said Rico, with murderous clarity, "and get in the car."

"Why?"

"Because I thought you'd want a ride home. Was I wrong?"

I slid in the passenger side door, and she started the engine. "It's on Sentiment Street—"

"I know where it is."

"Of course." Resentment nipped at me. "You would."

After a few blocks, I asked, "Are we square? Can I stay home now?"

"What do you mean?"

"You're out of leads, aren't you? What do you need me for?"

She shook her head. For the first time since the roof had fallen, I looked directly at her. There was blood mixed with the plaster dust on her face, from a cut near her eye. She seemed not to notice. The Night Peepers were gone, possibly lost, and I saw the intensity of her gaze, the way it seemed to reach past the street and the city and into some place I couldn't see or imagine. "Did I say I was out of leads?"

"Aren't you?"

"I'll get Linn to take a crew and go over the building in daylight." She smiled suddenly, a harsh expression. Her hand went into her jacket, came out again. "And I have this."

In her fingers, a thick white sheet of paper, now rather crumpled: the note from the table.

"I'll come by for you tomorrow. Around noon," Rico said, just as if I'd responded.

"Stop here."

She did. "Something wrong?"

"I think . . . I think I'd like to walk the rest of the way."

She looked at me for long seconds, but didn't speak. She understood that much, at least. I got out and shut the door firmly behind me. "Tomorrow," I said, and walked away. I heard the engine pick up behind me, and the crunch of gravel under the tires.

Tick-Tick's motorcycle was parked in front of my building. Tick-Tick was sitting on it. When I was close enough for her to tell that the sorry object walking toward her was me, she vaulted off the bike and ran toward me. I let her do it.

"Mab and sprites and imps of Hell," the Ticker burst out. "What in all their names did that copper bitch lead you into?" She'd grabbed my shoulders; now she let them go, as if afraid she'd break me.

"It was a mistake."

"I think that goes without saying."

I tried running my hands through my hair, but I hit a sore place and stopped. "It'll probably happen again."

"Why should it?" she asked ominously.

"Because she's not done."

"Might I suggest that you *are?*"

I shook my head.

"Why not?"

I thought about it, about the things the Ticker didn't know. About a car, and an act of violence. "Because it would be a bad idea."

She looked down the street; not at anything, just not at me. "I tried to follow you from Chrystoble Street," she said after a moment, with less heat. "I got too late a start. I'm sorry. All I could do was come here and wait."

I looked up into her moonlit face, at the deep dismay there, and touched her arm. "I'm all right. I just need a shower."

Her fine-carved mouth worked; then she said, "Do you need to get out of town, too?"

"If I did that, I'd never be able to come back."

She understood. She knew that, in all the wide world, one could run out of places to run to.

"Go on home," I told her. "I'll stop by tomorrow."

I went straight upstairs, picked up a towel and a bar of soap, and went down again to the backyard. There's a solar shower there, an old black plastic fifty-gallon drum full of water with a hose and a shower head at the end of it. It loses heat slowly, even well after dark.

I rocked the drum—plenty of water, nearly full, in fact. Maybe my fellow squatters had left town because of the heat. I pulled the shower curtain closed, peeled off my filthy clothes, and flung them out on the grass. Then I opened the spigot. Warm water. I scrubbed down; then I just stood, letting the water pour over me and away, as if rinsing off more than soap. I had an angry-looking gash down one arm, pulled muscles in my neck and shoulder, a darkening bruise on one hip, a painful lump on the back of my head, and another on my shin.

But I was alive. That was nice. I hadn't realized that before: that events could have turned out such that I wouldn't be there, and they hadn't done that. I could almost feel the other path, the one where I'd died. Suddenly, standing naked under running water was the most wonderful experience I'd ever had. So I did it for a long time.

When I was finished I tied the towel around me and pumped water to fill the drum again. Then I carried my clothes upstairs to my squat, dropped them on the floor, and crawled under the covers. I must have fallen asleep almost immediately.

I sat up. No, that's not what I did. That's not even close to what I did. Like some machine part, like a bolt being shot from one position to another, like a single-pole switch toggled from off to on, like a tractor-trailer jacknifing on the ice, I found myself vertical in the dark, sweat already cold, stomach and heart like trapped birds flapping, flapping, and a sound, not really a scream, escaping the back of my throat.

They do it in movies. Gunshot on the soundtrack, and a fast cut to an actor, sitting up in bed. It's real. I did it.

"Easy," said someone next to me in the dark. "Easy. You were dreaming. Tell me about it." There was a hand on my shoulder. I snapped my head around and stared at the silhouette barely visible between me and the darkened window.

Lightning flashed behind, and a match flared in front of her. Sunny Rico. She sat in one of my kitchen chairs near the bed. Light sketched the outline of the fingers on the hand that sheltered the match; light rolled over her impassive face and lowered eyes and made her look like a statue in a Mexican church. A Madonna with a brush cut. She lit a candle on the nightstand as thunder cleared its throat outside.

Terror is a long-lasting, mind-numbing drug. I sat amid the ransacked bedclothes unable to identify them, or to make sense of anything, dragging air in and out through my constricted throat. Then half-thoughts fell over each other: what was *she* doing here, or if she was here, where was I? Memory began to settle out—Rico, her car, the building, Charlie, the dream I'd just—

"How'd you get in here?" I gasped.

"Tell me about the dream, before you forget it."

"Not likely—"

"Tell."

I slumped forward and leaned on my knees. "Don't be a ghoul," I said, muffled against the sheet.

"You can charge me for the time. *Please?*"

I turned away, back to the rucked bedclothes, settled my chin on my knees and let my eyes unfocus. I spoke fragments aloud as I remembered them, and as I spoke, the pieces shifted into a reasonable order. The hot blue sky, and low walls of crenellated brick. Tar bubbling up, sticking to shoe soles; the smell of sweat, mine/his. The belfry empty; someone to meet there, but it was empty. Looking around, out over the rooftops, the street, way down, no fear. Sound behind. A thing—not clear, something awful, leaping at my face—screaming, arms up, a step back and the wall comes up hard below my knees and what's coming is more terrible than the thing I saw on the roof . . .

I stopped a little before the nightmare had, and my fingers dug into the mattress for security's sake. A decent silence had been in place for a few seconds before I said, "He was set up."

"Yeah. I'd thought so, but now we're sure. And there was no one else on the roof, so we can quit looking for a hitter. Here." She held one of my glasses out to me, and I smelled whiskey. Since I didn't think I had any whiskey, she must have brought it with her. I drank it off and shuddered at the silken burn of it.

"So how did you get in?" I asked, as soon as I had my breath back.

"You left the door unlocked. It's a bad idea."

"I leave it unlocked all the time. Usually there aren't any cops in the neighborhood."

"Very funny."

"Did you just drop by to see if I was having a nightmare?"

Rico said, "Actually, yes. When I got home, I found Linn waiting for me. He'd been thinking about what happened when you laid hands on Charlie's body. According to him, the theory is that elves can make stuff like that work because they've . . . God, what did he say? . . . *integrated* their conscious, subconscious, and unconscious minds better than we have. He said if you couldn't remember what happened when you touched the corpse, you'd probably passed the whole trauma straight into your unconscious, and there was a good chance you'd get a nice little package delivered in your dreams tonight."

I stared at her. "Tell your partner to quit the cop business and take up psychotherapy. So you came to hold my hand?"

"I came because he said that, depending on the quality of Charlie's last moments, there was a good chance you could take major damage from it."

"Oh."

"And to find out if Charlie took anything with him to the Happy Hunting Ground that will help me find his goddamn boss." Her words were so measured and fierce that I had to look at her. Still a statue, but not a Madonna. Her face was hard and still, with only the eyes alive.

"Ah. Not to hold my hand, but to pick my brain. Well, do you know anything more now than you used to?"

"Not very damned much."

"What about the thing I saw? That jumped at me—him."

Rico sighed. "An illusion. Hell to do in full sunlight, but it only had to be convincing for a second. Still, it's beginning to seem like our friend is finest-kind illusionist."

"Sounds like an elf."

"You'd think so." Rico smiled at me, another of her humorless ones, and stood up. "But you can find things you've never seen and do psychometry with corpses. I'd say the species stereotypes are going to hell in this town." She crossed the room, turned in the doorway, and took something out of a jacket pocket. "Catch," she said, and tossed it. When I caught it, I found it was a flask, black leather over silver. "Don't waste it. It's Tully. Probably older than both of us."

I remembered the taste over my tongue: honey on fire. "I don't need—"

"Yeah, you do. And lock the damned door behind me. If for no other reason than that a guy who sleeps bare-assed should be more concerned about who might walk in."

She closed the door behind her. There was only the one candle; I don't think, even if she'd waited for it, that she could have seen me blush.

This time the thunder cracked before the lightning's afterimage started to fade. It sounded like the World Tree had been split, and to say it made me jump would not quite cover it. Maybe tomorrow it would be cooler.

*You can do psychometry with corpses.* As if it were now part of my permanent repertoire. Well, it wasn't. It had been traumatic, dangerous, and not even particularly useful. And embarrassing, besides. To hell with it, and to hell with Sunny Rico. When next she asked me to find something, I'd pretend to come up zero, and live with the resulting discomfort.

I lay back, closed my eyes, and found the pavement of High Street rushing up at me behind my eyelids. Rico had been right. I spent an hour in intermittent conference with her flask before I could sleep again.

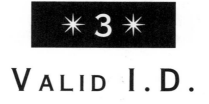

# ☀ 3 ☀

# VALID I.D.

I WOKE OF my own volition, more or less, at nine in the morning. From the feel of it, someone was tearing my brain tissue down the middle like a piece of paper, and my mouth tasted like an old felt hat. I decided that I must have been drinking, but I couldn't remember having any fun. I lowered my feet carefully to the floor and sat up. I'd once put the stub of a candle in a jacket pocket and forgotten it was there; when I found it a month later, it was covered with lint and hair and all the unidentifiable stuff that makes its way to the bottom of a pocket. According to my stomach, I had swallowed something remarkably like that candle. I lay back down.

The sight of Sunny Rico's flask on the bedside table jump-started my memory. Oh boy, oh boy. And we were to start all over again at noon. I had three hours in which to do something about the state I was in.

This time I managed to get all the way to my feet and across the room to the kitchen, where I worked the pump and stuck my head under it. Then I drank a lot of water, stumbled down the hall to the second floor toilet, and returned feeling, if not better, at least different. And hungry, in spite of the candle wax in my stomach. Well, of course; Rico had spoiled my appetite for dinner at the Hard Luck, and after that things had been a little busy. I knew what I'd find, but I looked anyway. In the bread box, one heel of whole-grain, rigid as ceramic tile. In the cupboard, a half-tin of cocoa, a box of peppercorns, and the dregs of a bottle of soy sauce. In the icebox, the last three bottles of homebrew out of the dozen Hawk had given me for finding him a copy of Pinkwater's *Fat Men from Space*. For a moment, I thought about one of those—carbohydrates, after all—but only for a moment.

Well, I had told Tick-Tick I'd stop by today. I hadn't meant it to be quite so short a distance into today, but if she wasn't up yet, I knew I could trust her to tell me to go away. I pulled on a T-shirt and cutoffs, combed my hair with my fingers, grabbed my sunglasses, and headed downstairs to the street.

Last night's storm hadn't lowered the temperature much, but it had given the humidity a serious leg up. All the potholes were full of water, unstirred by so much as the threat of a breeze. Above the ragged, ambling rooflines of Soho I could see the sky over the Border. It looked as if someone there had seen a few animated fairy tales and meant to duplicate the style: improbable pastel clouds came streaming out, toward the World, against a watercolor turquoise backdrop. It's stuff like this that makes it impossible to predict the weather in the Borderlands.

I wasn't the only thing awake, but I was close to it. On Desire Street I saw an auburn-haired girl hanging out laundry from her fire escape, singing something about a smiling Trojan horse to a lilting, scampering sort of melody. A calico cat teetered on the top pipe of a chain-link fence and regarded me gravely. "I'll live," I assured it. It lashed its tail and leaped down to investigate a storm drain.

Trudging uphill to Tick-Tick's sweated some of the hangover toxins out of me. Still, when I yelled under her window and she leaned out to look at me, she shook her head. "Back to the pit that spawned you," she said.

"That bad, huh?"

"You should have a mirror in that little hideaway of yours. Then you could at least try to turn degradation into a fashion statement."

"This isn't a fashion statement?"

"The young Lou Reed on a three-day bender? No, my dear. Or at least, I hope not."

"Who's Lou Reed?"

Tick-Tick covered her eyes with one slim white hand. "Blessed isle. So much for the notion that only cool people come to Bordertown. Would you like some breakfast?"

"Nah. I figured I'd hang out here some more and we could wake up *all* your neighbors."

Tick-Tick yanked on an iron ring mounted next to her window frame. The latch on the green-painted double doors to the building said *clack,* and I shouldered my way in. The Ticker was the only tenant in the building who didn't have to come to the front door to let her guests in. It wasn't selfishness; she'd promised to set up remote mechanical latches like hers for at least three of her neighbors, just as soon as she got around to it. But having solved the problem and implemented the solution once already, she'd found the thrill wasn't in it anymore.

I slid my sunglasses off as I passed through the lofty

center room. The grubby skylight two storeys above me dropped morning sunshine grudgingly over someone's unfinished project: a tapestry woven of dyed jute rope. On it, a young man sat under a tree in a forest, his arms at odd angles and his mouth open. Three other figures could be seen from behind, in the background. Ravens sat in the trees above, and the beginnings of two wolves showed at the working edge of the weave. There was a lot of detail in the thing, considering that it was made of rope, and the finished effect was obviously going to be disturbing.

The tapestry was already twenty feet long, and seemed to be no more than two-thirds done, if that. I wondered where Tick-Tick's neighbor planned to hang it ultimately. Just then, it was suspended from the railing that ran around the room on the second floor, from an artfully twisted Volkswagen bumper, a wrought-iron garden bench, and a street-sign post whose sign read, "Yellow Brick Rd." The found-metal balcony rail had been another neighbor's project two years before.

The elevator was passenger-powered; I stepped into the cage and hauled on the rope. The pulleys it ran over squeaked just enough to let the second-floor inhabitants know someone was coming. By the time I stepped out, the Ticker's door, further along the balcony, was open and letting out kitcheny sounds.

The Ticker had half the second floor. It was one of those cavernous warehouse rooms that everybody wants, but hardly anybody knows what to do with. Tick-Tick refused to divide hers up with walls; she claimed that the whole point of a space like that was being able to see from one end of it to the other. Since there were windows on three sides, it was a little like living in an open field. Instead of walling them off, she'd defined the "rooms," or at least, the areas devoted to particular activities, by turning the floor into a series of connected plywood platforms, each one about a foot and a half higher than the last, and devoting a different level to each room. Inside the door, at the former floor level, she had her workbench and tools, the table saw, the drill press, and all the other equipment that was neither too big to get through the back door, nor too dangerous to keep indoors. I think the reason her workshop was the first thing you came to was that Tick-Tick was convinced that ideas are fragile, and when she came flying upstairs in pursuit of the execution of an idea, she was afraid the mere sight of creature comforts would drive it clean out of her head.

The next level up was the kitchen, with cabinets with carved doors and a countertop under the windows. The indoor necessary plumbing was on this level, too, but on the opposite side of the room from the windows, where the walls that made it private wouldn't interfere with the sight lines. The platform above that was the area that in anybody else's place would be called the living room. This meant you had to go through the kitchen to get to it, but as Tick-Tick pointed out, everyone goes to the kitchen first anyway, so why not design for it? The two levels above that served as library, study, guest bedroom, and whatever. Beyond them were the front windows, and the Ticker's bed raised like a treehouse in a loft above the window frames.

So the first smell that greeted me as I came in the door was engine oil, and the first sight a disemboweled gear box on her workbench. But beyond that, Tick-Tick, in a red silk kimono that contrasted startlingly with her dandelion-yellow hair, was setting a waffle iron on her gas stove. (The Ticker is one of the few people in B-town I'd trust with a gas stove. Sometimes, touched by the passing

of one of the Border's logic-devouring eddies of magic,
the gas doesn't flow, or won't light. Some people forget
to close the gas cock when that happens. A few hours
later, they light a cigarette and find out that the gas has
come back on. Several blocks in Soho have undergone
sudden urban renewal because of that.)

"Waffles would be nice," I said.

"Fresh out. Will you settle for waffles?"

"Ugh. I'm too tired to keep that up. What can I help
with?"

"Wash your hands first, my chick. There's no saying
where they've been."

I went to the kitchen sink. "Where's the soap?"

"Oh, that's right, I used it up. Unwrap another bar,
do; they're in the drawer."

I opened the drawer she'd pointed to and found an
impressive stash of soap in about twenty different colors,
wrapped in about as many ways, bearing labels from out
of the World, the Elflands, and from here in town. The
smell was pleasant, but staggering. "I took out a pale purple bar. "How about this one?"

The Ticker looked, and sighed. "Not in the *kitchen,* my
dear. That's lilac. There should be a rather nice lemon in
there, somewhere."

"Why not lilac? It smells nice."

"Very. But not in the kitchen. Fruit or spice or, possibly, herb for the kitchen. Flowers and the strong perfumes, like patchouli, for the bath."

I stared at her, and tossed the bar of soap and caught it
a couple of times. "There's supposed to be some kind of
internal logic to that, isn't there?"

Tick-Tick gave me a wide smile. "I'm sorry; I'd quite
forgotten that wasn't your long suit. Now wash your
hands."

I used the lemon.

"Now, slice those," she said, pointing at a cutting board heaped with ghost-white Border strawberries each the size of my thumb, "and pour some of that on them."

I uncorked the That bottle and sniffed. "Hey-*yah*. I'm already hung over."

"Fear not. We're going to set breakfast on fire before we eat it."

There was a label on the bottle, a brown, brittle, faded paper one. It was about as legible as a fallen leaf. I sniffed again. The fumes breathed out memories of seasons past, spring in strawberry beds, summer among raspberry canes, autumn in orchards full of plum and peach and apple. " 'Sweeter than honey from the rock,' " I murmured. Then I remembered the source of the quote was Christina Rossetti's "Goblin Market," and that it was one of a class of stories that wasn't exactly complimentary to the Fair Folk.

But the Ticker laughed. " 'Men sell not such in any town.' Just so, my lad. It's from over the Border."

I looked up quickly, and the liquor slapped the side of its bottle with a little chiming note. "I thought—" And thought better of asking, and shut up.

She didn't. "That I'd not go back? I haven't, and I won't. I took this in payment for fixing Mother Mayeye's sewing machine. I believe it began life in my father's cellars, and when I think of how little pleased he'd be at where it is now and what I did to earn it, I treasure it even beyond its deserts. Blessed Isle, my father would rather have cut my hands off at the wrists than see them used to make and mend foul Worldly machinery."

"He'll never know."

"No, indeed he won't—I'd heard he died a year or two ago. My brother, I think, still lives. And if my brother

objected to the provenance of that bottle, I doubt he'd
have the backbone to say so to my face. So there; time
has robbed me of these childish pleasures."

It made me uncomfortable, to hear her speak of the
past. "You don't have to talk about it."

She turned away to pour batter on the hot iron, and
over the hiss she said, "I know. If I had to, I'd fight it like
death itself. But with you, I don't have to. So I can."

"Ah."

The Ticker cast a look over her shoulder. "Nor do you
have to reciprocate."

I knew I should. She was my friend, and even if she'd
just said that I didn't owe her the story of my personal
road to Bordertown, who the hell else did I owe it to?
Rico?

I sliced strawberries with all my attention. They were
particularly fine ones, large and white clear through
without a hint of pink. (Wild Borderland strawberries are
one of the Border's little jokes. They form bright red, and
fade as they ripen. No strawberry has ever been so
sweet.)

"So, can you tell me about last night's adventures?"
Tick-Tick said.

"She didn't say not to." I told her about Charlie in the
morgue, and how the keys worked, and how the ceiling
fell on us at the derelict apartment building. As I'd expected, she made me go back over that part.

"Rico thinks it was the light?" she asked, intent.
"Then why assume the trigger was magical, and not pho-
toelectric?"

"The thing in the corner was. Magical, I mean." I driz-
zled liqueur on the strawberries—sparingly, however
glad the Ticker might have been to squander the stuff on
mortals. The smell made me want to lie down in the

bowl. "Oh, and so was the other thing, that scared Charlie off the roof."

She stopped in the middle of plucking a waffle off the griddle and raised her eyebrows at me.

"Oh, sorry. That was the rest of the night, after you went home." I described the dream, and, sourly, Rico reappearing in my apartment.

"That was well done of her," said the Ticker.

"It was? It didn't feel like it at the time."

"Hah. You're only ashamed to have been caught in a moment of weakness."

She was probably at least partly right. I decided that trying to think of the other parts would make my head ache.

Tick-Tick handed me a bowl and a whisk, and pointed at the milk bottle. "Pour the cream off the top of that and whip it, would you?"

"Wait a minute. That's work."

"It's exercise. Do you good before breakfast. Linn is right, you know. These dreams can harm the dreamer; I've heard of it happening even over the Border, where one might expect people to know how to prevent such things. If Rico knew the signs, then she would be able to wake you if she saw them."

I remembered the end of the dream, suddenly and for the first time. It had been as if something had reached past Charlie's memories and tapped mine on the shoulder. It could have been my own ego, denying death for all it was worth. Or it could have been someone in the room, doing or saying the right things, whatever they were. Nothing that happened after I woke up told me which it was. If Rico had saved me from unspecified damage, she'd been self-effacing enough not to tell me so. I wondered, while I whipped the cream, if that made me feel less nervous, or more.

"Ideally, *not* butter," Tick-Tick said. She was standing next to me, unlit match in hand. In front of her were two gilt-edged plates bearing waffles and strawberries. "Whatever your flaws, my bonny boy, you've always been reasonably alert. This sudden tendency to fall into abstraction—" (the liqueur gave off a satisfying *foomph*, and a toxic-looking blue-green flame) "—is not like you. I put up with it in Wolfboy because I can't tell when his eyes aren't focusing anyway."

"Um."

" 'Um,' indeed. And I would love to know whose face you were seeing in that poor cream." With that, she used it to put out the last scuttling bits of flame.

I thought about it. "Mine, maybe. Probably I was just spacing out."

We sat at the round table that was just the right size for two; I don't know if the Ticker ever has dinner parties. If she does, she can probably find another table. This one was made of some highly-polished golden wood in high Art Nouveau style. Heaven only knows how these things come into Bordertown, or, once they have, why they should land on Tick-Tick's doorstep instead of in some parlor on Dragonstooth Hill.

The alcohol was gone from the liqueur, the strawberries were warmed and softened, and some of the sugars had caramelized. The waffles were crisp all around the edges and soft in the middle. And the Ticker had stopped me just in time on the whipped cream. There was hot tea to wash it down with, which tasted something like Darjeeling and something like not. It was related to last night's shower: It was a meal to make me grovellingly happy to be alive.

So I was grateful that Tick-Tick waited until I'd finished before she said, "And who did you kill?"

"Pardon?"

She looked patient. "That was two syllables, so I know you're stalling. If you really didn't know what I was asking, you'd have made do with 'Huh?' Or is this Richard Paul Somebody not you after all, in which case, what does he have on you, my lad, that you'll go out and get ceilings dropped on you rather than tell Rico to go bother him?"

On second thought, it would have been useful to have some food to push around the plate, so I could pretend to be distracted. "I thought I didn't have to reciprocate."

"Of course not. But that was in matters of confidences freely given. This is a direct question. I ask because I want to be of use, and I can't trust you, once you're fully sunk in misery, to recognize when I *can* be of use."

I wanted to say, "Nobody you know," and let her figure out if it was the answer to her first direct question or her second. Stylish, if the Ticker would have let it stand at that. "It's all from before I came here. Tick-Tick, you know every stupid thing I've done since I got to Bordertown. Aren't those enough? Can't I leave the rest back in the World?"

"Well played. You've been going to the movies again. What would Rico's answer be?"

"She hasn't asked about it." I remembered then that she had, in the car at the stop sign. But she'd apologized for that. "I don't think she cares about the details, as long as I help her find this guy."

Tick-Tick shook her head and reached for my empty plate.

"No, you cooked. I'll wash."

"In your present state, do you really believe I'd give

the good china over into your hands? No, you'd jump at a falling leaf, and there I'd be with fewer plates than saucers. Go home, you ninny. But by the holy trees, do remember that I'm here, and good for something.''

I stood up, feeling at once ashamed of myself and obscurely comforted. ''I'll remember. Thanks for breakfast, Tick-Tick. And if . . . if I told anybody about it, I'd tell you.''

'' 'If' would make water run uphill.'' She followed me to the door, out of the reflexes of the perfect host, I thought. But at the door she took hold of my shoulder, her thin fingers almost cool through my T-shirt, and turned me gently around. She spoke carefully in the language of the other side of the Border, putting all the endings on as a courtesy. ''You do what you are, and you become what you do.'' She looked away swiftly, then back at me. ''Wear fortune as a coat, true friend.''

I wanted to reply in kind, but my accent is terrible. I looked her in the eye and nodded, and saw that she understood.

Downstairs, the artist was up and working on the tapestry. It was Luigi, Weegee for short, a halfie who lived on the first floor.

''Morning, Weegee. How's Clarice?''

He grinned, showing the gap where one of his upper front teeth was missing. ''Cool. We're back together.''

''Congratulations.'' Since Weegee and Clarice broke up about once every seventy-two hours, sometimes for as much as a whole day, I didn't feel bad about not knowing they'd done it this time.

He finished a row of the tapestry, and pressed the new work up tight against the old with his hands. One thin lock of his carrot-colored hair swung braided in front of his right ear. He was wearing cut-offs and a pair of leather work gloves, and seeing the film of sweat on his white skin and the bunching and rolling of his shoulder muscles, I realized the weight of the rope he was working with, and how much effort it was to push and pull it through the weave.

"Looks good," I said, inadequately.

"Uh? Oh, thanks."

"What's it about?"

"This? It's 'The Death of Young Andrew.' "

"I don't know that one."

"No?" He squinted at me thoughtfully. "D'you like movies?"

"Yeah."

"Well, it's kinda the Brian De Palma flick of ballads. Great betrayal and vengeance stuff. And generation versus generation, too, 'cause this girl's father lets her die 'cause his pride is wounded, but her brothers avenge her. Anyway, they leave this guy Andrew with his arms and legs broken and Dad's gold in his lap and tell him he can count the money 'til the wolves come for him. It's great."

"Yum," I agreed. "How much longer 'til it's finished?"

"Couple days. The weaving goes pretty fast, but I haveta find some stuff for the edging. Like, I want to get a skull. Human or elf, doesn't matter."

"In this town, it's either easy or impossible. Good luck." I settled my sunglasses on my nose and went out into the sullen heat of midday.

When I got to my building, the Spitfire was in front of it. I could see the top of Rico's head past the driver's side seatback, and both her feet, crossed at the ankles, propped on the passenger's side door. When I came closer, I saw that she was lying with her arms crossed, and that she'd substituted very dark shades for the Night

Peepers. I couldn't tell if her eyes were closed, which I suppose was part of the point. She looked pretty comfortable for someone trying to nap sitting sideways in two bucket seats.

She was wearing a gray tank top, and I still couldn't see any tan lines. There were freckles on her collar bone. It suddenly occurred to me that cops tan by the same method the rest of us use—by lying in the sun with little or no clothing on—and it was as if all of reality shifted an eighth of an inch to one side and snapped back. I swallowed the lump in my throat before I spoke. "I'm surprised you didn't just wait in my apartment."

Her mouth twitched. "I'm sorry, I'm sorry, I'm sorry. I was housebreaking without a warrant. I'll never do it again. Any more baggage?"

"Baggage?"

"It's too hot to snipe at each other."

I stood on the sidewalk staring down at her. Last night Sunny Rico had been a tough, driven cop in a sleek, strange car, with a grip on the scruff of my neck. Now she was . . . still that. But her smile was relaxed, her body loose, and her damned car showed its age with the glamour of darkness off it.

"You're off duty," I hazarded.

Rico slid the sunglasses down her nose and frowned at me over them. "How did you know?"

"If I told you, you'd be annoyed. What are you doing here if you're off duty?"

"I feel a strong urge to say, 'If I told you, you'd be annoyed.' I may be off duty, but Linn isn't. And Linn's combing over last night's apartment building even as we speak. I don't know about you, but I'm crazy to find out what he's found out."

"Huh." I tried to look nonchalant. But after telling

the Ticker about the night's adventures, and hearing her speculations about the mechanics of dropping ceilings with magic, I actually did want to know.

"You should put on a pair of pants, though."

*You better not be blushing,* I warned myself. "I'm wearing pants."

"No, you're not. You're wearing the oldest pair of cutoffs in the known universe. If I'm seen in public with you, people will think I've gone back to living on the street."

"Jeez, nobody likes the way I dress this morning." I left her waiting in the car and went upstairs to put on jeans. I did it because I wasn't sure where we were going or how long we'd be there. It had, I was certain, nothing to do with how cops get tans.

We laid a little rubber leaving the curb; Rico drove like a reckless motorcyclist, which caused me to wonder what she'd driven before she'd dedicated her free time to the Spitfire. As the dusty trees of Liberation Row flicked by, she asked, "What's the going rate, anyway? I said I'd pay you for this."

"It's usually by the job. I'm beginning to think I ought to charge by the hour for this one."

"By the day, anyway. Why can't I just ask you to find the guy responsible for making and distributing this shit?"

"I don't know. It just doesn't work that way."

"What way *does* it work?"

I shrugged. "I don't—I'm not sure," I finished, since no matter how stupid this line of questioning made me feel, at least I didn't have to repeat myself. "I know there's a certain amount of . . . specificity involved. I mean, you don't know if the one you're looking for is male or female or human or elf or halfie. You don't even know if you're looking for one person or a whole crew. How do you know the person who makes it is the same one who distributes it? One of us, at least, has to know what we're asking me to find."

"But once it works, it's guaranteed?"

I spent a city block rolling my answer around in my mouth, deciding whether I was going to say something I'd suspected for a while, but hadn't quite wanted to hear out loud. It seemed like the right time. "I think I'm sort of like a polygraph. I think there's an illusion of—there's a word I want—lack of bias, objectivity, I guess—that isn't necessarily there if the thing I'm looking for is a little . . ." I shrugged. ". . . Subjective."

Rico gave me a sideways look from behind her sunglasses. "Uh. Give me some help here. Got an example?"

"Yeah. In the end, when we were trying to figure out who was the real, no-shit mastermind behind the murder at Danceland, Wolfboy asked me to find the person who met two different sets of qualifications, because he knew that the person who met both was the one behind the killing. So I found that person. But Wolfboy was already pretty sure she had done it; he was just looking for confirmation. Did I find the person who fit the specs, without bias? Or did I just locate the person that Wolfboy had in mind?"

"In that particular case, it was the same thing," Rico reminded me, but she said it slowly, as if examining my theory as she spoke.

"Yeah. I was lucky that time, wasn't I?"

We took a corner as if Rico expected the car to be hinged in the middle. "You're telling me you don't trust this gift of yours."

"I'm telling you it's not trustworthy. You should keep that in mind."

"Fine. I'll do that. Just don't let it screw you up."

I slid as far down in the passenger seat as the harness allowed—not far—and sighed. I don't think she could hear me.

She turned at last onto the street where we'd parked the night before, across from the apartment building. Former apartment building. In the brassy light of midday, I couldn't imagine anyone having left the top floor under his own power. Certainly not me. Then I remembered last night's storm, and realized that things like the spill of bricks into the street, casual as a drift of sand, might be new since I'd been here last.

Rico said something fierce and explosive that I didn't catch; then she seconded my thoughts. "Linn must have been biting the heads off nails. No telling how much the rain washed away last night."

"Then why wasn't he out here last night?"

Rico gave me a look. "Unless you want the Vulcan Nerve Pinch, don't say that to him."

She slung herself over the top of the door and strode across the street, and I followed her.

Linn met us on the sidewalk with no sign of rust stains on his teeth; if he was angry, it was some kind of incalculable emotion that I didn't know how to read. He wore a faded red sweatshirt with the bottom half and the sleeves lopped off, mud-stained jeans, and, twisted up and knotted around his waist but still recognizable, the official silver jacket.

"Such things as might have been here, the sky only knows," he said, making all the syllables crisp. His partner knew him pretty well, after all. "Sweet Nature herself wipes away this devil's tracks." There was a chalk line on the pavement in front of the ex-building; Linn stepped over it absently, like a kid who'd trained himself not to walk on sidewalk cracks. Rico did, too, just as I walked into the thing it delineated.

The sensation faded fast, but I said "Ow," anyway, and felt like a dog whose master has forgotten to hold the door for it.

"Your pardon," Linn said, on a note of genuine apology. He held both hands over the chalk line about a door's width apart, and spoke a sweet, ringing sentence. "You shall have passage now, anywhere along the line."

He led the way into the still-soggy front hall. All the doors to the apartment units stood open now, and several people in various quantities of silver were moving chunks of brick and second-storey floor joists and scraps of faded wallpaper and frowning over them. One woman with crisp black hair and long almond eyes looked up at us and shouted, "Dammit, Linn, put hats on 'em!"

"They're ours," he told her.

"Never mind, then," she growled. "Nobody cares if the public servants get brained with a brick."

"Mind your footing on the stairs," Linn warned us. "We've bound what we can, but the Border is an unchancy place for knots."

Rico started up the stairs after him, but I lagged in the doorway and asked the black-haired woman, "Don't the public servants themselves care?"

"Huh?"

"About being brained with a brick."

"Oh." The dust on her face cracked with her sudden grin. "But if we did anything about it, people might think we were scared of dying."

There was a scuffed yellow hard hat propped rakishly on the newel post. I put it on as I went up the stairs.

The sun was beating down in the apartment where Rico and I had found the note. On first look, I thought the mess we'd left behind us the night before was undisturbed. Then I recognized that the whole business had been shifted just enough to form a grid, which had then been examined with downright archaeological sensibilities.

"Your apparition," Linn began, "manifested here, by the inner doorway?"

Rico nodded. "Table with the note on it over there, in the middle of the room."

"The remains of it are there still. We found nothing by the door; if there was some small thing to serve as vessel to the spell until it was freed, it was destroyed or carried away."

Rico clenched one hand, as if she would have liked to whack something with it.

"But see what we did find, in fallen plaster." Linn handed her a clear plastic bag, and she frowned. I leaned over her shoulder for a better look.

"I'll be damned," I said. "The Ticker was right." I snagged it out of her hand without thinking, for a closer look.

Before Rico could object, Linn asked sharply, "You know its nature?"

"It's a photocell. Tick-Tick does things with 'em now and then. This one's smaller, though, and the part that picks up the light looks sort of burnt."

"Indeed. It was made to use only once, to close the contact in a circuit. In *that* circuit." And he pointed at the remaining ceiling above my head.

His excavations in the plaster had exposed it, or enough of it: the light-gauge covered wire, the battery holder that now dangled empty, and the four terminal ends, only one charred black where something explosive had been attached and gone off. Three more that hadn't fired.

"Had the wind not turned and brought a fey spirit with it, we'd have taken your bodies from out of this wrack."

Four ceiling beams blown loose at once could have dropped the whole top of the building into this room. Linn's assessment seemed pretty reasonable. A quick image crossed my mind: Charlie's broken body wearing my bloodied clothes. I felt as if someone had twisted a stick in my guts.

"I don't get it," Rico said. "Why the indirect route? Why not just plant a bomb and blow us up?"

Linn looked startled. It was an expression so much like one of Tick-Tick's that I smiled. He'd been so busy unravelling the fine points of "how" that "why" had never come up. The Ticker was the same way, given some complex puzzle to work out, or some delicate structure to assemble—

There are times when the light bulb goes on over your head so emphatically that you can hear the pull chain click. "Because it wasn't meant for us."

They both turned to stare at me, but it was Linn who said, "So sure?"

"Well, it couldn't have been. Charlie's keys led us here. But Charlie's keys wouldn't have done jack if I hadn't been involved, and I wasn't involved until maybe an hour before we showed up at this place. And that," I finished, pointing at the wires and battery holder, "wasn't set up in an hour, was it?"

"Indeed, no. The ceiling was patched after the trap was laid, and there was no sign that the fallen plaster was still wet."

"So who was it for?" Rico asked.

I shrugged. "They were Charlie's keys."

She thought about that. "Okay. This starts to make sense. Assume our illusion-maker doesn't realize that I'm watching Charlie already. Also understand that if somebody blows up a building, even in Soho, we all kind of notice, but that a building falling down from rot and old age is common enough that we wouldn't think much about it. Whoever it is wants to dispense with Charlie *and* not attract too much attention to him *post mortem*. So, a shame about him being in that old building when it collapsed, or, gee, his friends warned him about being stoned on top of tall things."

"So this was just the leftovers." I fingered the photocell through its plastic bag. "But why was it still here? Once Charlie was dead . . ."

"You already explained that. They thought they had plenty of time. They didn't know we had you."

Linn was contemplating me with a sort of interested pity, much like his reaction when I'd passed out in the morgue. "You have led us to a place we should not have found. You have brought Charlie's last moments out of the past, and with them, the proof that his death was not an accident. Our quarry will know soon, if he does not yet, that you are a danger to him."

I suppose I'd already figured that out. Or at least, I would have shortly, just as soon as I could have seen past the puzzle itself to the consequences. I was getting to be as bad as Tick-Tick.

"Why the note?" Rico said, and I tried to concentrate on that. "There wasn't anything like it on the Pigeon Cloisters roof. And why a melodramatic, "So long, sucker" message, anyway?"

"Let me see it," said Linn.

I left them with their heads, sandy-brown and silver-

white, bent over the battered square of note paper, and
picked my way through the rubble to the stairs. I sat
down on the top one. I didn't know what I felt, besides
afraid, and even that didn't seem to have any shape or
direction. No, not true. There was one direction that always seemed to attract fear and anger, and it could be
best described as: If I wasn't able to find things, I wouldn't
be in this mess. It was almost comforting to have such a
familiar cause for my problems.

The black-haired woman appeared at the bottom of
the stairs. "You mean they're still at it?" she said when
she saw me.

"Whatever it is. Yeah."

She climbed the stairs and dropped down next to me.
"You're not ours, are you? No matter what the hell Linn
says."

"Well, I'm scared of dying and I don't care who
knows it."

"I mean, you're not a cop."

"No. No matter what Linn says."

"Didn't think so. Civilians get kind of a look in the
presence of the constabulary. You know, more of the
whites of the eyes showing."

"No, I didn't know that."

"Hey, nothing personal. It's a reasonable reaction,
anyway. I mean, Jesus, who comes to Bordertown to be a
cop? It makes sense to figure all the Silver Suits have a
spoke loose."

"Do you?" I asked. I half expected to see a bottle la-
belled "Drink Me" on the step at my feet. "Have a spoke
loose, I mean."

"Oh, yeah, but just barely. I've only been in it for a
year and a half. But you have to wonder about Linn—

hell, I never heard that the elves have anything like police, when they're at home. So why would he do this?"

"He probably started with crosswords," I said, "and got hooked on the harder stuff as he went along."

She frowned at me.

"Sorry. He reminds me of a friend of mine, is all."

"Would your friend become a Suit?"

"She'd be anything that gave her enough of the kind of problems she likes to solve. I don't think she has a choice."

"Maybe that's it. But his partner—that was her, wasn't it—she's got *two* spokes out."

"How's that?"

"I hear her father was a cop, back in the World. I mean, if you've seen this job up close, you've gotta be crazy to want it. And who the hell ever heard of somebody coming to B-town to be just like her *parents?*"

I thought about that one. Certainly nobody I knew had run away to join the family business. But maybe it was something that happened when you got older. Which made me wonder how old Sunny Rico was, anyway . . .

"By the way, I'm Kathy Hong."

I shook her extended hand. "Is there a rank with that?"

"Nah. Some stations use 'em, especially on the Hill. Maybe they're cops because they all miss ROTC or something. And sometimes down here you'll tack a rank onto your name if you think it'll scare somebody into being helpful. But mostly if it's anything, it's job description more than rank. Detective, Patrol, stuff like that. And you're . . ."

"I'm called Orient."

"I've heard of you! You're the Finder, right? You

found a Taylor twelve-string for a friend of my room-
mate's, once."

"I vaguely remember that." I shifted a little on the
stair tread.

"I always figured from your name that you'd be, you
know, not a round-eye. No offense."

"No offense. It's the other meaning of 'orient,' as in,
'to find a direction.' "

She smiled, a strangely acute and piercing expression.
"Have you found one?" she asked.

"Yes," I said. "Yes, I have."

Rico came out of the apartment then. "Linn says
there's nothing fancy in the note—paper, ink, and no
clue about the writer. Would you mind doing your thing,
here, and seeing if there's anything you can pick up?"

Kathy Hong looked first at Rico, then at me as I stood
up. Her eyebrows were raised; the corners of her mouth
were raised and compressed as if something about the
scene at the top of the stairs was terribly funny. *Yes, I have
found a direction. Yes.* From out of the empty spot in my
chest, I said, "It's twenty-five bucks a day, or the equivalent, in currency or trade goods. Thirty in credit. And I
don't charge you for days you don't use me."

There was no reading Rico's expression. "That's fair,"
she said at last.

I pulled off the hard hat, handed it to Kathy Hong,
and combed my fingers once through my hair. "Let's see
the note."

# AND MILES TO GO
# BEFORE WE SLEEP

S OMETIMES IT SEEMS as if any trick will work once, in the Borderlands. Unfortunately, there are so many times when you can't make them work again. "Where does this belong?" seemed to be one of those. The piece of paper in Rico's hand sat like a—well, like a piece of paper, and didn't tell me anything more than what was written on it. I even took it from her and held it, though contact had never made any difference before.

In daylight, it had more character. It was a thick sheet, the surface not perfectly smooth, with one thin and ragged edge. Between the creases and dirt from last night's mistreatment I could see threads, hairs really, of red and blue, that seemed to be part of the paper. And the writing, of course. It was still densely black; none of those perfectly-made letters had smeared or scuffed. Very crisp, clear, careful.

And inert. If this piece of paper belonged anywhere that it knew about, it wasn't talking. I wandered across the landing and leaned on the stair rail. It quivered ominously, so I gave that up.

The direct approach? Not to be scorned. I fingered the paper and wondered where the person was who'd written on it. Nothing, nothing.

Rico cleared her throat behind me and said, "Progress report?"

"Garbage in, garbage out. I warned you. This is a little subjective."

"Could have fooled me. What's subjective about where a piece of paper came from?"

I wondered if she could tell from my face that she'd just made me feel a right idiot. I shouldn't have been embarrassed; "Where did this come from?" could have been the wrong question just as easily as any of the ones I'd already asked. It wasn't, though.

"Thataway," I said.

"Oh, goodie. Let's go there."

"Criminy. I might have a fix on a paper mill," I warned her.

"Very true. Don't you want to know?"

"I don't have a lot of choice now. Silken cord goes yank, yank. It's a compulsion."

"And it might not be a paper mill. It might be a nice box of stationery in someone's desk drawer, and I would be one happy copper. Wouldn't you like that?" She clattered down the stairs without regard to their structural integrity.

Kathy Hong looked after her and said cheerfully, "Two spokes."

"Oy," I replied, and followed Rico out into the sun.

My guidance system was suggesting we head uphill. It was too soon to tell if it wanted us to go Up Hill. I let

Rico's idea of how to leave the curb press me back into the bucket seat and said, "So your father was a cop?"

I got a sidelong glance from Rico that wasn't quite long enough to affect our trajectory. Eventually she said, "I take it Ms. Hong is a busybody."

"Is it supposed to be a secret?"

A moment's pause. "No."

"Did he just make it look like fun? Why did you become a cop, too?"

"I don't suppose it's occurred to you that it's none of your business?"

"Just making small talk," I said, while realizing that this was, maybe, not the smallest subject in the world, after all.

"I had a teddy bear in a policeman's uniform. It affected me deeply."

Something about the voice she'd said that in suggested that she didn't want to hear so much as an "Oh" out of me. But silence didn't seem like the right response, either. "Oh," I said.

Rico braked hard and pulled the Spitfire to the side of the road, which made the motorcyclist behind us yell something as he gunned past. I saw my face twice in her sunglasses as she said, "I didn't ask you about your childhood."

"Only once."

"I apologized."

I felt like slime—not all at once, but with a steadily growing conviction as I thought back over the last few minutes. "That's a fact," I said at last. "I'm sorry. Try turning right at the next street."

Right was good; in fact, all of my directions were good, which was the only good thing in the car for about a quarter of an hour. In that time, we drove out the side

of the city proper, into a formerly residential tangle of
streets that were too close to the Border to survive un-
touched when Faerie came back. Most of the neatly grid-
ded lots had gone back to wilderness. A few still held the
ruins of ramblers and two-story Colonials, the kind of
houses I could tell you the floor plans of without ever
going inside. And there were, occasionally, structures
that had been changed by whatever non-human agency
turned off the lights periodically even now in Bordertown. I saw a tower, bent over like an old woman,
wrapped in mauled vinyl siding and topped with the remains of asphalt shingles. One house seemed to be in
perfect condition, if you can say that about a house that
appeared to have been turned inside out like a T-shirt in
the laundry. Its exterior materials were compacted in a
tidy cube from which all its rooms radiated. The chenille
bedspread in the master bedroom was white, unmarked,
and smooth.

"I hate neighborhoods like this," Rico said suddenly,
breaking our long silence. I jumped because of that, and
because I'd been thinking the same thing.

"Too weird?" I tried to keep my voice perfectly neutral.

"Not weird enough. Is it much further?"

Did that mean that she hated them as I did, for the
memories they evoked? I'd never lived here; but I'd lived
in that place just like it that existed in every North American town, all those places named for trees that had never
grown there, for features the terrain had never had.
Maybe Rico had lived there, too. That would mean we
had a lot to say to each other, or nothing at all. "I can
never really tell how far. Just direction. Make this left."

She did. It was a dead end, but that was all right; I
knew we were there. Something had been grandfathered

into the zoning here, to allow for the neat little farm that had once occupied the end of the street. Now all that stood was the barn, set far back from the road, its white paint nearly gone, and a scramble of weathered board fence. The "KEEP OUT!" painted on the barrier across the overgrown drive was more recent.

"Ping," I said. "You Are Here."

"Can't argue with that," Rico replied. Her voice had changed. It was familiar, though, a peculiar intense calm, and I remembered it suddenly from last night, when we'd arrived at the derelict apartment building. I looked, and found she had her revolver in her hand, broken open to check the chambers. To judge from her face, she'd never had an emotion in her life.

"Is this going to be dangerous?"

The sunglasses swivelled to reflect me again. "We hope not."

"Damn straight we do."

"Do you know how to drive a stick?"

"What? What does that—"

"If you don't get a signal from me one way or another in fifteen minutes, or if someone comes out of there who isn't me, drive back to Chrystoble Street and tell 'em what happened, where I am." She had a shoulder holster in her lap, with her copper card fastened to it. She shrugged into it as I watched.

In other words, I was supposed to stay in the car. I should have been relieved, and I was, really I was. I was also offended. I resolved to ignore that.

I watched her go, bent low and moving quickly along the fence line. Her gray tank top and faded fatigue pants blended pretty well with the scenery. There was a row of trees behind the barn that I thought she might be making for. The trees weren't evenly spaced, or all the same age;

they looked as if they were growing there because they felt like it, and not because someone had planted them. Trees sprouted up like that beside creeks and riverbeds.

The sun drilled down on me, and I wished Rico's taste hadn't run to convertibles. Of course I could drive a stick. Though she wouldn't know that from her police report, that the damned enormous Chrysler had had a manual transmission. I remembered the awful grinding sound when I tried to yank it into reverse too fast, in the tight space between the ditches, and the way the tall grass had stood colorless and shivering in the headlight glare.

At the barn door, something moved, and slapped me back into the present. I flinched; then I saw it was Rico. My heart banged away in my chest anyway. She made a quick, short gesture with one hand that I finally figured out was "come here." I thought for an instant about traps, before I realized how stupid that was, and climbed out of the car and over the barrier.

Halfway there I smelled it, and thought of wet laundry. Steam and starch and a whiff of bleach. There was a steady thumping sound coming from inside, and an odd mid-range hum, and a sudden clang of metal. I came up to Rico with my eyebrows raised. She just nodded me in the door, her face impassive.

I was sun-dazzled, even after I took my shades off, and it took me a moment to register what was being done in the barn. Then I murmured to Rico, "I win."

"Close only counts in horseshoes," she answered. She had taken off her sunglasses, too.

"What do you mean? It's a paper mill."

"Don't tell that to him," Rico said, jerking her head at the figure coming toward us.

He was very large. Not just tall, but with shoulders big even in proportion to his height, and with great thick arms poking out of his T-shirt. His hair was thick and black, and even damp went every which way; his eyebrows formed a single unpruned hedge across the field of his forehead; his moustache bristled further forward than his nose; and his beard seemed to continue over his throat, down the neck of his shirt, and out the armholes to his wrists. Beneath the hair, his exposed skin was apple-red. For a moment I wondered if he'd dyed it. Then I remembered the big vat behind him with its cumulus cloud of steam, and realized he was just lightly parboiled. His T-shirt read, "Art doesn't kill. Artists do." He was scowling at us.

"You a copper, too?" he said to me as he came up, in a voice that shook the cross-timbers.

"No," Rico answered for me. "He's an independent contractor. Orient, this is Dave."

"Just Dave?" I asked, probably unwisely.

"Orient. You're the one who finds shit." He said it with a little snort. "Anybody who loses something deserves to be without it."

"That's kind of harsh."

"I don't owe anything, and nobody can make me do anything. You know many people in this town can say that?"

I was careful not to look at Rico.

"Did you make this?" she asked, and handed him the mauled piece of paper.

Dave took it to the door we'd come in. I noticed that he barely glanced at the writing; he turned it over to its relatively unmarked side, rubbed his thumb across it, then held it up to the light. "Yeah, I did. I remember this batch, with the silk fibers in it. And it's got part of my watermark. See?" He held it up for me, because I was closer. "Somebody cut this in half, but you can see the fish head at the edge."

The irregular pale areas, like reverse shadows cast on the paper, resolved themselves into pouting mouth, an X where the eye would be, the curve of cheek and gill. "How do you do that?" I asked him.

"Huh?" Dave said. Rico widened her eyes at me. Even I was a little surprised, actually.

"The watermark. I've always wanted to know how they're done."

Half an hour later, I knew that. I'd also had a short history of watermarks, and what Dave assured me was a quick description of the ancient Chinese method of papermaking, and an explanation of the differences between that and the process used in Europe during the Renaissance, which Dave assured me was very close to what he was doing, and who the really great papermaking artists were and why, and how a high percentage of cloth fibers in the pulp made better paper, and that a deckle was the wooden frame in which the pulp was confined to form sheets, that the stretched screen the pulp was spread on was a mold, and that the rough edge on the piece we'd brought him was called a "deckle edge" because it was just as it came out of the deckle, without trimming.

I got a tour of the equipment, with Rico following along, looking bemused. The steaming vat was full of a heaving white porridge of broken-down cloth and old paper. The heat from that, and from the wood fire burning in a stone-lined pit underneath it, kept me from getting close, but I craned my neck. In the vat a four-bladed wooden paddle went round and round, attached to a wooden shaft turned by a cluster of enormous wooden gears (they seemed to be the source of the humming and clunking), which were themselves turned by another wooden shaft that disappeared out through the back wall. The shafts looked like young tree trunks, hand-hewn.

"Got a water mill out there in the stream to turn it," Dave explained. "If I had to stir the stock by hand, it'd slow me way down. This way I can mold and roll one batch of stock while another one cooks."

There was another vat, not as hot, where the stock was thinned with water before it was scooped into the mold, and basins for sizing and starch. There was a press made from what looked like the timbers of another barn, with a huge hand screw on top, to force the water out of a stack of formed sheets. Another press was mounted with a cylinder that would squeeze the surface of a sheet down to a smooth finish. The cylinder bore the slightly raised double-dead-fish logo at regular intervals on its polished face. On the other side of the room was a wide table with a heavy draw knife mounted in a frame, to trim the sheets to size.

My hair hung damp and curling in my eyes. I wiped it back and asked Dave, "Is there anybody else in Border-town who makes paper?"

"A few people. Nobody with this big a setup. And no-body as high-quality as me."

"Why are you doing it all the way out here?"

"Takes lots of water," he said, waving one platter hand at the vats. "Got the stream right back of the barn to pump from."

"There's the Mad River, in town."

He made a face. "I make white paper. Nothing but. You don't make white paper from water the color of cherry goddamn soda. I'd have to put all kinds of bleach in the stock, and that's bad for the paper, and bad for the river. The little bit I use, I don't like. That's why I got the dead fish watermark, to remind me not to fuck up."

I'm sure there have been drug dealers and serial killers with environmental consciences, but I couldn't make myself believe that Dave had any active involvement in the plot Rico wanted to bust. For the first time I recalled that this was where the paper was *from*, and I understood that someone like Dave could make paper that, no matter what its subsequent history, would always bear his magical imprint, would always name him, and this place, as its origin. In spite of his opinion of my talent, I wanted to tell him that his paper remembered him. Then I looked around again, and decided that he already knew that.

In an elaborately patient voice, Rico interrupted. "I don't suppose you remember who you sold this particular kind of paper to."

Dave lifted the awning of his eyebrow. "That batch was five hundred sheets. That's two thousand quarter-sheets, which is my usual trim for writing paper. A little under fourteen reams, if anybody bought it by the ream, which nobody does. I sell it a couple hundred quarter-sheets at a time to shops around town, then some to the big merchant families and business houses, and to individuals sometimes in quantities of maybe twenty-five or fifty. Hell, the town council's bought stationery from me. Do you want the whole list?"

Rico sighed. "Not really, but I'll take it, anyway. I have to check 'em all."

Dave looked closely at her, for the first time, I think. "What the hell is this about?"

"Somebody is making and distributing some stuff that kills people, and I want to find and stop the somebody. That note on your paper was part of a trap laid to kill a guy who might have talked about it. Instead, it almost got my associate and me last night." She nodded in my direction.

"My paper?" Dave echoed, his voice surprisingly small. He looked as if someone had told him his kid had shot a liquor store clerk. He shook his head slowly, twice. Then he glowered at Rico. "That's the other reason I live out here. I forget it sometimes."

"Why?" I asked.

"Because people suck." He turned his back on us and headed for a flight of wooden stairs up to the loft. "I'll get you my customer list. Then you can get out of here."

Conversation was formal and drastically limited after that, until Rico and I got back in the Spitfire. Then she made a U-turn in a spray of dust and gravel, and I said, "Now what?"

"Now a lot of boring flatfoot police work, unless another lead turns up." She tapped the sheaf of papers tucked between her seat and the gear shift. "I go around and talk to all of these. Which means you're out of the cop biz for a while."

We shot past the bent tower. Ahead, through the heat haze, I could see the buildings on Dragon's Tooth Hill, and past them, the suggestion of Faerie's rolling meadows and forested slopes. The Ticker had assured me that the view was a glamour, part of the barrier of the Wall, but she'd never described what it really looked like. "Different," she'd said, and we'd both changed the subject.

"Happy?" Rico's voice cut across my thoughts.

"Um? About what?"

"About being out of the cop biz."

"Oh." I shrugged against the shoulder harness. "Neutral."

"Well, that's an improvement."

"It's a job."

"Some people like their jobs. Especially people who get to be their own bosses."

I thought about that. "I'm self-employed. I'm not exactly my own boss."

"I don't get it."

"Putting this thing to work so that it feeds me, that's good. It's better than the reverse, which is when it feeds on me. But when I use it, *it's* calling the shots."

"Uh-huh. As in, 'Yank, yank.' You could quit."

Except that I didn't know any way to turn it off. Once I'd had a concussion, and my talent had gone away. It would have been a wonderful couple of days, if only the events surrounding the concussion hadn't been such a nightmare. I shook my head. "If you're already a geek, you're better off joining the sideshow and biting the heads off chickens, because at least it's a regular paycheck."

"Don't tell that to your pal Lobo. He might part your hair for you. Where'd you get the idea you're a geek?"

"I grew up with it," I said, looking at her profile. "Sort of like your teddy bear."

We were back in town; I recognized the edge of the Scandal District. She said, "I didn't mean to push your buttons."

I don't know what I would have answered, because that was when the big Norton, painted metalflake olive and cream and brilliant with original chrome, slewed out in the street next to us. Rico said something sharp and pulled over.

The motorcyclist yanked his helmet off to reveal Linn's ascetic pale face. It was bloodless to the lips this time, lines drawn sharp between the eyebrows, eyes a little wide and mouth laid tight closed.

"Sunny! There's another one," he said.

"Hell," Sunny Rico breathed, and it sounded less like an epithet than a description of the circumstances.

"Bolt Street emergency, and not much time." Linn pulled his helmet back on and throttled the Norton into the street and around the corner.

Rico turned to me. "I can't take you home right away. I'm sorry."

"It's all right," I said, suspecting that whatever was going on was not all right for somebody. We sped off in pursuit of Linn.

The clinic on Bolt Street was almost a real hospital, certainly as close as you were likely to get south of Ho. Sometimes they even charged patients for treatment, when it seemed like they could afford it. Four doctors kept their offices there for outpatients, but there were also a few recovery rooms and a surprisingly well-outfitted ER. It was outside this that Rico bumped her front wheels up over the sidewalk. I hadn't exactly been invited, but when she came flying in the door, making everyone in the hall leap back with startled looks at her shoulder holster, I was pretty close behind.

She grabbed the first person in white she came to, a middle-aged woman in tunic and trousers, and said, "You had an O.D. admitted, very recently. Where?"

"You're with Detective Linn?"

"Yes. Where?"

"That hall, third door. And who the hell are you?" she said to me, straight-arming me in the chest.

"I'm with her," I answered, and dodged past.

By the time I reached the door, the place had caught up with me. There was the smell, of course: alcohol, disinfectant, the spoiled-yeast smell of some medication; and under those, the frightening scents, the smells of sickness and wounds and fear. There was the relentless, bright light that bounced off surfaces that were easy to clean but hard, hard to look at. And the sounds, of people trying to hurry quietly, to talk of urgent things calmly, and to muffle the noise of pain as if it were a germ that could spread. I bit my tongue against a familiar twinge of anxiety and slid into the room before the door closed behind Rico.

There was a human girl in the bed. Or maybe she'd been a woman, before whatever this was had dragged her back to the helplessness of childhood. Her hair was white and thinning, but the face beneath was unlined. Her skin was the color of old paper against the pillowcase. Her eyes seemed to be retreating down blue-black tunnels in her skull, and her cheeks might have been hollowed out with spoons. Under the sheet, her body was long and bony, and the proportion of leg and arm to torso seemed wrong. She had a tube down her nose and an IV drip in her arm.

Linn was already there, his helmet on the deep windowsill, his notebook and pen out. I stopped at the foot of the bed and he looked at me, but I'm not sure he quite registered my presence.

"Is she awake?" Rico asked.

He nodded. "She's not given her name. Three other children brought her in an hour ago, left her in the hall, and ran away. She was taken straight into emergency, and has only been out these few minutes."

Rico leaned over the bed rail. Her sunglasses hung by one earpiece from the neck of her tank top, and I could see her whole face fixed on the girl in the bed, on the closed sunken eyes, as if sheer concentration could accomplish whatever it was she meant to do.

"Miss, can you hear me? Miss? I'm sorry to disturb you, but I want you to talk to me. Miss?"

The eyelids shifted, fluttered, opened. I took a step back before I could stop myself. In a network of ruby-bright broken veins, the girl's irises were the color of slightly muddied water, as if the pigment had been rinsed out of them. Her pupils were barely visible.

The girl muttered, and struggled to see Rico. Finally she said, "Oh . . . no, you're . . . oh, you're just . . . what d'you want?"

"I need you to answer some questions. Do you think you can do that?"

"A few. I'm in a hurry. I have to go soon."

"Where?"

The girl's face crumpled into a frown, and her eyes closed again. "Through the Wall. I'm in a hurry."

A muscle showed suddenly under Rico's ear, but nothing else changed. "You've been taking a drug lately. Sky-blue liquid. Where did you get it?"

A long, harsh inhalation from the pillow. "So I can get across."

"Yes. Where did you get it?"

"Come . . . follow me over. To . . . follow . . . Charlie. His name is Charlie."

Rico's eyelids dropped for a moment. "Do you know anyone else who's taking this drug? I need to find them."

The girl smiled. Her gums were bleeding. "They'll never let *you* across."

"That's all right. Just tell me who else is taking it."

"We're *all*—" the girl burst out, and stopped to swallow. Her voice was much weaker afterward. "Humans are over. Dinosaurs . . . we have to change. We *have* to . . ." Suddenly her eyes opened again, very wide. "Lady? Are you still there?" She didn't wait for Rico's answer. "Did I change? You can see, right? I changed, didn't I? Please?"

It wasn't her gums bleeding, after all. Linn jerked the cord that would call in help. I wanted to look away, but I couldn't. "Yes," Rico said. "You changed." Rico was holding her hand, and both sets of knuckles, Rico's tanned ones and the girl's papery skin, were white, white.

"I have to go soon. When I'm better. Then I can go across? Can't I?"

"Yes," said Rico. I could barely hear her. "Very soon." Three people in hospital uniform burst through the door, armed with apparatus that wasn't going to be of any use.

I bolted from the room, followed by the frail bubbling sound of the girl's breath.

I fetched up hard against the opposite wall of the hallway and slid down it, and sat on the floor with my face on my drawn-up knees. Almost immediately a man in white was crouched next to me, saying, "Do you feel faint?"

I shook my head without raising it.

"Stay here." I heard his footsteps move away, blend with others, come back. "Drink some," he said, by my ear.

It was a paper cup of water. I felt desperately guilty for attracting attention, for seeming to need care in a place where other people really did, where in a room across the hall a girl was hemorrhaging— I knocked back the water and croaked, "Thank you."

"It's what I do."

"I'm fine. I'm not really—"

"She's the third one we've had," he said, as if he thought I needed to know why he could still stand up, and talk, and think.

"They can't know," I muttered.

"They do, though. They don't care. They take it anyway, because they think maybe this time, for them, it'll work."

For one bleak, cyclonic moment, I hated elves. I hated Tick-Tick, and Linn, and every elf I knew and didn't know, for existing, for being there to envy and long for so fiercely that someone could think a lingering, ugly death was not too great a risk.

It was only a moment; I knew too much for it to last longer. Tick-Tick, if I told her about the dying girl, would find something rare and precious, take it to her second-floor window, and let it drop. Then she'd stand and stare at the wreckage. I'd seen her do it; it was what she did with a grief too big for crying. No elves I'd ever met, no matter how haughty, would believe they were due such unspeakable homage.

But someone else, who didn't know any elves, might hold that hatred for a long time, let it grow strong, and pass it on. For the first time, I began to understand the size and shape of the thing that Sunny Rico was trying to head off, in Bordertown.

"I'll be all right now," I told the nurse, and my voice was steady. "If I'm not in the way, I'd like to stay here, though."

"Were you a friend of hers?"

I shook my head. He stood up, said, "If you need anything, flag somebody down," and disappeared down the hall.

The emergency team left the room first, wheeling a gurney with an elongated shape under a stained sheet. It was a surprisingly long time after that that Rico and Linn came out. Both of them had that absence of expression that took a lot of work to achieve.

"Out of chairs?" Rico asked, when she saw me folded on the floor.

I was angry—and then I wasn't, just like that. Tick-Tick broke valuables. Rico said things like "Out of chairs?". It amounted to the same thing. I stood and kicked the cramps out of my legs.

"Want to go home?"

"Yeah."

We didn't say anything to each other between Bolt and Sentiment streets. It was a slightly different kind of silence than any of the ones we'd indulged in before. When she stopped in front of my building, I said, "Let me know if there's anything I can do."

"I will."

I scrambled over the car door and trudged up the steps. Behind me, the Spitfire moved off in what sounded like an almost sedate fashion.

I went upstairs to my apartment, pulled the uphol-stered chair over in front of the window, and sat down. After a few minutes, I got up, took one of the bottles of beer out of the icebox, and took it back with me to the chair. Then I just sat, and drank until the bottle was empty, and stared blindly at the outdoors until the light was gone.

I lunged up out of sleep in the ink-dark room, the bed-clothes tangled around me. I was sweating and making odd little noises as I breathed.

"Déjà vu," I said, and the sound of my voice in the darkness made me wish I hadn't.

It was Charlie's death *again*. Nobody had told me this would keep happening. This time I didn't even have a sympathetic cop and a flask of whiskey. I'd dreamed an-other backwards-and-headfirst dive off the belfry, the street very close and clear. Something rising up off the hot tar roof, leaping at my face. The bright, silent day, with the heat muffling everything. It was cooler on the winding stair up to the belfry, but before that, on the sidewalk, the sun bounced painfully off the paint job on a bike—

It had started earlier. It had rewound further, the replay had started earlier, and there had been a motorcycle at the scene, before Charlie went up the stairs. Not Charlie's bike, which would have been behind him as he came up the sidewalk. One with a matte-black-tubing chopper frame, and a dark-red teardrop gas tank—that was what the sun had reflected from.

*Where was that bike now?*

I groped in the dark for my clothes and pulled them on. Then I thundered down the front stairs to the street and turned north toward Chrystoble. I could find Sunny Rico, but depending on what incredibly stupid hour it was, she might not appreciate that. At the station I could tell them my news, and they could take responsibility for waking her up. Then she or someone like her could come along to help follow the invisible string that already stretched taut before me in the dark.

# SPECIAL DELIVERIES

S ENTIMENT STREET TO Chrystoble is a long walk. I had plenty of time to wish I was back in bed, and to congratulate myself for not dashing off alone to track down the mystery bike. Tick-Tick would be so proud of me; she'd once described me as the sort of person who'd try to sell magazine subscriptions where angels fear to tread.

I could feel the bike, though: My brain seemed to be leaning outward, yearning toward something off the port bow. I had real trouble keeping myself moving in the direction of the copshop. Also, not being able to scratch the ongoing itch gave the issue an artificial urgency I couldn't shake. Reasonably speaking, I could have gone back to sleep 'til noon, then trotted uptown to tell Rico (who would also have gotten a whole night's rest), and we'd still have found our next clue waiting for us when we got there. After all, why suddenly dispose of the bike three days after the deed was done? Particularly, why dispose of it in the only way I could think of that would keep me from finding it again: namely, destroying it entirely? Assuming the motorcycle had anything more to do with Charlie than having been reflected off his retinas the day he died.

As I said, that's reasonably speaking. My talent doesn't care how reasonably it's spoken to, unfortunately. I'd never have gotten back to sleep anyway.

For all the bustle and activity around the Chrystoble Street Station that particular middle of the night, it might still have been a library. I went up the broad concrete steps two at a time, which got me through the big front doors at a sufficient clip that the copper on front desk graveyard shift jumped out of his chair and dropped his book.

So I opened with "Sorry," and segued into, "I don't suppose I'm lucky enough to find Sunny Rico here?"

He sat back down, warily. "If she was still here, neither of us would be lucky. She was on until two a.m., and when she left, the whole shift believed in the Evil Eye."

I added it up for myself. If Rico had gotten up just in time for our noon meeting, she'd been awake for fourteen hours. Not so bad, if she hadn't spent all of them working. I hadn't really expected to find her there, but it would have been so easy if I had; and suddenly I wished things were a little easier. I dropped into the nearest chair, a straight one drawn up to one of the long oak tables by the wall, and hoped that my strength would catch up to me. Must have left it out on the steps.

"I'm sort of . . . I'm helping Rico with this thing she's working on." It occurred to me that she could be working on more than one thing, but the cop on duty nodded. "I've got something that might be a lead. So I thought I'd let you guys know, and you could take it from there."

"I can take a statement, but . . ." He made a paper-tossing gesture with both hands. "I've got three people out sick tonight, and I've got to hold down dispatch. I hope like hell it's not an emergency."

"It won't spoil," I assured him. I really *should* have let it wait until morning.

This guy was part of the proof that there's no such thing as a typical B-town cop. He would have looked right at home in the clothes of a working cowboy, except that his hair might have spoiled the effect when he took off his hat. Even that, I wouldn't have sworn to. For all I know, lots of cowboys have black hair an inch long, except for the horizontal strip at each temple left long and braided with seed beads close to the scalp, from the hairline to the back of the head. There was no gray in his hair, but his face had been crossed by a lot of weather. If I ran that sort of carnival booth, I'd have guessed his age at someplace in the late twenties.

"You're Orient, right?" asked the point man on the dawn patrol.

I nodded, a little surprised that he knew.

"Toby Saquash. Pleased to meet you. A lot more pleased if you help solve this fucker before Rico reams us all new assholes." I must have looked startled. He shrugged. "Sorry. She got in my face last night, is all, so it's kind of fresh. But she's been going off like a push-button lighter for the last couple weeks."

"I don't think I'll be much help with that."

"Maybe not. She should take a goddamn vacation. Ah, it's not that bad. Sorry, if she's a friend of yours . . ."

I had the feeling this had all been weighing heavily on his chest. "Not exactly."

"Yeah. She and I haven't ever been buddies, but she's okay. She's a good cop."

That hit my ears with the force of novelty. "Good

cop" wasn't a phrase in heavy rotation in Bordertown, and even Saquash used it as if he didn't use it much.

"Good, how?" I asked.

He seemed momentarily baffled. "Well . . . you know. You do your job—once you figure out what it is. It's not like there's a police academy in B-town. And you stay straight."

I wanted to tell him, no, I didn't know, but we were interrupted. The front door swung wide on the newcomer in regulation silver. He wasn't big, but the outline of him, on first glance, suggested he worked out. The second glance supplied a little softness around the belt and under the chin, but I still thought I wouldn't want to hit him in either place. Over his brown hair he wore a black baseball cap with no insignia. The hair was tied up in a ponytail that poked through the opening at the back of the cap. His face was sunburned.

"It was a tree branch," he said, in a tone of deep disgust. "Jesus Christ."

"Well, you gotta check," said Saquash.

"Hell with *I* gotta check. Let *them* check once. Practically hidin' under the counter with that goddamn empty shotgun when I got there."

"If they were that scared, you oughta be glad it was empty. They might have shot you otherwise."

"Probably would've shot themselves. And good riddance."

That was when he noticed me. A quick flush came up under the sunburn, which produced a really impressive color on his nose. Then he gave me a harder look, and turned to Saquash. "You been out bustin' 'em, or did this one turn himself in?"

Saquash shot me an apologetic glance. He replied, "He's working with Rico on her drug shake."

The sunburned cop came over and squinted at me as if I were an illegible postcard. For want of anything else to do, I stared back. He had very pale blue eyes, and the shiny streak of a scar running from the right side of his nose to the corner of his mouth. He turned back to Saquash and asked, "Snitch?"

"Jeez, Vickie, mind your manners and get a brain. Informers don't hang around at the police station."

"Goddammit, don't call me Vickie," he said mildly, as if he'd had to do it a few times before this.

"Pleased to meet you," I told the sunburned cop, in as neutral a voice as I could manage. "I'm Orient."

His brows drew together. "Ori—wait a sec. You're the mutant who finds stuff, right? How 'bout finding me a blonde babe about 38–24—"

" 'Fraid not," I said. "It doesn't work that way." The awful thing was, it did work that way. I hadn't had to field that particular joke since back in the World, when I'd had an arsenal of snappy comebacks to it. Just as well I couldn't remember any; I was sure one or two of them had gotten me hit in the face.

"Jeez, I bet Rico's even paying you. You do this for money, or dope, or what? I bet you'd find me a blonde for enough dope."

I gave up. "I'm holding out for gold, spices, and slaves. Are there more at home like you, or did your parents replace the lead water pipes?"

He thought about taking offense; I watched him do it. In the end, he laughed. "You punks down south should be more careful. Some cops don't have a sense of humor like I do."

I wanted to tell him I was relieved about that, but Saquash intervened. Probably just as well for the sake of my appealing profile.

"Vic," he said, "if you don't haul ass, you're gonna be late on the dock check. And I don't want to hear about it from Apollonius."

Vic scowled. "Pointy-eared tightwad. Wish he'd hire a security guard."

"He did. Us. Be glad it's not raining."

"Jesus. Why don't you go?"

"Because I'm catching tonight, and you're on patrol. Next week you can sit here and listen to me whine about my job, okay?"

Vic blew through his lips like a horse and tramped back toward the door. He turned when he got there and waved to me. " 'Bye, Mutant Boy. Give my love to Sunny-honey."

I thought of a good many observations I could make to Saquash, but once the door closed behind Vic, I found I was too tired to make them. I propped my forehead up in both hands.

"You okay?" Saquash asked.

"Tired. Guess I used up my second wind getting mad."

"He might have been taking it out on you; he's scared shitless of Sunny."

I would have answered, but I was occupied with a huge yawn and a violent shiver.

Saquash leaned over the table to give me a close look. I didn't feel like a postcard this time. "When did you last eat?"

I thought back. "Oh," I said wisely.

"Sheesh." He shook his head. "I'll be right back."

He swung through the door that I knew led back to that deer track of offices and the morgue. Now that I'd been reminded to add it up, I noticed that since Sunny Rico had walked into the Hard Luck, oh, maybe thirty-six hours ago, I'd had a total of seven hours' sleep and one meal. Next time I saw her, I was going to ask if she was required to display a Surgeon General's warning.

The motorcycle was now behind and to the left of me. Its nudge for my attention was beginning to feel less like a nudge than a scrape.

I was involved in some elaborate eye-and-bridge-of-nose massaging and missed his entrance; but when I opened my eyes, the tall, fatherly elf with the tightly braided hair, the one I'd seen here on my original visit with Rico, was sitting across the table. He wore a classic furrowed-brow Fred MacMurray nice-guy expression, and the immaculate silver jacket.

"Hawthorn," I said. I was pleased with myself for remembering his name. Then I was a little alarmed, thinking that there had been a rank attached that I couldn't remember. But Kathy Hong had said that they never really used them—no, she'd said they did, up on the Tooth, which was where Hawthorn hailed from. . . . That took less time to think about than it looks, but not much.

Hawthorn, thank Mab or whomever, smiled. He had really good teeth, and cross my heart and hope to die, laugh wrinkles around his eyes. Had I ever seen an elf with laugh wrinkles? "Captain Hawthorn, actually."

Well, there was my answer. "Captain. Sorry."

"No offense taken. I saw you here with Detective Rico—night before last, wasn't it? Did she introduce us?"

I certainly wasn't going to tell him that I remembered his name because Rico and I had talked about him behind his back. "No. I'm Orient." I stuck out my right hand, which is not something one usually does with elves, but I had the feeling it was appropriate with this one.

It was. He had a good firm handshake, which fit the role. Bingo—now he made sense. He might be older than most elves I knew, and have a more responsible job, but Hawthorn was as much a sucker for playacting as any of them. Darn good at staying in character, too. Wolfboy would have asked him if he'd seen Robert Preston in *This Gun for Hire.*

"I think I've heard of you," he said. "You can find things for people, can't you?"

I nodded. "That's what I've been doing for Rico. I've got a fix on something right now that might be useful."

"I see. Failing Detective Rico, will I do?"

"Nicely." I explained to him about the dream, which took considerable backtracking; he was as surprised as Linn had been that I'd snagged a memory off a corpse, and wanted all the irrelevant details. Then I told him about the black-framed bike with the red teardrop tank. He stared over my shoulder, abstracted.

"Sound familiar?" I asked.

"Possibly. Possibly . . ."

I made a reflexive gesture toward the breast pocket of my T-shirt; then I remembered I hadn't put my smokes in it before I tore out of the apartment. My lighter was in my jeans pocket, but my cigarettes were on the windowsill at home. I made a little disgusted noise.

Hawthorn missed neither the gesture nor the sound. He pulled a packet of cigarettes out of his inside breast pocket, shook one out for himself, and held out the pack.

"Herbal?"

He nodded. "Take a few to tide you over."

"Captain—*is* there an elven equivalent for a saint?" I took two, and put the extra in my T-shirt pocket.

Hawthorn smiled and lit for both of us. "I don't think so, but I understand the sentiment. You say you know where this bike is now?"

"Mmm. Thataway," I told him, with a swing of my head.

"It would help if you could be more specific." He sounded a little chilly, and I realized he thought I was withholding information.

"I can't be more specific. I only know direction, not location. I have to go out in person and find the sucker. If somebody here can go with me and do cop things when we get there, there might be something useful in it."

Hawthorn sat with his long, bony chin on his hand, looking thoughtful. "There might, indeed," he said at last. "Unfortunately, Officer Saquash can't leave the dispatch desk, as I'm sure he told you. And I'd need approval to act outside my jurisdiction. I can get it, but it will take a few hours."

"The bike should keep. And even if somebody does move it between now and then, I'll be able to follow it."

"Well," Hawthorn said. He seemed impressed. "Well. Is this feeling of yours something that wears off? Can you wait a little?"

I rubbed the bridge of my nose again, in reflex. "It wears off eventually, but eventually isn't for a while yet. In the meantime it's sort of uncomfortable. If you happen to have two aspirin and a pint of dark beer it would help a lot."

"Won't that—" He seemed to scramble for a phrase. "—make the feeling go away faster?"

"Won't matter if it does. I'll just find the bike again."

The door at the back of the room swung open to let Saquash in. He was balancing a bowl and a cup, both giving off steam. When he saw Hawthorn he stopped and stared. "Hullo, Captain. Didn't know you were still here."

"I was working too hard to make any noise, I'm afraid. What's that you've got?"

Saquash set his load down in front of me. "Food for the kid. He was starting to look fuzzy around the edges."

The food was vegetable soup, and the cup was full of genuine coffee. Well, I suppose if anybody knows where to get it when the rest of the town is short, it'll be the police.

I hope I didn't salivate visibly. I slid an ashtray over from the end of the table and snuffed my cig. "You didn't go out of your way for this, did you?"

"It was all we had left. We already ate the donuts. No, we keep a pot on pretty much all the time, for when we're too busy for breaks."

"Good grief. Thank you."

"No prob. If we run out, next shift can make their own damn lunch."

Hawthorn had watched the whole exchange closely, as if he were looking for tips on his intonation. "We can also manage some aspirin and a beer, I think. Can't we, Saquash?"

"Yes, sir. Beer's in the icebox, and aspirin's in the first aid cabinet."

Hawthorn pursed his lips faintly, eyeing Saquash. Saquash was rummaging industriously in the table's long drawer for, it turned out, a spoon. Finally Hawthorn's shoulders rose and fell a little, and he ambled off through the door at the back as if he'd always meant to do it, anyway.

Saquash gave a contained snort of laughter. "Old Prickly's a swell guy, actually," he said, and handed me the spoon. "But you have to make him run his own errands, sometimes."

I dug into the soup. It probably wasn't as good as it

seemed at the time, but that still leaves some room at the upper end. "Hawthorn's a Dragonstooth Hill guy?"

"Yep. But we let him hang around just to show how broad-minded we are. Actually, I think he's interested in Rico's illusionist, this guy you're helping her chase down. Maybe they haven't forgotten, up on the Hill, that Soho is full of their kids."

"I hadn't thought B-town cops had so many regulations."

Saquash cocked his head. "Like what?"

"Hawthorn said he had to do something to clear working outside his jurisdiction."

"Eh. That sounds like Old Prickly. It's more a courtesy than a regulation. Nobody would give him shit for pitching in, but his conscience'd bother him for months."

Then Hawthorn came back, and we had to stop talking about him. He had an unlabelled, sweaty beer bottle in one hand and the aspirin bottle in the other. From a pocket of his silver jacket he produced a ring of keys so big I wondered what he weighted the rest of the pockets with in order to get the jacket to hang so well. There was a bottle opener on the ring, with which he popped the beer. "No dark, I'm afraid," he apologized.

"Lager works, too. Thanks, Captain." I washed the aspirin down with what turned out to be a perfectly presentable pale ale. A little heavy on the hops for my taste, but I wouldn't have sent back a case.

The door to the hallway opened a little, and Vic stuck his head around the edge of it. I was startled, until I realized there was no reason why the copshop wouldn't have a back door. He took a quick survey of the room, spotted Hawthorn, made a face, and drew his head back again. The door closed behind him. I don't think Hawthorn noticed.

"Make yourself comfortable," Hawthorn said. "I've radioed for my authorization. If the call went through, there should be no trouble about it, and we can go after that motorcycle in about an hour."

Saquash caught my eye over Hawthorn's shoulder and winked.

Before Hawthorn could turn away, I asked, "Do you think this might be it?"

He raised his eyebrows.

"I mean, that the owner of the bike might be the person Rico's after."

He thought about it. "Frankly, I doubt it. This fellow seems to be too good at covering his tracks to have risked being anywhere near High Street when his trap was sprung."

"Good." When Hawthorn looked surprised, I added, "Rico would be ticked if this turned out to be it, and she wasn't there."

I finished the soup, the beer, and the coffee while Saquash popped in and out of the room on various errands, and finally disappeared altogether. Hawthorn sat at another table with a pile of paper. I felt much better after the food. Relaxed. And after all, who'd mind if I put my head down and caught a nap? Surely they'd give me a poke if I started snoring.

I closed my eyes, and opened them on a different room, with a window across from me that was letting in the commotion that birds make just before dawn. I was lying on a cot in a room the size of Rico's office. The rest of the furniture was a stack of cardboard file boxes along one wall. I was only slightly alarmed, because I couldn't think fast enough or well enough to figure out what there was to be alarmed about. When I sat up, my head did the breast stroke, but the rest of me was fine. I stumbled to the door and out into the hall.

It looked as if I was still in the station house, so I tried drawing a bead on the front room. I managed to follow the trail without actually running into any walls. At last I pushed through a familiar-looking door, and the tug on my brain went dormant again.

The first of the morning shift must have just come in; a blond, slightly chubby guy in his thirties and a halfie woman with forest-green hair and a Chinese dragon tattoo were passing papers back and forth while they dunked their tea bags. Vic was there; he was sitting backwards on a chair talking to the first two cops. I couldn't tell from what I caught if he was filling them in on the night's events or airing his prejudices.

Hawthorn was at one of the big oak tables, cradling a coffee cup. Just for a moment, he wore the closed, stony expression that highborn elves sometimes slip into, when they're not being social. Then his eyes met mine, and grew wider.

"Sun and shadow, you're awake! Are you all right?" At the alarm in his voice, the other two looked up as well.

"Hey, Sleeping Beauty!" Vic called out. "You movin' in here, or what?"

"Bad cop," said the green-haired woman without looking up from her papers. "No promotion."

I ignored them both. "I'm fine," I said to Hawthorn. "Why didn't somebody wake me up?"

"We tried," Hawthorn said. "We couldn't."

I frowned at him, trying to make sense of that. I'm not a heavy sleeper, particularly.

"We tried quite hard, in fact. Finally Officer Saquash and I carried you in and put you on the cot, and he headed for home. I've been trying to wake you every hour or so, but it wasn't doing a bit of good. I'd nearly resolved to get a doctor."

"No, I don't think I need a doctor." No question, though; I still wasn't exactly firing on all cylinders. I once heard that it takes four hours for a bear's body temperature to get back up to normal after a winter in hibernation. I felt as if I were about two-and-a-half, maybe three hours warmed up. I sat down in one of the straight chairs.

Hawthorn checked my pulse in fine professional style. "Have you had reactions like this to alcohol before?"

"Ye gods, it had better not be a reaction to alcohol. No. Maybe I'm allergic to something. Maybe it's just that I was so short of sleep."

He shook his head. "I suppose it could be. Look, there's only an hour or two before Rico comes in. At this point, I think the best thing for you to do is go home and get a little more rest. I'll send her to you as soon as she comes in."

"I don't know. I . . ." To be honest, I was a little scared. Those of us who are rarely sick are inclined to panic whenever our bodies let us down. But somewhere out there (I didn't ask for it; I was careful not to) was a motorcycle. It might not have anything to do with anything. Except, except—Oh, hell. Hawthorn had spoken with the Wise Voice of Benevolent Authority, and besides, he was right. I would wait for Rico at home.

I stood up. "As soon as she gets in, okay?" I said.

Hawthorn nodded. "Immediately. She'll say you did exactly the right thing."

"I hope so," I muttered. As I went out the door, I made an acknowledging gesture at the other three cops. The two new ones raised their teacups to me. Vic said,

"See ya, Mutant Boy." I blew him a kiss, but I didn't have the nerve to wait for a reaction.

Dawn was just about to spill over the edge of the horizon. The sky was battleship gray, and if there wasn't yet enough light to read by, there soon would be. The air was moist with a little cutting edge of coolness. It was like menthol in my throat and lungs, and I took in lots of it. That, and the exercise of walking, brought me closer to awake. The more awake I was, of course, the more the sense of unfinished business nagged at me.

I *had* to go find the damn motorcycle. If I found it, I could give Rico the address when she came 'round to my place, and go back to sleep. I wouldn't do anything about it by myself; in fact, I would try not to be seen in the vicinity of the bike, for fear someone would get nervous and make the thing disappear before the cops got there. Nothing too demanding. Just locate it and go home. That seemed to dispose of every objection I could think of. I hoped it covered the ones that Rico or the Ticker might have, on the grounds of either good police work or my personal safety.

Now, where . . . ah. Thataway. I turned off Chrystoble, following my muse. I felt better already.

I know, I know. Any reasonable person (and even I, now) will look at the decision to go find the bike and think, "Hey, what was that funny noise? Guess I'll go down into the dark basement alone and check it out." And that's not the only decision I've ever made that would cause one to think that. In this case, I plead exhaustion and obsession, and can only tell you that it seemed like a swell idea at the time.

It was a long walk. Still, I'd had some food, and by whatever cause, I'd had some sleep. I felt a little drowsy and inattentive, but even that was fading away. So I hiked into what was once the warehouse district, before Faerie came back and changed everything about who lived in B-town, and where, and for what reasons. I was passing under one of the old freeway ramps, looking up through a hole in the concrete at the pearly gray of the sky, when I realized I'd seen that hole before. Tick-Tick and I had come this way, in search of her stolen wrench. How long ago? A couple of days?

The further I went on the string that tied me to the black-and-red motorcycle, the more things I recognized. *Nah, couldn't be,* I thought, just before I turned the corner and stopped in sight of Walt Felkin's bunker-like house.

Well, how unlikely was it? One unsavory Townie (Charlie) had associated himself with Rico's illusionist. Why not another one? Especially one like Walt, with a reported eye for the main chance and the fast buck, and no reported qualms about anything that might have to be done to lay hands on them. In short, a lot like Charlie.

While I thought about all that, I did have the sense to step off the pavement into a pass-through between two buildings, across the street from Felkin's place. I'd resolved not to be obvious about this, after all.

I leaned against the bricks under a broken fire escape. Water ran down the middle of the passage, headed for a storm drain in the street. Too much to be left over from night-before-last's rainstorm; someone on the block was emptying a holding tank. That meant someone was around, and awake, and I should be careful about being seen.

Of course, I couldn't be sure that Walt had any direct contact with the illusionist. He might be fencing the bike for a friend of a friend. He might be repairing it, or repainting it. He might have bought it from someone. Hell, the blasted thing might just be parked next to his property. An actual sight of the bike might tell me more. And whatever Walt's relationship to Rico's case, he was at least a real, live person who could answer questions.

I went further down the pass-through. There was a sort of courtyard, that was really only a widening of the alley, at the heart of the block. Old loading docks yawned open above the street, their doors long ago broken down, their head-high concrete aprons crumbling. The only signs of habitation were three cardboard boxes of empty beer bottles stacked in one doorway, and the water, which was rushing out a drainpipe that climbed the side of the building to a tank at the edge of the roof. I stayed close to the wall, in case someone was up there and attentive.

I followed the alley out to the street, and followed that to circle around Walt's place. The house itself, I decided, might have been a garage originally. It was a single-storey building with a flat roof and a few long narrow windows set too high in the walls to look into, their glass painted white. It also had a big paved area in back, walled with ten-foot chainlink and two strands of barbed wire. On the oil-stained paving I could see untidy stacks of old tires, rusting heaps of auto body components, and piled lumber warping in the weather.

I also saw a black-and-red motorcycle parked inside the fence, by the back door. The string connecting us dissolved.

As ambivalent as I was about my talent, I had to admit there were times when a find gave me a near-adrenal rush. This was one of them. My grin was involuntary, my whispered "Gotcha!" nearly so. There was an empty building next door, with a back yard full of scrub trees and high grass. I declared that "cover," and moved in closer. I should have known I wouldn't be able to get my motorcycle sighting and go home. Too much cat in my ancestry.

I'd expected the black finish on the rod frame to be primer, from my dream glimpse. Instead, it was either dense matte-black paint or some kind of rubberized coating. It looked phenomenally expensive. It was the metal-flake red on the teardrop tank that seemed a little cheesy; it didn't have the depth or gloss of the pearlescent midnight-blue lacquer on Tick-Tick's bike, and was a little battle-scarred, besides. Where most bikes would sport chrome, this one had black anodized metal. "The Stealth Chopper," I muttered, and realized that, whether functional or attitudinal, that's exactly what it was. Except for the gas tank. A replacement, waiting for a new paint job? Or were the black parts left over from better days and a previous owner?

It was a shaft-driven bike, which was surprising; chain drives are cheaper, and easier to fix, which means they're more common in Bordertown. The Ticker could have given me a rough idea of the engine size just by looking. Lacking her presence, I guessed 750 cc or larger. I couldn't tell how recently it had been driven, but the engine wasn't hot right then; there was no telltale ticking from cooling metal. There was what looked like a custom security cable running from the ignition, under the gas tank, and connected to something in the high weeds along the pavement's edge.

Unfortunately, there was no monogram on the seat upholstery, no tag that read, "If lost, please return to," and no way to tell if the bike belonged in Walt Felkin's back lot. It was not, in other words, as easy as I'd hoped.

That was Rico's problem, I acknowledged irritably. I pulled the cigarette out of my breast pocket and lit it while I thought. Rico would have to push past Felkin's front door manners (I tried to imagine her using a piece of tailpipe, and couldn't; possibly I didn't know her well enough) and ask him lots of questions about illegal things. And Walt, from what I knew, would close up as if he'd been welded shut. The Ticker had been confident that the mere naming of me would get her wrench out of him, but that was different. We were Townies, after our own. We weren't cops.

So. I crouched in the long, dew-wet grass behind the building next door, stared at Walt Felkin's painted-over windows, smoked my herbal cig, and let my stupid idea hatch. Maybe I was even less awake than I thought I was. Still, it seemed good then, and better the more I looked at it: Walt knew who I was. A Soho fixture, a friend of Tick-Tick's, an adamant neutral in the choosing of sides that went on among gangs and races in the territory south of Ho street. I began to compose my line of innocent enquiry. I didn't stub out my cigarette in the dirt and rise up out of the undergrowth until it was nicely polished.

Walt's front door was actually at the corner of the structure, recessed a little under a projection just big enough to keep the weather off while one fumbled for the key. One would have to, every time; there was a lock, but no doorknob. The door faced the wrong way for morning sunlight, but the current owner didn't strike me as the sort to have noticed. Though it was still barely dawn, the difference in the light between the back of the building and the front was enough to make the porch seem dark. I knocked with enough enthusiasm to wake someone up, which I knew I was doing.

And when I was done, my eyes had adjusted to the gloom. Now I could see the roughly twisted strands of wire taped to the doorframe, the connector that would separate when the door opened, the cardboard box set against the doorsill, big enough to hold a basketball, to which the wires ran. The last vestige of fog left my brain in a great cold rush.

From beyond the door came the sound of something falling over.

*"Don't open the door!"* I screamed. A steel door full of insulation; could he hear the words? "Walt, this is Orient! Don't open the door!"

"What the fuck?" If I could hear him, then he could hear me. Thank you, God.

"There's a bomb wired to your door! It'll go off if you open it. Stay there until I get someone to disarm it!"

"There's a *what?*"

"A bomb—don't touch the door! The cops'll have somebody who can dismantle it. Walt, do you hear me?"

He was right next to the door now. "Is this a joke? Did that goddamn elf broad put you up to this?"

"What?" Oh, he meant Tick-Tick. "It's not a joke; there's a box out here big enough to—I don't know. Just don't open the door. It's got something to do with the motorcycle around back."

There was no comment from the other side of the door.

"Walt?"

"Who sent you?"

"Nobody. Walt—"

"Who the fuck sent you?" He'd stepped back a little.

"Walt, calm down—"

His voice rose in volume and pitch. ". . . Backstabbin' sonofabitch! Well, fuck him!" The last was a shriek. I could hear the mingled fury and terror even through the steel.

"Walt?"

No answer. In the room beyond the door, something clattered.

In one sickening instant, I knew what was happening. "Walt, no!" I screamed, and launched myself toward the back of the house. I couldn't have been fast enough if I'd teleported.

Felkin, you idiot. Did you think he wouldn't rig the back door, too?

The blast from it, when Walt tried to bolt, blew out the windows in a hailstorm of glass. I remember that: over my head, three sparkling gouts of glass, like water spat out by someone surprised by a joke. Surprise, Walt.

The contents of the cardboard box at the front door went off immediately, when the first blast warped the door. I felt it more than I heard it. The third explosion, though—I heard that one. The one set off by what I'd mistaken for a security cable on the motorcycle. It sounded like the Devil himself was laughing.

The weather saved my life. If it hadn't poured rain two nights before, and if the dew hadn't been heavy that morning, the parched trees and tall grass next to Walt Felkin's house would have kindled from the flaming debris and burned like a grease fire, and me with them. As it was, they smoldered, and the smoke from the field, the house, and Walt's old tires kept anyone from spotting me for a while. It would have been longer yet, except for Sunny Rico. According to stories I heard later, she refused to listen to the suggestion that I might never have been there at all.

"Drunks would pass up free beer first," she said through clenched teeth, and began to comb the site for me or my remains.

The first I knew of this was Rico's voice, saying, "No, don't move. There's a stretcher coming."

Everything I'd found out flooded my mind and clamored to be reported. I couldn't sort it. I opened my eyes and shut them again immediately; the sun was painful, and the smoke. I'd caught a glimpse of Rico's face, daubed with soot and with a bleeding scratch across the bridge of her nose, her hair soaked with sweat and sticking to her forehead. Now that I paid attention, I could hear the rushing noise of flames, and the firecracker explosions of things caught in the fire. The heat was buffetting.

"It's a he," I said.

"What?"

"It's a he," I said, more carefully this time, and louder.

"I can't hear you. Don't worry about it now."

"Felkin said 'he.' The bike was here. I can describe it."

Inside my head, the words had been half shouted and clear. But Rico shook her head, frowning. I finally realized that I was only half conscious, and even that wasn't guaranteed.

"I can't tell if you've broken anything," she said. "The blood's just from the cut on your head. I'm worried about things like your spine. So when we move you onto the stretcher, if anything hurts, scream like hell right away, okay?"

That seemed funny. She might even have meant it to be. "Helper of men," I murmured.

She raised one eyebrow.

I didn't recognize the two people with the stretcher, when I squinted up at them. They were probably with the neighborhood fire watch. They were both as grubby as Rico. At that point I lost the signal again, if not consciousness altogether. I tuned back in as the sky was being replaced by the roof of an ambulance. "Sunny!" I said with all the force I could manage.

"Yeah?" She was somewhere close by.

"Tell Tick-Tick." I hoped she'd understood; I hadn't the strength to stick around and find out.

# THE CONSEQUENCES
# OF THATAWAY

A ND THAT'S HOW I ended up in Bolt Street Clinic myself. It could have been the same room as the one I'd
been in the day before, the one in which I'd watched a
girl die. I don't know; I hadn't paid much attention to it
then, and I wasn't going to ask.

At Bolt Street, the medical hierarchy wasn't any more
elaborate than the law enforcement equivalent at Chrystoble Street Station. Anybody who knew how to handle a
problem, handled it. I wasn't, the staff assured me, much
of a problem. I was attended to by the man who'd
brought me water in the hall, the last time I'd been there.
He sewed up the gash between my right eyebrow and my
hairline, shone light into my eyes and ears, prodded my
battered limbs and asked "Does this hurt?" (the answer
was usually "Yes"), and told me I was going to be there
for twenty-four hours, for observation, whether I liked it
or not.

I told him I didn't. I also told him I'd climb out a

window sooner than spend the night, no offense meant.

"Good of you to warn me," he said. He sounded tired. "How about if you stay away from the windows for eight hours, and we'll renegotiate then?"

"I'll try." I didn't really feel like standing up yet, but I wasn't making an empty threat. The hospital surroundings were already making my nerves flutter. It had been four years since I'd lived in the World, since I'd lived with this ambience at second hand and come to associate it inextricably with everything that happened at home. Some things take more than years and distance to escape, I guess.

He cleaned me up and left, warning as he did that there was probably somebody waiting to see me; at least, there had been, on and off for a while. I propped my pillow and me against the headboard and tried to look competent and unfazed.

I don't know why I was surprised when Tick-Tick came in. I was expecting her, of course; I just wasn't expecting her first. Her back was very straight and her face was calm. She shut the door behind her and sat down in the chair beside the bed. She crossed her legs. She folded her long white hands, right over left, on her thigh.

"I'm sorry," I said. I didn't think I looked competent and unfazed.

"I know that." Her voice matched the rest of her. "So?"

That was when I understood just how hard this was going to be. "Do you want me to promise never to do it again?"

"Never to be foolish? Of course not. What good would that do? You might as well promise not to blink. Or were you proposing to promise never to go to Walt

Felkin's in search of . . . *clues*?" She coughed the word out as if it had stuck in her throat. "I believe you could keep that one, but it's precious little protection from anything now."

"I thought I was doing the right thing at the time."

"Did you?" Think, I mean. Or did you simply put your nose to the ground and chase along behind it, like a dog after a skunk?"

The Ticker actually stopped, then, looked at me, and waited, as if the question weren't rhetorical. I said, "Don't let me interrupt you. You're barely warmed up."

That was meant to make her overtly furious, which would have been easier for me to take. It failed. "It seems I was nearly called upon to identify your body."

"Oh, for God's sake. Three stitches, all right? Three. I had worse falling off a swing when I was five."

"I spoke at length with Linn, Rico's partner. From his reconstruction, you must have been about halfway down the length of the concrete wall of the house, which means only about four long strides from the center of either blast. A few strides, and the chance durability of concrete—does that not seem like a near brush to you?"

It would eventually seem worse than that, I knew; but I also knew that the real knowledge of it would have to catch up to me at its own time. "Walt's dead, I suppose?"

"If you can assure the police that Walt was present at the time of the blasts, I know they'd appreciate it. There was certainly someone present, but dental records are few in Bordertown."

"Oh."

"Linn is an excellent source of information, if one has the wit to ask him for it." She sounded positively pleasant now, but I knew her; there wasn't anything in that for me. "For instance, did you know that the explosive used in the ceiling of the apartment building was Astrolite?"

"I don't even know from Astrolite." She knew I didn't.

"Ammonium nitrate and hydrazine."

"Why does that sound familiar? Wait—rocket fuel?" I asked, appalled.

"Different hydrazine. Not so viciously toxic, nor so difficult to lay hands on, though it must be sought assiduously and worked with caution. But once combined with the nitrate, it is dependably stable outside the presence of fire or spark, even under the influence of magic, and powerful in very small quantities. I have used it and made it and traded it, as have many other people in the Borderlands with the knowledge and the need." Her voice, and her eyes, which didn't waver from mine, were steady and cool. The clinic could have air-conditioned the whole building with her. "But the gifts placed at Walt Felkin's house were not that. No, my dear. They were gelignite. Gelignite contains nitroglycerin, which cannot be made dependably stable in the Borderlands no matter what you dope it with. Anyone who uses it here is either an unlettered fool, or a lettered one of appalling *hubris*. I would sooner keep a polar bear than I would a corn-kernel of gelignite."

"If it's that bad," I said, "why would anybody have it here at all?"

"Because there are, without question, fools in Bordertown. Sensible people, when they find caches of unstable explosives, have them confiscated, thus reducing the communal price of folly by a few pennies."

The dissertation on explosives was entirely Tick-Tick-like. The apparent change of subject in mid-rant was not.

"This has something to do with why you're so angry, doesn't it?"

She stared at me and chewed the inside of her lip. "Yes," she said finally.

"Can you explain it?"

"To a thoughtful analyst like yourself? Probably not." Her gaze left mine, finally, to consult the ceiling. I could have told her it was blank. She folded her hands the other way, left over right. "Astrolite requires some know-how and experience to use efficiently, and time and care to set up at the site. Whoever blew the ceiling of the apartment building had all those. What was done at Walt Felkin's was not unlike deer hunting with a grenade. I'm sure Linn will squeeze all the relevant details out of you later, but he's assured me that the most cursory observation of the site indicates a woefully inefficient use of materials. The blast at Felkin's and the demolition of the apartment building might have been done by two different people. Under the circumstances, that seems so unlikely as to be laughable."

"So that's not what scares you."

She shot me a glare, as if I wasn't supposed to notice that she was scared. "What *is* likely is that someone with the knowledge and experience to use explosives wisely and well has, under pressure, used them sloppily and without regard for the wider consequences. Such a person, under pressure, will make no distinction between targets and bystanders."

My fingers had closed on the blanket, gathering it in two knots. "I don't know if this person believes in the concept of bystanders."

Tick-Tick stood up with a sharp exhalation, and paced to the foot of the bed. (*Was* it the same bed? If so, that was where I'd stood.) "And that's why you won't leave it be."

Until then I hadn't considered whether or not I meant
to leave it be. I'd still thought of myself as having been
pressed into service by Sunny Rico. But I hadn't behaved,
the night before, like someone who was working against
his will. Maybe I was as bad as the Ticker herself was,
when faced with a puzzle. Whatever my motivation was,
I didn't feel up to analyzing it immediately. "I don't
know."

She stood erect at the foot rail, as if behind a lectern.
She looked, in fact, like a preacher who wasn't very fond
of the congregation. "Your duty as an honest citizen of
Bordertown is to deplore evildoing. You are not obliged
to tie a cape over your shoulders and search the alleys for
it. You have a job, which you should do well, and leave
others to do theirs. You did what you could for Rico.
Then you did what you shouldn't have, which harmed
you and muddied the waters generally, I suspect. If so, no
doubt you'll hear it from Rico." She leaned forward, her
forearms pressing down on the railing. Her expression
was noticeably less composed. "Leave it, Orient. Let it go.
The police will take over."

I had a headache banging at the front of my skull, and
the smell of antibacterial soap was making me a little bit
queasy. "I sort of thought you'd mention the consequences of my actions right off. You left out getting Walt
killed and the evidence destroyed."

Tick-Tick shook her head irritably. "Linn thought the
doors were wired. Were they?"

I nodded.

"Then he would have opened one with or without
you. Wallowing in unearned guilt won't save you. Will
you give it up now, or not?"

I hadn't thought about it, and I wasn't going to think
about it then. "I'll think about it," I said.

"I do hope you'll practice on something else first."

I might have said something unforgivable, if Rico hadn't appeared in the door to the room. I felt like a kid caught waging a name-calling fight. Rico looked from the Ticker to me, and said, to neither of us in particular, "This is a bad time, right?"

"That depends entirely on what for, and for whom," Tick-Tick said, making all the consonants count.

Rico blinked. "I'll figure that out and get back to you." She turned her attention full on me and nodded. "My, you look lousy."

"But I feel terrible," I assured her.

"Guess that proves you can't tell by looking."

Tick-Tick's eyes went back and forth between the two of us; then they stopped at me, and she raised one eyebrow. "Have you been studying Insouciant Copspeak?"

"He's a natural at it," said Rico. And to me: "The guy in white out front says you don't want to stay here."

"I don't, much."

"They can't check for internal injuries if you don't hang around. And the city's picking up the tab."

"I'd rather go home," I said. At the same time, Tick-Tick said, harshly, "He doesn't like hospitals."

I stared at her. I'd had no idea she knew that.

"Nobody likes hospitals," Rico replied. "Grit your teeth."

The Ticker straightened abruptly. "He can go home with me. I'll take responsibility for him."

Rico looked at her—looked up at her, where, absurdly, she stood with feet planted and chin a little outthrust. You tend to forget the relative ages of elves; now I remembered that Tick-Tick was the elven equivalent of my age, more or less, and Rico was older than me. I wondered again by how much. Now Rico said drily, "And what does he say to that?"

"I'll go home with her. But I'll take responsibility for myself, thank you."

Tick-Tick bent a look on me that told me exactly how she would have responded to that if Rico hadn't been in the room.

Rico shrugged. "Take it up with his repairman."

I got another look from the Ticker, this one harder to read. Then she said, "I'll do that now." She gave the impression of gathering herself up, though she hadn't brought anything in with her. Then she stalked out of the room like the Queen of the Veldt. Grrr.

Sunny Rico sank her hands in the pockets of her trousers. She was in formal dress again: black suit jacket and pants and a maroon Edward II T-shirt. "Criminy," she said, gazing toward the door where Tick-Tick had gone out. "Why do I feel like I've been dismissed?"

I took the question seriously. "Force of personality. She has an awful lot of it."

"And all of it ready to launch in your defense. When I came in I thought she was kicking your butt."

"Yeah, but that doesn't mean anybody else gets to. You know: Your sister can punch you, but heaven help the neighbor kids if they try it."

"It's a sisterly sort of relationship? I wondered if it was anything closer."

"God, I've never *had* a closer relationship. Including with my mother." Which reminded me of my surroundings, of course.

It must have shown on my face; Rico saw something, anyway. "Anything you want to mention?"

"No." Then I changed my mind. "My mom was a nurse. She went back to it after—after my father left her.

Us. She was second shift ER staff. Things were pretty grisly for us, and I still associate the whole thing with hospitals."

I didn't sound very coherent, even to me, but Rico nodded. "Money problems?"

It would have been easier to say yes, but that wasn't, I discovered, what I wanted to say. I struggled with it for a moment, and shrugged, and looked out the door, since there wasn't anything to see out the window except the wall across the alley.

She said, "Kids always blame themselves when their parents get divorced."

I was startled enough to stare at her. Her expression was bland, but I think she made a mental note.

"Okay, let's get some work done," Rico said, and pulled a notebook out of her inside jacket pocket. "Before the medical professionals decide you've had enough social life." She let her pen hover over a clean sheet and looked at me.

I drew a long breath, by way of organizing some brain cells, and began by summarizing the director's-cut version of the dream, as I'd had it the night before. I explained why I had gone to Christoble Street with the new information instead of finding her, and she shook her head.

"Should have woke me up."

"Fine. If it ever comes up again, I'll remember that."

"What time was all this?"

"Ye gods, I wasn't really—wait, when I got to the station, it was pretty close to four a.m."

"Which side of four?"

"Maybe ten, fifteen minutes short?"

"Okay. Keep going."

I tried to do it in order: talking to Saquash, being interrupted by Vic's entrance (Rico nodded and muttered, "Vickie, God's Gift to Third Shift"), Hawthorn's entrance, telling Hawthorn about the dream and the bike, eating, waiting for authorization, falling asleep, Hawthorn sending me home . . .

"You fell asleep?" Rico repeated, a textbook example of skepticism.

"It wasn't something I'd been doing much of, until then."

"Didn't they think to wake you up?"

"They tried, I guess. I don't know if Hawthorn ever got his authorization, come to think of it."

Rico shook her head, and said, "Go on."

So I explained, or tried to explain, why I thought at the time it would be a good idea to track the bike down myself. Rico didn't make all the faces Tick-Tick would have; she just wrote things down.

"Time," she prompted again.

"Um. Just before dawn. What's the legal definition of dawn, anyway? The sky was getting light. Call it somewhere around six."

I told her about recognizing where I was, when I got to Walt Felkin's, and explained how I knew who Walt Felkin was. Then I described the bike with great care, knowing that it didn't exist anymore. "I really did think it was a lock cable," I sighed.

"And then?"

It seemed strange, suddenly, that she didn't know what had happened at Walt Felkin's place, that she hadn't deduced everything I'd done from evidence at the scene. That made me wonder how much evidence was left there, of anything. "You're going to hate this," I warned her.

"Probably. But right now I'm getting down what happened, not how I feel about it. Keep going."

"I knew Walt would do his double-damnedest not to tell you anything. I mean, you or any other cop. And I thought that might not be true if it was just me he was talking to. So I went 'round the front and knocked on the door."

At the pause, she looked up from her notebook and waited.

"Then I saw the bomb wired up to go off when the door opened. I yelled through the door and told him about it. He asked—after I told him I thought it had to do with the motorcycle, he wanted to know who sent me. And then he said something about . . . a backstabbing son of a bitch, and 'Fuck him.' "

I raised my hands to rub my head, which ached, and my fingers brushed against the bandage on the right temple. I settled for rubbing the left side. "After that—before I could stop him, he tried to get out the back door. Boom."

Rico didn't comment. Instead, she flipped back a few pages in the notebook and began to re-read what she'd written. I stared off into space, consoling myself with Tick-Tick's observation that Walt would have opened the door eventually, that that had been the bomber's original intention, in fact.

I was brought back to the room by a new intensity in the silence. Rico was looking across the top of her notebook, not quite at me, and I could see a muscle appear and disappear in her jaw as her back teeth worked. "Tell me again," she said quietly, "about what you did at the station."

I started to, and she said, "Slow down." I did, and she still stopped me with questions like, "Was that when

Toby came back in?" and "Did you see Vic again after he left to check the dock?" and "Did Hawthorn leave the building while you were there?" and "Was that the first time you'd seen the two morning shift officers?"

I'd been hit on the head, but I still wonder why it took that long before I said, "You think it's a cop."

The blood had backed away from her face and left her tan gray. "Yes," she said, a little hoarse. "I think that."

After four years in Bordertown, one would expect me to have given up being a nice suburban kid. But in this, at least, I'd held onto my roots; the idea that Chrystoble Street Station had not been a safe place to talk about the motorcycle was very hard to accept.

Rico must have seen that. "You were right the first time," she said. "Why destroy the motorcycle now? Why do anything about it now, as long as someone isn't looking for it? Unless, that is, you find out someone *is* looking for it. The only people who could have known that, going by your testimony, were in Chrystoble Street. Unless you told someone else about it, and forgot to mention it." Her voice was determinedly flat, but I could still hear the hope that lay under the last sentence.

"No. But one of the cops might have said something to somebody."

"When?"

"Hell, *I* don't know. Rico, I can't see it. I can't picture any of those guys . . ."

She waited for me to try to find the words, and when I didn't, she offered, ". . . Killing people? It's the last resort in my job, but I have to be prepared to do it if the last resort comes around. So do they."

"Not like that. Which of them could do that?"

"Just at a guess, I'd say the one who doped your soup."

I stared at her.

"Oh, come on. You're not going to tell me that never occurred to you?"

When I found my voice, I said, "You bet. Every day. My God, of course it didn't. Where am I supposed to get all this practice at being paranoid?"

"I don't know, but you'd better start looking." Then she closed her mouth sharply, and after a moment added, "No, scratch that. You won't have to. Beyond developing a certain base level of practical street smarts, which is my parting recommendation to you."

"What does that mean?"

"It means you're off it. You're out of here. Done. I need to pick your brains about a few more things that happened last night, and then these last couple days can fade like a bad dream." Just too late she must have recognized the appropriateness of that; she winced.

I was surprised to find that everything inside me seemed to have stopped happening; I had a feeling of suspended time filling my ribcage. "I screwed up," I said. "I know that. It won't happen again."

Rico slapped her notebook against the arm of the chair. "God damn it, this is not a punishment." She sprang up out of the chair and paced to the other end of the room, stood there for a few seconds, and walked back to my bedside. "Not negotiable. You're out. Sorry if it cuts into your income."

I had my mouth open to tell her off, when I realized it was another of those characteristic sentences: *Sorry if it cuts into your income.* It built a cofferdam around the thing she didn't want to talk about, and let the discussion run safely around and on. And she expected me to respond in kind. This time I had no idea what she didn't want to talk about.

I took a deep breath and nodded, and said, "I won't starve."

I saw a small relaxation in her face. She poised her pen over the notebook again and asked, "Toby brought you the food?"

"Anybody could have been in the back and added something to it. Except—while Saquash was getting the food, Hawthorn was out front talking to me. And once it was in front of me, nobody had a chance to do anything to it."

"What about the beer and the aspirin? Hawthorn brought those."

"The aspirin was in an aspirin bottle, the pills were stamped 'aspirin,' and I shook them out myself. That would have taken a hell of a lot of planning to set up."

"The beer?"

I reconstructed my memories. "No. The beer had a crimp-on cap. I watched him pop it off with the opener. I think you have to leave Hawthorn out."

"Maybe. Christ, this is going to be fun. I have to question everybody without making it look as if anyone's under suspicion. You say Hawthorn got on the radio?"

"He said he radioed for authorization to do stuff outside his turf."

"I'll check that. If he mentioned the motorcycle to the dispatcher, the field of suspects opens up like a sonofabitch."

I knew what she meant: The cops on Dragonstooth Hill would have the news. So would anyone in B-town who'd monitored that frequency in the frail hope that radio transmission would, even temporarily, be working in the Borderlands the way it worked everywhere else. If I were the illusionist, I would try to keep an ear on the police band, if I knew there was one. It was still possible that Rico wasn't looking for another cop.

Except for the suspicious circumstances of my falling asleep in the police station. "I might not have been doped," I said.

"Of course not. And the Elflands may have disappeared again while we've been standing here, but it's not what you'd call likely." This time her expression reminded me a lot of one Tick-Tick might have used.

"Could it have been a spell?"

"I assume you would have noticed if anybody in the room cast one." She asked it as if it were a serious question.

"I've lived here for four years."

"Some people are thick enough that four years won't even make a dent. *Would* you recognize the casting of a spell if you saw it?"

"Thank you," I said pleasantly, "yes, I would."

"All right, then. That would rule out anything but a spell to put the whole station house to sleep, and according to what you've said, Chrystoble Street didn't turn into Briar Rose's country house last night. I could have someone sniff around the place for lingering traces of hocus-pocus, but there usually *are* some. We use it ourselves, any time it makes life easier."

She flipped her notebook closed and stuffed it back in her breast pocket. "I'm going to go before they throw me out. Thanks for giving me the rundown on last night. And don't be in any rush to get back on your feet."

I had forgotten. I really had, just for a minute, because we had gone on talking about the case, picking it apart. I hadn't realized that she was just questioning a witness. "And that's it?" I asked her.

"Linn may come around to ask you more questions."

"That's not what I meant."

"Oh, right. Send me a bill." And before I could repeat myself, she turned and walked out.

It seemed very quiet, in spite of the clinic sounds in the hall, in spite of the dry-grass sound of my breathing. Nobody was doing anything much today. I certainly wasn't. Nothing to do but get out of the hospital and go back to my slightly-interrupted life, which offered blessedly few opportunities to court disaster. What a relief.

The room was darker when Tick-Tick came back in. "I talked them into letting you go. Do you need help dressing?"

She plunked what she was carrying on the foot of the bed, and I recognized the component parts; she'd gone to my place and brought back some clothes. I wondered if the clinic had thrown out the ones I'd been wearing. There wouldn't have been anyone around to tell them that most of my wardrobe looked like that anyway.

"I think I can do it. Thanks."

"I promised you'd stay overnight with me."

Well, that was that, then. Tick-Tick was scrupulous about promises. She left the room to give me some privacy, and I slid out of bed. I was shaky, but it was nice to contemplate leaving the clinic, and that gave me the strength of purpose to get my clothes on. I was sore enough to be reminded of what it felt like to have a ceiling fall on me. No more of that, thank you, and no more of this. Relief was the word for it.

"Are you decent?" Tick-Tick called through the door.

I said what I was supposed to: "No, but I'm dressed."

She stuck her head in as I was limping cautiously toward the door. She didn't offer to help, because even if I had behaved like an idiot and betrayed every intelligent piece of advice she'd ever given me, she was still my best friend and a damned considerate fey wight.

My nurse waited in the hall. "Need a chair?" he asked us.

Tick-Tick shook her head before I realized that he'd meant the kind with wheels. "We'll do very well," said the Queen of the Veldt, and offered me her elbow with a dashing air. I took it as if the gesture were mere gallantry between friends. Besides, she was too tall for me to throw an arm across her shoulders to hold myself up.

The moon had come out of its corner, silver on turquoise, and the sun was expiring under a count of ten. I'd missed the whole boxing match for the sake of Rico's stupid case. Good riddance to it and her.

I slumped in the sidecar in relative comfort, while Tick-Tick drove with decorum and a sixth sense for avoiding potholes. When we got to her place, she worked the elevator rope. There wasn't enough light in the atrium to see how far her neighbor had gotten on the tapestry. Besides, it had only been a day—two days—since I'd seen it. In a normal life, that wasn't long. I wondered if he'd found his skull. Heck, maybe he could get Walt's.

Tick-Tick had a fainting couch about two levels up from the kitchen platform. I hobbled up the risers and sprawled on it. "Did you tell 'em, at the clinic, that you lived in a tree house?"

"Ho. Ho. Wait until morning, when you're stiff as bricks and have to come down for breakfast. Which puts me in mind of dinner. What do you want for it?"

"No vegetables. It'd be cannibalism. Actually, I don't think I could eat right now. Do you mind?"

"Gracious, no. Waste away to nothing. We'll hang

you on a pole with your mouth open and use you for a wind sock.''

A little later she called softly, "Are you asleep?"

I turned my face away from the window, where the outlines of buildings against the navy blue sky made such pleasant, cool geometry. The Ticker was sitting at her workbench in a spill of light from a kerosene lamp, a book open in front of her. I don't know what it was; it had tiny, closely-spaced type, thin yellowed pages, and occasional illustrations that looked like Victorian engravings, dense and scratchy.

"No, I'm awake."

"I shouldn't bother you."

Pretty tentative, for the Ticker. "You're not bothering me. I'm not doing anything." Well, I was breathing, and my heart was beating. But the rest of me wasn't busy.

"Ah. Then . . . have you thought about it yet?"

"What do you mean?"

"I said you should give up Rico's puzzle, and you said you would think on it. I wondered if you had, or if you cared to think aloud."

"I don't have to." Her head came up rather sharply when I said that. "I've been laid off."

For a moment she sat still as a painting. Then she said, in a changed voice, "Oh. Oh, bother."

"Huh?"

"Sleet and snow, I'd never thought Sunny Rico was a fool."

"I'm not following this," I said. I hadn't expected the news to make her angry and amused and resigned, and all of them at once.

Tick-Tick folded her arms over the back of her chair, rested her chin on them, and looked at me. "I, at least, know that the surest way to make you want to do something is to tell you that you absolutely may not."

I thought about it. Then I said, "Not this time. It's a relief. I can get back to real life now. Hell, maybe I'll find a steady girlfriend and learn to play the guitar."

She glared at me. "You are my dear friend," she declared, "and you lie like a rug."

"No, honest."

She snorted delicately and turned back to her book.

But I really wished that I hadn't taken the time to think about it. Because as soon as I did I realized that, of course, she was right.

# STREET SMARTS

L INN DID COME around, the next day. He looked tired, which doesn't always look the same in elves as it does in humans. His eyes weren't bloodshot, and there were no shadows under them, and heaven knows he couldn't have been paler than normal and not be dead. He just seemed dimmed, like a candle flame flickering in its own wax.

I was sitting in the kitchen window (that is, the window closest to the level the kitchen is on) nursing a cup of tea when Tick-Tick showed him in, so I had a nice vantage point to watch him from. His gaze bounced from level to level around the room like a runaway Superball, starting and ending at the Ticker's workbench. I couldn't tell if he was trying to look unalarmed, or unimpressed. I was pretty sure it was one or the other.

"Good morning. Tea?" I asked, sliding down off the windowsill.

"Thank you, no. I'm pleased to see you well, or seeming well."

"Not bad, actually." What I wanted to say was, "Have
you found out anything? What's Rico up to?" and, oddly
enough, "How is Rico?" though nothing suggested that
she should be any different from the way she'd been
when I'd seen her last. But the words were hanging in
off-the-case limbo, and it seemed important to pretend
that that didn't bother me.

"Have a seat," Tick-Tick said, pulling up a Louis XIV
side chair with dairy-cow-print cushions.

He turned his head aside and coughed. The hand he
covered his mouth with was nicely manicured; the
Ticker's hands usually had something black under the
fingernails. "I will, if each of you will take a seat, as well."

Tick-Tick shrugged. "You want to talk to Orient. I can
get out of the way."

Tick-Tick's verbal style usually slid easily from fey to
human idiomatic and back, but I'd noticed this about her:
in the presence of another elf, one she didn't know well,
her language was adamantly human and embarassingly
graceless. It was her version of a Brooklyn accent, I guess.
I also had a few guesses about why she felt the need to do
it when she did it, but that was her business, very little of
mine, and not a bit of anyone else's.

Linn made no sign that he'd heard anything unusual.
He shook his head. "You know of these devices, I believe.
If you will, sit and listen, and what I neglect to ask, speak
out upon. I would be glad of it."

"I guess I can do that."

Honestly, she sounded as crass as me. Which was
probably where she learned a good bit of it. I scrunched
my mouth up at her, which she pretended not to see.

Linn asked questions like paleontologists dig up

bones. It's hard to accurately describe catastrophe after you've taken part in it; each successive loud noise tends to obscure the last one, until the only thing you're sure of is that everything came unglued, somehow. But Linn demanded, patiently and politely, every tiresome detail in order, from the time I arrived at the corner down the block from Walt's. He did it by the steady application of "What happened then? No, before that." Except, of course, that when Linn said it, it sounded better.

The Ticker seemed to relax as the questions progressed; things that explode were, after all, one of her areas of expertise. Several times she rephrased Linn's questions, when she caught on to what he wanted to know and had a better idea than he did how to get it out of me. I think she was impressed by his attention to detail. I certainly was.

When he finally had everything out of me that I could remember, Linn said, "So we may have a witness to the act."

"We may?" I asked, startled.

"The early riser, working on the roof, the one you sought to hide your presence from. There is some chance the one who set the blast was o'erlooked as well." He coughed again. He'd done it several times during the round of questions, but this time it went on a little longer.

Tick-Tick rose, filled a glass with water from the jug by the sink, and set it down in front of him. He drank the whole thing, with great concentration, and thanked the Ticker in the language of their mutual homeland. I think if he hadn't been distracted he would have picked another language.

The Ticker smiled and said, *"De nada."* Linn looked up, startled and, I'd swear, apologetic. The sudden motion made him cough again, and Tick-Tick refilled the glass.

To forestall a repeat performance of the whole thing, I said, "That sounds awful."

Linn shook his head. "It is only smoke, I think, from Felkin's house. And little sleep, and some distress of mind."

I could count my acquaintance with Linn in hours, but admitting to distress seemed completely out of character for him. I stared. Tick-Tick ambled away, down to the first level and her workbench, and that made me stare, too. Had I missed something? I must have, because Linn was visibly relieved when she passed out of earshot.

People in the World may claim that in Bordertown, all bets are off when it comes to manners, but that's ridiculous. Etiquette is much more complicated here, and the residents learn it faster, because we'd all go crazy otherwise. Bad enough in the World, where one culture's respect for privacy is another's standoffishness. Toss in the customs from over the Border (various and contradictory), plus the lot of us who came here from one culture or another too young to have been properly socialized anyway, and it's a zoo. Anybody who's fit to stay in town figures out in the first fifteen minutes that good social skills are worth more than a late-model tank in most neighborhoods, for defense *and* offense. And the first and last rule of B-town etiquette is, if all else fails, keep your mouth shut and your eyes open. Having mastered that one, I waited for Linn to give me a hint.

He contemplated the glass of water, his lean face grave. "This is difficult," he said at last.

I decided that wasn't my hint.

He pursed his lips, as if he'd come to an unsavory decision, and raised his eyes to mine again. "You see, I'd ask a boon of you, but there I'm stopped. I cannot frame its nature. How may you grant what I've not craft to ask?"

After working that one over for a second, I said, "I see."

A quick, surprising smile lit his face. "Or at least, you see you cannot see, if I cannot be more plain. This touches on my partner."

I jumped, but only internally; and I wondered why I had. "I don't think there's much I can do for you there."

"You have done, if not much, then some at least already."

"I have?"

Linn shook his head, impatient, and coughed again. "She will not have you longer on this case. She will not countenance it, even to discuss. And yet, I think she held great hope of you, of what your skills might bring into the light. She seems now as if all her hope is fled, but will not, when I ask her, have it so. She is my friend; I cannot see her thus."

I wanted to tell him how many times I'd seen friends with troubled minds, and felt I had to do something about it, and did, and made it worse. But that was one of life's little lessons that was best learned through on-the-job training, anyway. And maybe in this instance he was right. "So you want me to go back to work for you and not let her know?"

"I'd not serve her such a turn. She has forbidden it, and I'll not go behind her to have it done in secret, nor above her, to have it ordered done in her despite. Still, if it were done, and no one had the ordering of it . . ."

"Except me, of course," I said, because I really did see, this time. "You want us to have never had this conversation, and me to go on sticking my nose into places where it's likely to get blown off in the hopes of finding this illusionist, and Rico to have nobody to yell at for it, if she finds out I'm doing it, but yours truly."

Linn smothered another cough and studied the tabletop. "Put so, I would deny it if I could. But no, that is the meat and bone of it."

"You could have saved yourself all that scansion. I never meant to quit on Rico's say-so." All right, I'd thought I meant to, for a few hours the day before, but nobody but me believed it anyway, so I wasn't counting it.

He stared at me. I think he was halfway between grateful and guilty, which is an unenviable piece of real estate. "You will . . . the danger will be great."

I quirked the eyebrow that didn't have stitches in it.

He looked away and rubbed his eyes. "If I can, I'll help. Take no foolhardy chances; you're to seek information, not to act."

I stood up. "If I'm not working for you, it's not your business how the job gets done. Your partner would understand that."

Linn stood up, too, more slowly than I had, as if he were the bruised and battered one. "She does, I think, and the reverse as well, which may be why she will not now employ you. Good day, and thank you for your help."

I watched him go. He took polite leave of the Ticker as he passed the workbench.

She stayed where she was until we heard the elevator squeak. Then she ambled up to the kitchen level and put the heat on under the teakettle. "How are you doing, my dear?"

Except for the head wound, and feeling mostly as if I'd been kicked down a long flight of stairs, I was fine.

When I said so to the Ticker, she sighed and asked, "Very well, then; what's the plan?"

"I haven't made one yet," I said, since I knew denying it would be a waste of time. I hoisted myself back onto the window sill.

"Tell me when you have, then. Because if you try to tiptoe off and indulge in heroics by yourself, I shall have you changed into something. Something slow." She considered. "Which wouldn't be so much of a change, now that I think on it."

"Ha. Ha. Did you hear any of the stuff that Linn said to me?"

"I very carefully did not."

"Did he send you away? I didn't notice him doing it."

"Not really. He was uncomfortable, so I made to wander off, and he didn't stop me. If he'd asked me to sit back down, I would have tried to make you go away, unless he made it clear that he was simply uncomfortable with what he had to do, and that we were both welcome to attend on his discomfort."

"Well, there was some to attend on. Rico officially tossed me off the job. Linn has unofficially asked me if I couldn't find it in my heart to be curious enough about the case to go on working on it privately."

"Did you tell him you didn't need a hobby?"

"No. I told him I had every intention of continuing to dig up dirt on this. Which you already knew, so don't try to look surprised."

"I am much too lazy to feign anything so difficult as surprise at what you'll do next. You're angry, aren't you?"

My forehead itched under the bandage; I pressed it a little, knowing that wouldn't really help. "I guess I am."

"Linn made you so?"

"It's—yeah. I don't—I can't really explain why, even."

"No, I expect you can't, though you would never consider doing what he's done, and if you were accused of doing so, you would think it a blow to your honor."

I haven't hung out in Tick-Tick's company for so long that she can't, now and then, make me gape at her. "I would, would I?"

"You wouldn't put it so. But indeed, my cabbage, our fine policeman's actions don't bear much scrutiny." She sat down on the chair Linn had occupied and stretched her long legs out in front of her. "His partner has forbidden you to dabble further in this—the most probable reason being that she doesn't care for the thought of waking up some morning and finding that all your recoverable parts can be stored in a space the size of a post office box. She, at least, recognizes the difference between choosing to risk her own life and choosing to suggest someone else risk his.

"Now here's Linn, who doubts his partner's judgement. Instead of confronting her with his doubt, arguing the matter over with her, and abiding by the decision, he comes away in this furtive fashion to undermine what she has done. He does not hide from you that he doubts his partner. He does not want to accept responsibility for it if you defy Rico and continue the search. And he has offered you nothing but a share in his guilt. Your successes will be the hole-in-corner successes of the informer; your failures will be described as just what one would expect from an amateur; and your death, if it happens, will not be called a hero's death but the sordid result of your own folly."

The teakettle was working up to a good kazoo-like hum. I grinned down at Tick-Tick and eased myself off the window sill. "You're pissed at him for reminding you you're an elf."

"You think I'm too hard on him?"

"Yeah." I turned the gas off and peered into the teapot. "Are these leaves okay to use again?"

"Blessed Mab, they most certainly are not. You may be as slovenly as you like in your own house, but in mine you'll make a decent pot of tea. Use the last of the Darjeeling."

I scraped the old leaves into the compost, rinsed the pot with a little hot water from the kettle, and left the new leaves to steep before I returned to the question of Linn. "Okay, he's running roughshod over a couple of my principles, but he's doing it in the interests of the public good, at least. He wants to get this guy."

"Bring the pot to the table, or you'll forget it, and we'll have cold paint thinner to drink. 'Good' is a somewhat differently-shaped concept on the other side of the Border. One may pursue one's own good: that is simple wisdom, a care for one's own well-being. If one extends that care to the well-being of those one loves—the good of friends and family—one is admired as above the common in honor and in duty, as having an ardent soul. But the public good? There is no ardency in that, no romance; the well-being of unknown persons does not touch upon fey honor nor the fey heart."

"It touches you."

"I am a changeling."

"Mmm. But Linn *does* want to catch the illusionist."

"Of course. As he would want to win at tourney. And he does have an ardent soul; the distress of his partner causes him distress. But there is no abstract desire in him, as there is in you, or in Rico."

"You think he's not a changeling, too?" I asked her.

"Why would he be?"

"He moved to Bordertown."

Tick-Tick raised her hand, acknowledging the point. "We are all changelings. All the more reason, however, not to judge him or anyone by yourself."

I looked out at the ragged line of buildings, trees, and fences that made up the town as seen from Tick-Tick's kitchen window. "Hey, does it work the other way?"

"Pardon?"

"If people don't think much of the concept of a general good, over the Border, does that mean they don't think in terms of public evils, either?"

She frowned and poured out the tea. Then she answered, "Some do. Changelings of another sort, my chick."

And changelings, as I'd pointed out, gravitated to Bordertown. I sighed. "I wish I knew what to do next."

"Have you tried simply looking for the wretched stuff?"

"Huh?"

"This drug. Have you been on its trail long enough to know what it is, and *that* it is, so that you can simply lock on and find the nearest sample of it? Well, it might be a start," she added, when I stared at her in what must have been a pretty blank fashion.

"No—I mean, of course it would be. I just feel so stupid for not—except I probably couldn't have done it until recently." What I'm trying to find has to be real to me. What the specifications of "real" are varies from item to item, but I knew the drug Rico was worried about was real to me now, because I'd seen the girl in the hospital bed. All I had to want to know was where to find a sample of the drug that had killed her. So I wanted that.

Nothing happened. It was as if I'd tried to find the

man in the moon; there just wasn't anything. Tick-Tick was looking at me, hopefully.

"Maybe I'm broken," I offered.

"What?"

"Do you have any chocolate?"

"Yes, it's—"

"Don't tell me." Question. Answer. "If it's in the cupboard over the spoons, on the shelf next to the honey, I'm not broken."

"Then you don't know this drug well enough to find it after all?"

I shook my head. "I know it. Has the supply dried up? This is creepy."

She gazed out the window past my head. She looked irritable—unexpectedly so, and I realized that she'd decided this really was her business. "How do we find out?"

" 'We?' "

"Yes, 'we.' Don't make trouble for yourself."

I knew that voice; I knuckled under. "We find out the hard way, I guess."

"Which is?"

"We tramp around town asking until we find somebody who'll tell us."

"And if we find a great many people who *don't* want to?"

"That'll tell us something right there."

Neither of us mentioned that there might be people who didn't want us to ask.

I know Bordertown isn't Utopia, and never has been. It's riddled with old hates and grudges that people have brought to it from wherever they came from in the World, no matter how pointless and outdated those grudges might be in the strange new world of the Border. Worse, sometimes; sometimes old prejudices are as comforting as old clothes when you're up to your lower lip in elves, in magic, in all-bets-are-off B-town weirdness. Some people, faced with the perfect opportunity to give their lives a complete makeover, turn tail and do everything they can to identify "our kind" and stick to it. This is why Dragontown exists, for crying out loud, and the whole silly two-block area stubbornly referred to by its inhabitants as "the Barrio," and even the desperate attempts at suburbia that crop up in pockets around the outside of the city proper. Give them the choice between the familiar—even if the familiar is *terrible*—and the unknown, and they'll take familiar any time.

And there are people who think they *have* brought their lives up to date, simply because they've put aside hatred of whoever or whatever it was they hated back home and replaced that with hating something they can only find in Bordertown. Once we started asking questions, I began to wonder if both kinds of immigrants were deeply and personally involved in the issue of drugs that promised to turn humans into elves. I suppose if I'd thought about it beforehand, I would have realized that the answer was yes.

There was the fierce, black-haired human girl with the broken nose, who glowered at Tick-Tick while she told us that if she did know where to get hold of something like that, she'd turn herself into an elf and cross the Border and beat the shit out of every elf in Faerie.

There was the round-faced brown-skinned human boy who laughed heartily and wanted to know who the hell would want to become an elf fag anyway, and then made it even more disconcerting by looking conscious and apologizing to Tick-Tick.

There was the tall, slender, silver-haired beautiful girl whose only sign of her halfie blood was a pair of undisguisable honey-hazel eyes, who looked down at me with haughty amusement and asked if the people who'd developed the drug had started by turning sow's ears into silk purses.

There was the elfin knight with thin features and a brush cut, who thought the drug sounded like a good idea, since it could make it possible for Bordertown to be entirely elven without having to force anyone out, thus allowing the inhabitants to make a start on achieving a golden age of civilization. Then his brushed-aluminum-colored eyes widened as he realized what he'd said, and he apologized to *me*.

Those were only the most articulate ones. I'm leaving out the people who glared, who mumbled, who had something they had to do somewhere on the other side of town—not because we were asking uncomfortable questions, but because one or the other of us was the wrong species.

We were sitting on the wall outside the Antler Brewery at the corner of Ho and Wildwood (I was swinging my feet; Tick-Tick's reached the sidewalk) when I finally said, "I don't think I'm stupid. Or naive. Am I?"

Tick-Tick thought about it. "I suppose it depends on the subject, really."

"Thank you very much. No, I've always known that B-town has its share of dipsticks. I just didn't think they were as high a percentage of the population as this. And in my line of work, I've met a lot of people in this town."

She looked at me, a little aslant and rueful. "I was afraid you were noticing the miscellaneous lapses of manners."

"Whatever subjects I'm naive about, racial and ethnic slurs aren't among 'em. What's happening here?"

The Ticker was silent for what was, in the context of

the conversation, a long time. "You know," she said at last, "a human who truly hated and feared fey things, or one of my folk who hated and feared humans, might prefer to leave misplaced things misplaced, than to come to you." After a moment, she added, "I don't say it to hurt."

"I know you don't. Fact of life, and a very wise observation. Besides, it only hurts a little. Except—remember the one in the gray leather vest? He *has* come to me. About six months ago, I found seeds for some kind of antique tomato for him, and everything was fine. We even compared notes, a little, on what it was like to grow up weird in the World. Now he's about as friendly as an ice sculpture. Hell, the cops get better treatment down here than that."

Then I looked at her, and she looked at me. "Uh-oh," the Ticker said, summing it up for both of us.

"What Rico was afraid of has started, hasn't it?" I asked, just to be sure.

"This drug—even the rumor of it—is a divisive force. My people can view it as a threat to the safety of the Border. Yours must hear of its failures and think it a murderous fey trap."

"Excuse me. What is this 'my people, your people' stuff?"

She opened her mouth, and closed it, and finally said, "A very wise observation, my chick, in spades. Didn't I say it was a divisive force?"

"Well. So the rumor's out, and the wedge is in. No wonder Linn's worried about Rico's state of mind. She's probably cancelled Christmas until this gets solved."

We sat in silence for a minute, our elbows crossed over our respective knees. Then Tick-Tick said, "You like Rico, don't you?"

I frowned at her while I thought about it, so she

would know that I wasn't ignoring the question. Also so I could pretend that the question hadn't thrown me into more confusion than I could account for. "I respect her."

"Perhaps that's it," the Ticker replied inscrutably, and stood up. "Then let's return to our quest, my dear. After all, if we can help solve her case, the respect will be mutual, won't it?"

I almost said it was already; she'd seen fit to hire me, hadn't she? Of course, she'd also seen fit to fire me. I hopped down from the wall, and followed her around the corner onto Ho Street.

Two blocks later we found Camphire. No, actually, two blocks later we found Camphire's advance guard, in the form of a grid of chalk lines on the street, the sidewalk, and up the sides of buildings as high as a medium-sized person could reach. Already outlined on the grid were shapes and figures that looked random to me—but if they were random, why grid them first? Then I looked further ahead, and saw the filled-in color that didn't yet extend to where we stood, and how it made sense of the design. The two blocks ahead of us were filled, walls and street, with chalk-drawn animals, plants, and people elongated, geometricized, and abstracted into a knotwork that was part Celtic, part Aztec. Some of the people were elven, some human; some of the animals were real and some were fantastical. I couldn't vouch for the plants. It seemed at first as if we couldn't go any farther without walking on the art. Then I noticed the path that wound through, as non-random as the art itself, calculated to bring you to just the right viewing distance for each major group of figures.

"This must have taken weeks," Tick-Tick breathed.

"Two and a half to do," said a sweet, breathy voice behind us. "On paper, though, designing it, that was a

couple months. I think. Getting there is half the fun, or
maybe it's that packing takes longer than travelling. One
of those things that's supposed to be broadening, anyway."

It was Camphire, of course. She was stunningly ordi-
nary to look at: middling height for an elf, collar-length
hair dyed brown and tucked untidily behind her peaked
ears, eyes more like gray than silver, regular but undis-
tinguished features. There was a smudge of indigo chalk
dust on the side of her nose. She wore a T-shirt that was
much too large for her, and a wide denim skirt that didn't
seem to have ever been hemmed, and a carpenter's
apron with the pockets full of colored chalks.

"Of course," she went on, with a not-exactly-
focussed-on-anything smile, "a journey of a thousand
steps begins with a single mile, unless they're really small
steps. Here," she said to me, and handed me a length of
dark green chalk. "Fill in that stem. Start at the bird's tail,
and don't do the leaves yet." She held out a handful of
chalks to Tick-Tick. "Over there, that's a sunflower.
Make it whatever color you think sunflowers are."

"Yellow?" Tick-Tick ventured, not as if she thought it
would help. Horticulture isn't Tick-Tick's subject, either.

"If you want them to be," Camphire told her, nodding.

"We're sort of . . . in the middle of something," I said
to Camphire.

"Of course!" Her grin was big and bright and not
vague at all, and she directed it at me as if she were a
third-grade teacher and I had just correctly spelled "aard-
vark" out loud. "You're in the middle of green. You'll
like it."

Much as I hesitate to admit it, she was right. For the
next three hours, she placed the Ticker and me like a

general places troops, while she skritched furiously away herself, filling in color with a speed and certainty that baffled me. She seemed to hold the finished work in her head; she never referred to a drawing, and she never seemed to have to think about the next step.

Wolfboy, only—how many days ago had it been? Too much had gone on between then and now—not long ago, had told us that Camphire had said, "You have to break an omelette to make eggs." I wondered if he'd been in the middle of this when she'd said it. Camphire was a byword in Bordertown for not having the firmest grasp on reality; in fact, most of the time one could feel pretty certain that she had both hands full of something else, and reality, if she had any contact with it at all, was slipping out from where she'd tucked it under one elbow. We collected Camphire-isms as ultimate nonsense and non sequiturs, and didn't pay a lot of attention to what she did while she uttered them.

This, all around me, was what she did, and she was very good at it. She still smiled and nodded at the Ticker and me, and in that pretty, insubstantial voice said things like, "Is negative space the space you don't like, or the space that's not there? And if it's not there how can you tell?" and "I can see the light at the end of the candle. We're almost done." But she always knew where the next color went, and never smeared a grid line or dragged her skirt hem through the chalk.

I went from reluctant to absorbed in the course of those three hours, so it came as a shock when I looked up and found myself a foot from the end of the scarlet feather I was coloring, and the sun low on the skyline. Camphire straightened up from the figure she was working on and commanded, "Okay, stop. I have to end as I meant to begin. Actually, I *did* begin that way, but I meant it, too." She took the chalk from me and finished the feather in a dense, jagged polygraph line that jolted out of its border on both sides and trailed off like a tadpole tail at the end. She took the turquoise chalk from Tick-Tick and did the same thing to an elaborately outlined curlicue. She fished out a canary-yellow chalk from her apron and turned the pointed petals of a lily into a furious squiggle. Then she sat down, suddenly and hard, on the pavement, and dropped her forehead on her knees.

Tick-Tick reached her first. "What's the matter? Are you all right?"

Camphire raised her head. "I'm fine. It's just always a shock, that's all."

I stopped a little ways away from her and stared. Her voice, though still hers, had more decision in it, and her face didn't look as if it were waiting for its next expression. "Hullo?" I said.

She smiled (the smile was different, too). "This happens whenever I finish a really large piece. Don't worry, it wears off after a while. And a good thing it does, too, because I can't get a bit of work done in this state. I just can't concentrate." She stood up and dusted chalk and road grit off her skirt. "Thank you ever so much for helping me finish. I'd set my heart on winding up today, and I didn't think I could do it."

I got my voice back, sort of. "This . . . always happens?"

"Oh, yes. I suppose out in the World someone would say I was using my art as therapy."

"Seems to work."

"Well, yes, but do you know, I think my present state is the one I'm treating, because however *comfortable* it is to be normal, I find I can't really be *happy* like this."

"Mmm," I said, beginning to wonder if she was completely recovered after all.

"Don't you think so? I'm sure you'd be more comfortable if you weren't fey, but would you be happy?"

It was Tick-Tick, unexpectedly, who answered. "No. You're right. It's better to be happy than comfortable, if you can't have both."

"Artists hardly ever get both," Camphire said with a shrug. "The odd thing is, that if they don't choose happiness, they don't usually manage to be comfortable, either, because they're busy fretting over how unhappy they are."

"You're sure you're all right?" I asked.

"Perfectly. Oh, Mab! You were busy when I roped you in, weren't you? I'm terribly sorry."

"We're looking for something," Tick-Tick said. "Without much luck, so far."

Camphire's gaze moved from the Ticker to me, with a question in it. I realized that Camphire really did know who I was and what I did, and that the official town finder of things wandering around asking people if they knew where something was made as strange a picture as Camphire being rational. It would take too long to explain, so I told her about the drug instead.

Her frown made a neat pair of wrinkles over her nose. "Why does that sound familiar?" She interrupted her own thoughts with another glancing smile at us. "You see, when I'm in my usual state, people *will* be indiscreet, sometimes. And I can't think why, since it's not as if anyone believes I'm deaf. It had something to do with Bonnie Prince Charlie."

"That would be about right. He was probably a courier for whoever's responsible."

"Good riddance to bad rubbish in that quarter, I'm

afraid, though I know I shouldn't be so quick to say it. Oh, I remember! It was that poor wretched girl who calls herself Tiamat. Do you know her?"

Tick-Tick and I shook our heads in unison.

"Maybe she swims well. If so, it's more than one would expect. She's a lumpish, angry, red-headed girl—lives above that store on Woodruff that sells art supplies, and works at the counter there sometimes. She and someone I don't know were worrying over where to find a new source of something, because word had just gone round that Charlie was dead, and Tiamat said that she was, and I quote, 'damned well going to get it, because I'm planning on the Elflands for Christmas this year.' End of quote. I couldn't think why anyone would refer to the Elflands as if they were on a par with Cancún, but it makes sense now."

"It does, doesn't it?" said Tick-Tick. "Thank you very much. You've given us the first reasonable hint we've had."

Camphire laughed. "I believe stranger things have happened, but not very many of them. Oh, you didn't tell me what you think of the picture!"

What we thought of a piece of art that we'd had a hand in, and that had been indirectly responsible for a lead? We told her it was swell.


We found the art supply store on Woodruff. It was still open, and one of the people tending it was a red-haired human girl with a grim expression. She had been fat; her skin sagged, doughy and inelastic, on her upper arms and around her neck and chin, where the padding had disappeared too quickly beneath it. She walked uncertainly, as if her legs were new to her, and a little painful.

The Ticker studied her from across the store, frowning. I'd told her a little about the girl who'd died in the hospital, but nothing like all of it. "She is . . . there's something odd."

"It gets odder, if you let it."

"Mmm. Want me to mind the door?"

"I don't think she'll bolt. She might feel a little ganged up on with two of us, though."

"I'll be near by."

The red-haired girl was taking boxes of colored pencils out of a carton when I approached. "Excuse me," I said, and she looked up with an expression that suggested that I was not excused, and wouldn't be anytime in the near future if she could do anything about it. "Are you Tiamat?"

She nodded.

"My name is Orient. I'm . . . looking for some stuff that Bonny Prince Charlie used to have. A mutual acquaintance said you knew about it." It was surprisingly hard, this time, to talk about it.

"Who's the mutual acquaintance?"

Thick, Orient—you shouldn't have said that. "I don't think I ought to say. But the stuff—it has to do with crossing the Border."

"Humans can't cross the Border," Tiamat said, and turned back to the colored pencils.

"Not ordinarily."

"I don't know any Bonny Prince Charlie."

"Nobody does anymore, unless there's an afterlife."

"Does that mean he's dead?"

"You know he is."

"I don't know anything about him, and I don't know about his stuff."

"Yes, you do. You're taking it. I can see the effects."

Her hands stopped moving, stopped sorting. I noticed how long the fingers were, out of proportion to the palms and the thumb. What weird compound of ingredients would make your fingers grow and neglect your thumbs? Or was it even that predictable? I looked up, into her face, and found her staring at me with an unnerving mixture of hope and anger.

"What effects?" she said, and I understood. She wanted me to tell her it was working. The way the girl in the hospital had asked Rico if she could see it, could tell by looking that the transformation had happened. My stomach felt pinched.

"It's killing you," I said. "It doesn't work. You'll be dead before you see the Elflands."

Her chin came up, shifting the folds of pasty skin. "If it doesn't work, how come you can see the effects?"

"Sudden weight loss won't make you an elf. You could get the same result shooting smack. I swear to God, I just saw somebody die of this a little while ago. And she looked pretty strange, but she was still human when she died."

"You can't prove it won't work."

I was silenced; she was right. Being able to dispense truth is not one of the jobs of a finder.

"But I can prove it will work," she added.

"How?"

"By taking it until I'm changed and walking across the Border."

"And if you take it 'til you're dead, that'll prove it doesn't work, and much good it'll do you."

"No. That'll just prove it doesn't work on me."

We stared at each other again. Her grasp of the scientific method beat the hell out of mine, and her need to

believe trumped that. She needed to believe in this transformation, even if it killed her.

"Where are you getting it?"

"If it doesn't work, why do you care?" she asked,
with a haughty little smile that said she knew exactly
why I cared, and she wasn't going to tell me anything.

"He's right," said Tick-Tick over my shoulder, in an
unsteady voice. Not a voice I was used to from her. I
turned and found her face was pretty unsteady, too.
"You have . . . what's been done to you is unnatural. You
must stop taking this—no good can come of going on."

Tiamat gave the Ticker the once-over; the sullen
anger that seemed to be her most common expression
mixed with envy and a terrible wistfulness. "Where do
you get off?"

"I'm . . . I'm sorry. I can tell. . . . What could make you
do this to yourself?"

"Oh, you wouldn't know. Coming from the Elflands,
where everybody is so beautiful that nobody thinks it's
important. Well, in the World it's different. If you're not
beautiful, they make sure you know it's the most important thing ever. So what if you're smart, or nice? If you're
not pretty, they tell you to settle for what you can get,
and what the hell did you expect, anyway? So don't tell
me to settle, pretty girl. Pretty elf girl. I've tried that."
Tiamat bit her lip suddenly and grabbed up the rack of
pencils. For a moment I thought they'd spill, but she
righted them and slammed them onto a shelf.

I almost said, "I'm sorry;" I confess I was that stupid.
Not stupid enough to let the words get to my tongue,
though.

"Better think twice about trying to cut off the passport," Tiamat said, still with her back to us. "There's a lot

of us who think it's our big chance. People don't like los-
ing their big chance."

The passport. Well, everything had a name. "It's not a
passport to the Elflands," I said. "If you change your
mind, just ask around. I'm not hard to find."

I had to take Tick-Tick by the arm and propel her out
of the store, because she seemed to have forgotten how
to go by herself.

We were a block away and around the corner before
she dug in her heels (actually, grabbed the fender of a
gutted, rusted-out car that still stood by the curb) and
refused to be moved. "That was it?" she asked me, still
wearing that shaken face. "That was what had happened
to the girl who died?"

"Except that there was a lot more of it."

She rubbed her hands over her face. "That was—
blessed Isle. It was a parody of Faerie. A parody of *me*.
And yet—oh, surely not."

"What?"

"A part of it was true."

"What?" I said again, but in a different tone, because
there was something in her voice that scared me thoroughly.

"We are—the elven people are in a few ways more
like animal-kind than humans are. The wild canines
know in a dozen small ways which are members of their
pack and which not, and where they stand within those
groups. We can do that too, a little. We can sometimes
identify the blood of Faerie. And what that girl had, my
heart—it was not so, but it was very like. What can it be,
this thing we seek?"

I was just wondering if this latest piece of information
was news to Rico, when three people came around the
corner behind Tick-Tick. They weren't moving quickly,

but they were purposeful just the same. "Company," I said. "Three of them. I think they're looking for us."

"Five," Tick-Tick replied. "And no question of it."

It was almost a relief; I knew from the Ticker's face, anyway, that she'd set everything else aside for the moment to deal with whatever physical problem we might be about to have. The newcomers were all humans, and I wondered how many of them had applied for their passports. From the looks of them, if they had, none were as far along as Tiamat. Was that to our advantage or not? We needed some serious advantage. Neither of us was in the rumbling line at the best of times, and I wasn't at the top of my form right then.

They stopped and spread out—at least, the three behind Tick-Tick did, which was all I could see, since she and I hadn't changed position. Stopping was a good sign. In sane people, it means that they're willing to consider being talked out of pounding your face into the asphalt. Two male, one female, probably friends and/or roommates of Tiamat's. None of them had anything in their hands, but one of the guys had a baggy denim coat on, with pockets big enough to hold a lot of things I hoped they didn't. "It's all right," I said, trying for a soothing balance of calm and scared. "We're leaving. And we promise not to come back."

"Damn right you won't come back," said one of the ones behind me, and I had maybe part of a second to realize that one of them didn't want to be talked out of it, and that it only took one, before someone grabbed the back of my shirt. The Ticker's fist whistled past my ear and my shirt was free again, and I was sliding past her to deliver a stomping kick at the kneecap of the girl who'd come up behind her. I knew when I landed it that it wasn't in the right spot, but it stopped her anyway.

I left Tick-Tick to pay attention to things behind me. The guy in the coat was hanging back a little, but the other one, a boy with a long blond braid and a big purple bruise on the side of his jaw, waded right in. I made a feint at the bruise, which ought to have worked, so I didn't pay as much attention to defense as I should have and got a stiff one in the ribs. The girl whose knee I'd kicked lashed out at my ankle with the heel of her work boot and had her calf stomped on instead. But that put me off balance, and I couldn't do anything about it when her partner punched me somewhere in the vicinity of the kidneys.

One thing led to another, as things do if you let them. We ended up with me on my feet but pretty thoroughly immobilized by two people who, if they hadn't had a grudge against me when they came down the street, certainly did now, and Tick-Tick pinned down to the hood of a long-abandoned Buick Special by three people, one of them the guy in the coat, who was holding a pistol with the barrel end in the hair over her ear. Him and his damned pockets. We were all breathing hard.

I knew next to nothing about guns—it wasn't my job. Tick-Tick knew about them, though. The guy in the coat pulled the hammer back with his thumb. The Ticker's face looked as if it had never worn an expression in its life.

Guns are pretty rare in Bordertown. Ammunition is even more so. I kept my voice low and even, so it wouldn't startle anyone, and said, "Tick-Tick? Is it loaded?"

Tick-Tick, who knew about guns and what they did and how they did it, who had the acute hearing of her species, would have listened when the hammer went back; she would know, from the sound of metal on metal, if there was a round in the chamber. If there wasn't, I hadn't figured out what we would do, since there were still five of them and two of us. But we would probably think of something.

In a voice as blank as her face, the Ticker said, "Yes."

I hadn't been afraid until then, I discovered. "What do you want us to do?"

"Just wanted to make sure you knew we were serious," said one of the ones pinning Tick-Tick, a dark-skinned female one. "Don't come back. It's none of your business what happens to us."

I thought of the day's events, thought of saying that if the climate of public opinion got any worse, it would be everybody's business, that there were people who already considered it their business who had even less reason than I did. But all I wanted was to see the side of Tick-Tick's head undamaged and out from under that gun barrel. So all I said was, "It's a deal. We're going."

The guy with the gun stepped back first, keeping Tick-Tick covered. Then the other two let her go, and she straightened up slowly. "Go on," said the gun owner. I realized it was the first time he'd spoken; his voice was higher than I'd expected.

"What about my friend?" asked the Ticker.

"Start walking. When you get to the end of the block, we'll let him go."

For the life of me—maybe literally—I couldn't think why they'd do it this way. Pure harassment?

Tick-Tick turned around, leaned against the fender of the Buick, and folded her arms. "Maybe you'd better just shoot me and be done with it."

"Go on!"

"Not without my friend."

"Tick-Tick," I said, "go ahead."

She wrinkled her mouth. "I don't feel like it."

The two people holding me didn't loosen up, but I could tell their attention was caught. The dark-skinned girl said, "Are you crazy? We're not afraid to shoot you. What's your problem?"

"He's my best friend," Tick-Tick said to her, as if she were explaining why one shouldn't cross the street when there was traffic coming. "I'm not stirring without him."

"He's a human," said the guy with the gun.

Tick-Tick blinked. "No, really?" She didn't sound a bit sarcastic.

Still, the dark-skinned woman took a step toward her.

"No," said the Ticker. "I will not run, and I will not fight, and I will not leave here without my friend. Let him go," she told the two who held me, and they did. Probably out of surprise. Once they did, I stood where I was, and since I refused to do anything hostile, they probably felt it would look silly to grab me again.

We all looked at each other for maybe half a minute. Finally the dark-skinned girl said, "If you come back, we'll shoot you dead. We won't do any talking."

"Fair enough," Tick-Tick replied. I joined her by the fender, and we started up the road. Nobody said anything, so we kept going. After two blocks we looked back. They were gone.

My place was closer than hers at that point, so we headed toward it. Twilight had set in; everyone who lived south of Ho was finally awake and looking for something to get into. Now that I knew to look for it, I saw signs of pulled threads in the social fabric—odd, suspicious, sliding-away glances at Tick-Tick or at me from humans or elves, respectively, whom we didn't know. There were people around town, apparently, who believed that one or the other of us was letting the species down.

We didn't do a lot of talking until we got to my building. Then Tick-Tick said, "What now, my dear?"

I had been thinking about that, which was why I hadn't been talking. "I say to hell with Linn's little plan to keep this quiet. Rico needs to know all this."

She nodded. We made it to the first-floor landing before I remembered that I was out of beer.

"Go on up," I told her. I went back down and cadged two bottles of lager from my neighbor Yoshi, who looked like he'd just gotten up.

"I owe you," I said.

"Nah. I think I owe you. Anyway, don't worry about it." He scratched his scalp with both hands and yawned.

I tramped back up the stairs with the two sweating bottles. At the end of the hall, my door was open, and the room beyond was dark. I set the bottles down on the floor outside and bumped the door open with my arm at full stretch. Tick-Tick was sitting in the armchair by the window.

"You didn't light a lamp."

Her silhouette shook its head. "Hadn't the energy. And the dark is so restful—"

Her words stuck on a long and painful-sounding cough.

# TALKING HEADS

S HE WAS TIRED—reasonable enough, *I* was tired, it had
been a hell of a day—and said, if I didn't mind, she'd
as soon sleep in the armchair as stumble off home.

"I mind," I answered. "You can have the bed."

"Where will you sleep?" She really did look tired; her
eyelids drooped, her shoulders drooped, and her head
was carried a little crooked, like a rose beginning to sag
on the stem.

"Same place I slept before I got the bed. On the floor."

"Aren't you a little bruised and chipped for that sort
of thing?"

"Nah. Foam pad and a sleeping bag will take care
of it."

She protested a little, but only a little. She slid from
the chair over to the bed in one boneless motion, and
seemed to fall asleep as soon as she landed.

It didn't sound like a restful sleep. I lay on the floor in
my sleeping bag listening to her cough, because I knew

I'd wake up every time she did it, anyway. Not a familiar
sound. Tick-Tick had been hurt before, and sick drunk
once in my memory (tequila shots, immoderately taken,
will make even an elf sick), and mildly food-poisoned a
couple of times, from one cause or another. I couldn't
remember ever hearing her cough before, and the
strangeness of it, and the intensity, brought me fully conscious every time she did it.

When the light through the window got to be too
much to ignore, and the room warmed up too much for
the sleeping bag, I got up and put a kettle of water on. I
was out of peppermint tea, which the Ticker would have
liked, and out of licorice root, which she wouldn't have
liked but which would have been good for her. There was
purple coneflower, though, which according to Ms. Wu
was good for the immune system. Okay, better late than
never. I made a pot, poured out two cups (I had no idea if
I could catch anything she could catch, but a well-
groomed immune system is an ornament to one's life at
the best of times), and took hers to the bedside.

"Hullo," she croaked. Tick-Tick usually wakes up
quickly and gracefully, unlike yours truly. This was obviously not going to be one of the usual days.

"Tea. Do you want honey in it?"

"No, thank you. I'm sorry if I kept you up. I did,
didn't I?"

I thought about lying politely, but it would have been
pointless. "I think Linn gave you his stupid cold."

"I think you're right. Probably the day before yesterday; he was coughing at the hospital."

"I hope he's miserable."

"For shame, dear heart. I assure you, I'm not miserable. Indeed, once we finish this pot of tea, I think we
should venture out for breakfast. Oh, but I was *so* weary

last night, as if all the virtue had been drawn off from my blood!"

She spoke in a good, strong, lively voice, but spoiled it by coughing at the end.

"I can cook something here."

"Certainly. This from the boy who had to beg beer from his neighbor last night, and I know very well that if you have nothing else consumable in the kitchen, you have beer. I had something more sustaining in mind to break my fast than fried water."

She was right, of course. "I can go out and get something and cook it here."

"No, my dear, if I'm in a weakened state, the last thing I need is your cooking. Huevos rancheros at Taco Hell will set me up to a nicety, if it's open yet."

It was, for a wonder. Mingus, in fact, looked as if he hadn't been to bed yet, which didn't interfere with his cooking. I looked around for his sister Electra, without much hope; she's not the kind of girl who sees eight o'clock in the morning very often. If she was seeing it that day, she wasn't doing it at Taco Hell. One less compelling distraction. I had, suddenly, an urge to know what Sunny Rico was doing at eight in the morning. Idle curiosity.

The Ticker and I ate, and talked about nothing very consequential. We avoided the matter that had absorbed us all day yesterday as if we were under a compulsion. Tick-Tick explained to me that fresh salsa was the best remedy for a cold the world has ever known, and I wanted to know, if that was true, why hospital food was bland.

She laughed, and coughed, and, suddenly serious, said, "I'm sorry I told Rico that you didn't like hospitals."

I shrugged. "No reason why you shouldn't. I didn't think you knew."

"You've never said, all in one piece, what your life was like before you came to the Borderlands. But you've said bits of things. . . . I suppose it's like knowing who lives in a house by the washing they hang on the line. I've come to understand that your family thought of your talent much the way my family thought of mine." She began to pleat her napkin. "I believe that your mother didn't like you very much."

"No, she just had a lot on her mind." It still bothered me, though. You're supposed to be able to count on your mother putting in a good word for you in spite of everything. All those serial killers, down through history, whose mothers swore to the reporters, "He would never have done that—he was a *good* boy."

"Why?"

"Why, what?" I'd lost the thread.

"Why did she have such a lot on her mind?"

"Oh. Because I busted up her marriage. Or at least that's what Dad said in the message on the answering machine."

Her brows climbed up her forehead. "The *answering machine?*"

"He's a modern kind of guy. Mom picked me up after track practice, we came home, she played back the messages while I made us a snack, and there it was."

Tick-Tick sat with her mouth open, until another round of coughing seized her. She gulped water and croaked, "Mab and all attendants. What did he say?"

"He said," (and I knew exactly what he'd said, even after all those years, but I preferred to paraphrase it), "that he'd had his chromosomes checked, and they were normal, so it had to be her fault, genetically, that their only child was a mutant weirdo, and he was going to find a normal woman and have children with her before he was too old to father a proper son."

The Ticker thought about this. "I'm sorry to have to say it to your face, but I think your father was not the most well-spoken man I've ever heard tell of. What, then, did your mother do?"

"She'd been a nurse, before I was born. She got recertified, and got work in a hospital emergency room. Which, she found out, is a hell of a lot different from being some specialist's office nurse, which was what she was used to. I gotta tell you, in the list of jobs you should not take home with you, night shift ER is right up there. And it made her kind of . . . unstable. She started saying things to me, out loud, that she'd probably thought before, but at least hadn't felt the urge to share. So," I shrugged again, "I have bad associations with hospitals."

"Gracious," Tick-Tick said mildly. "Most of us simply go straight to the source and have bad associations with our mothers."

That made me sort of laugh, which was a better way to end the meal. Tick-Tick stood up from the table and said she was going home.

"Should I come along?" I asked.

"Whatever would I do with you underfoot? No, I believe you have an errand to run."

"I do?"

"I distinctly remember hearing you say that Rico needed to know about yesterday's events."

"Yeah. But . . ."

"But what?"

"I mean . . . will you be all right?"

"Good grief," she said, a little explosion in words. "I only have a cold."

"Okay, okay. Make some chicken soup or something."

"Yes, my keeper. Now do make yourself scarce."

We parted on the sidewalk. I heard, behind me, the sound of her cough.

There weren't a lot of people at the Chrystoble Street copshop. Shift change had been hours ago, and in Bordertown, as in most places, first shift is a relatively quiet time for the cops. The one with desk duty was the green-haired halfie woman with the dragon tattoo I'd seen the last time I'd been in the station, the ill-fated morning that Walt Felkin blew up. There was another guy I didn't recognize, who seemed to be filling out a claim for somebody, at one of the long tables; and there was Captain Hawthorn, who walked through the door that led to the back rooms just as I came in.

He was surprised, in a well-bred sort of way. "Orient! I had no idea you were up and around already. Are you certain you're not pushing yourself?"

"No, just walking like normal." That got me a blank look from Hawthorn and a little noise from the desk cop. "Is Rico here?"

Hawthorn looked to the desk cop, who told me, "Nope. I think she's at home. I suppose I can give you the address . . ."

"Don't worry," I said, "I'll find it." Thataway.

"Is there anything I can help with?" Hawthorn asked.

Rico thought we were looking, at least in part, for a cop. "No, just checking in. Almost a social call, actually. See you."

Rico lived in a nicer neighborhood than I did. Not that mine's a bad neighborhood, just that anyplace where you can live without paying rent won't be the aesthetic equivalent of Boardwalk and Park Place. And it wasn't that Rico lived on the Hill, either. Thataway said she was behind the façade of one of a block of red-brick row-houses. Their steps and mortar were in good repair, and none of the windows had blankets substituting for curtains, which told me that all of the people who lived there had done so for a while and planned to go on doing it. The row fronted on a street split down the middle by a broad median strip planted with grass and trees.

I triangulated a little and determined that hers would be the second door from the east end. Yes, four mechanical bells mounted in the doorframe, and "Rico" under the top one. Fourth floor. She probably chose it on purpose to keep in shape. I twisted the bell knob.

Just to my left I heard a distant bonging noise, like someone whacking a radiator at the far end of a pipe. It was a speaking tube, I discovered.

"Who is it?" asked the far-away voice, which was probably Rico's.

"It's Orient," I shouted back.

That produced a nerve-racking silence. It hadn't previously occurred to me that she might not *want* to see me, or that this might be a bad time, or that she might be annoyed that I'd found her doorstep and shown up on it. No, she'd said, next time come wake me up, but this wasn't the next time, exactly . . .

"I'll come down," the voice said, and I felt a wave of relief big enough to surf on. Then I wondered what I'd been expecting, since being told to go away wouldn't have done me any lasting damage.

As I would have expected, it didn't take Sunny Rico much time at all to come down four flights of stairs. I saw her through the heavy glass in the door; she came loping round the corner and down the last few steps into the little dim-lit tiled hall with the smooth, swooping motion of a good hurdler. Whatever stresses this case had put her under, they hadn't cut into her energy.

She opened the door and stood in it.

"Hello," I said, stalling for time.

"Hello. What's up?"

"I have a lump of new information for you."

"You," she said with a barely perceptible increase in force, "are not supposed to be concerned with information for me. At least, I remember telling you so. Do *you* remember?"

Ouch. "Could we go somewhere a little more private? And comfortable?"

"What for?"

"Oh, for crying out loud. Look, I have things you should probably hear. Is it going to do either of us any good for you not to hear 'em? Will that make it all right that I didn't do what you told me to?"

She breathed out, loudly. "No. But if I listen to you, it'll only encourage you. Christ, I have to listen to you, don't I?" She stepped back and held the door. "Come on up."

I would have loved to have known how long it ordinarily took Rico to go up four flights of stairs, but this wasn't a fair test; she climbed them at a staid pace out of respect for company. The stair layout suggested, as the doorbells had, that each floor was a separate apartment. The fourth floor certainly was. It had a tidy floor plan, probably not much different from the way it was when the place was built. The walls were mostly white, framed and bordered and vaulted in dark oak, except for the dining room, which was papered in a small-figured monochrome print of flowers and leaves in a light rusty-rose. A row of casement windows set into the front wall of the parlor were all open. Rico led me through the parlor, the dining room, and down a short hallway with a couple of closed doors in it to the back of the apartment, and the kitchen. This was mostly white, too, and none of the very few things on the countertop was purely ornamental. It was the kitchen—the apartment, in fact—of someone who couldn't spend a lot of time there, and when she could, didn't want to spend it dusting knick-knacks. Still, something about it made it strongly hers, and I was torn between feeling as if I ought to tiptoe, and wanting to sneak looks into cupboards.

Rico gestured at a little drop-leaf table under the back window, and one of the chairs pulled up to it. "Tea?" she asked. "Beer? Blackberry juice?"

"Beer, please." I got a look in her icebox as she opened it. It had lots more things in it than mine, and none of them seemed to have green stuff growing on them. She popped the tops on the beers and set one in front of me. It didn't have a label. I took a swallow. "That's familiar."

"Huh. My neighbor down the street makes it, but not for sale. I wonder where you had it. It's a nice summer hammock beer. Not very fizzy, either."

"A little heavy on the hops." Then I remembered. "I had this at Chrystoble Street! This is the same stuff Hawthorn brought out from the back room."

"That accounts for it—I take extras down to the station house, sometimes. Now, are you going to tell me what all the excitement's about?"

I told her about yesterday's adventures. I gave her a good-sized sampling of the reactions we'd gotten to our questions, which made her wince, but she motioned me to go on. I told her what Camphire had overheard from Tiamat, and I told her about my conversation with Tiamat, and our subsequent meeting with Tiamat's friends.

"Oh, good," Rico said at last. "Drug-crazed elf wannabes with a gun, *with* bullets. The town thick with paranoid-bigot rumors. And Linn sick in bed."

"In bed, is he? Whatever he's come down with, he's given it to Tick-Tick."

She frowned. "When did he have a chance to give it to Tick-Tick?"

Time to decide if I was going to give Linn away to his partner. I decided not. "He came 'round to her place yesterday to grill me about the bomb, but the Ticker says she probably caught it from him the day before, at the hospital."

Rico continued to frown, and stare at me. Her jaw moved, as if she were absently probing a tooth with her tongue. "That seems odd. Doesn't it?"

"Does it?"

"Have you ever seen an elf with a head cold?"

"No," I said, after a little consideration. "But you learn something new every day."

"I've never seen one. And forty-eight hours is pretty quick incubation, I think, for respiratory bugs. If it's that easy for elves to catch a cold, we ought to have seen an example of it before this."

"It must be a real beaut, anyway—Tick-Tick's never sick."

She shook her head. "This bothers me. You saw Linn yesterday?"

"Yeah. He seemed tired, and he had a hell of a cough, but he said it was overwork and the smoke at the bomb site."

"But of course, that's not what it was after all." Rico raked her fingers through her hair, across the top where it was shortest. She was sitting in a patch of sun from the kitchen window, and the light sparkled back from the occasional white hair amid the brown ones.

"How old are you?" I asked suddenly.

"What?"

"Sorry. Never mind."

"Not as old as I feel right now," she sighed. "Oh, and speaking of things that make me feel old, I consulted Milo Chevrolet yesterday about this stuff we're—I'm after."

Milo was one of the most powerful magicians in Bordertown; he'd used some of that power to carve out a magic-free space to live in, which he'd filled with three hundred volumes of nonfiction and a model railroad. He could make a fetus feel old. "And he says?" I asked, cautiously.

"He was annoyed when I kept calling it a drug. He says that properly it's a mutagen, if it's making permanent changes in the bodies of the people taking it."

"It's a who?"

"Never mind. Until somebody fails to die of it, there's no saying the changes are permanent, anyway. I reserve the right to save time and call it a drug. Unfortunately, he hasn't seen any of it."

"Well, Tiamat has."

"Mmm. Ordinarily, I'd have that art supply store staked out, and follow this Tiamat around until we found the next link up. But lately when I find people, they tend to get snuffed."

I considered this. One of the snuffed, of course, was someone I'd found, but I appreciated her restraint in not mentioning it. "Why?" I asked.

She looked at me as if I were a rare form of bread mold. "What do you mean, why? To keep them from leading me to the next link in the chain."

"No, I know that. I mean, why is it an unavoidable result?"

Rico's turn to consider. She scanned my face as she did so, but as if it might have been any face; she was just looking at me for something to look at. Still, I felt as if I might be blushing, so I concentrated on drinking beer. Yes, too hoppy. What a shame. Could have been a contender.

"Linn's the only other cop I can trust absolutely," Rico said finally. "The ones I don't really suspect of being in the trade, I can't be sure will keep quiet. They might trust people I wouldn't. And I don't know how long Linn's going to be sidelined."

"So why do you need Linn?" After his proposal to me the day before, and Tick-Tick's analysis of it, I confess I didn't entirely trust Linn, though I had a hard time imagining him involved with the bad guys in this case. "Take care of it yourself, and you don't have to worry who trusts who."

"Whom."

I frowned at her. "Are you sure?"

"Cross my heart." She made the gesture over the light green cotton of her very large shirt. I felt as if I were invading her privacy and looked away. "I need Linn or someone, because you can't stake out a place by yourself, *and* be prepared to follow any of the tenants if they leave."

"Oh." I finished my beer. "You'll find somebody to do it."

"What, no volunteers?"

"I've proved that I get in trouble if you let me out of your sight."

This time it was my face she was looking at. "If I

thought you'd done it on purpose, I'd give you free room and board in jail until this business was over."

"No, you wouldn't. Just think, there I'd be within reach of the corrupt mystery cop. He might do me in to keep me from interfering."

"I haven't been that lucky." She finished her beer. "And I don't think you get in trouble on purpose. I think it's pure natural aptitude. But do you think you could maybe curb it for a few hours at a stretch?"

"Excuse?"

"Don't be thick. I hereby invite you, grudgingly, to share my stakeout." She took up both bottles and carried them to the counter. Then she turned back and gave me a look that felt as if she'd grabbed the front of my shirt with both hands and picked me up. "But before you get puffed up about it, listen to me: This is not a God-damned Hardy Boys adventure. This is all live fire and real trouble, and more people's safety than just yours on the line. You do what I tell you, and if you do one thing more than that I swear I'll drop everything to deport you under police escort back to the World."

I was at a loss for what to say.

"Your line," she said grimly, "Is, 'Yes, Ma'am.' "

"No," I said at last, "I don't think that's it."

Her eyebrows went up. "Come again?"

"That's not how you and Linn work, is it?"

"Linn is an experienced professional. I know what to expect out of him, and he knows what to expect from me. We have a couple of years' worth of shorthand that allows us to react to surprises as a team. You don't have that, and if I were to count on you as if you did, I might as well stay home and play Russian roulette." I didn't think I reacted, but she was looking at me, and added, "Sorry. But that's the truth."

I folded my hands on the tabletop and looked out the window. It *was* a nice neighborhood; the wooden balcony was in good repair, and recently painted, and sported a wooden folding chair and a little table with a candle on it, any of which would have eventually wandered away from a back stoop in my neighborhood. From the distance between Rico's balcony and the one on the back of the buildings across the way, I suspected there was a small courtyard below.

"Whatever it is, go ahead and spit it out," she said.

Still looking out the window, I said, "I have a partner, too." Rico didn't say anything, so I went on. "We have that kind of relationship. We don't usually do anything as dangerous as you and Linn, but we break a lot of trail in the Nevernever, and travel rough, and we have to count on each other to decide the right thing pretty quickly. So I understand what you're saying."

"And?"

"And that's why I can't just promise to take orders. I know myself. I'm not in the habit. I just won't. That wouldn't bother me—I'd go ahead and promise, and do what had to be done, and explain myself to you afterward—except for one thing. You insist on taking responsibility for what I do. Linn said that was why you didn't want me to work on the case anymore. Which is okay, if you're the boss and I'm the lackey, and all I have to do is remember to ask, 'Do you want fries with that?' But that's not how it'll happen, and you won't be responsible for my actions, but you'll try to be. On those terms, I think I'd rather stay an outsider, and work with *my* partner, and spend another day like yesterday. It may have been uncomfortable, but you can't say it didn't work."

She didn't say anything for a few moments, so I turned to see what was going on. She was leaning up against the counter looking at me, with an expression that, except for a certain amount of amusement, was hard to sort out. "When you and Tick-Tick are working together," she began, gently, "don't you ever give each other orders?"

"I don't—"

"Duck? Hold this? Watch out? Grab that end, quick? And are you telling me that if something happened to Tick-Tick, especially when she was in your company, you'd say, 'Darn shame, but she wasn't my responsibility'?"

"No. I'm not telling you that."

"Good. Because I wouldn't have believed it. Linn and I give each other orders, and we're responsible for each other. That's what *I'm* in the habit of doing, and I'm not likely to change the way I work, either. I'm not asking you to shuffle and roll your eyes. I'm asking you to do what I tell you, when I tell you, in any potentially dangerous situation, on the off chance that my experience might tip me off to trouble before you spotted it."

"Does it work both ways?"

"I promise you, if you tell me to duck, I'll do it. Don't abuse the privilege."

I looked back out the window, but this time, not at anything particular. "I don't know," I said.

And I really didn't.

I'd thought I'd have to browbeat her into letting me help again, and I'd thought that without considering why it was I was so hot to do it. Then, when she'd turned high-handed on me, I wanted to prove to her that I deserved better—and I wanted to walk out after I did it, and wait for her to browbeat *me* into changing my mind and helping. I obviously hadn't thought about what I was doing, because nothing was less like Sunny Rico than that.

Now she'd presented me with an option that, somewhere in the back of my head, I realized was exactly what I wanted. Or had wanted, not so long ago. And I couldn't say yes.

What she was asking me to do was to be her new partner. She was asking me to be a cop. Unofficially, temporarily—but she'd as good as said that she considered what she was asking of me to be the equivalent of what she expected of Linn. She just didn't expect me to be as good at it, that was all. Maybe that was what rankled, though a second's worth of thought told me I wasn't, and wouldn't want anyone to believe I was. Maybe it was that I didn't, even temporarily, want to be considered police officer material. Well, that was true enough.

But it occurred to me that what I wanted her to ask was something different. I didn't exactly know what— maybe something with more of a sense of high adventure in it? No chance; she'd already pointed out that this wasn't the Hardy Boys, and I didn't think that she'd call it the Three Musketeers, either. This was her job—her hard, nerve-wracking, intermittently sordid job. No high adventure.

"You can think about it," she said. Her voice cut through my confusion and made me jump.

She was still leaning against the kitchen counter. In the huge shirt and a pair of skinny jeans with the knees worn through, and her brown hair rumpled, she looked younger than I'd ever seen her. Until I looked at her face. There were lines at the corners of her eyes, but her age lay in something other than wrinkles, in the sternness that set her features even now, when she was smiling a little.

"Twenty-five? Twenty-six?" I asked.

"Stubborn bastard." The smile widened. "It's something like that."

"Don't you know?"

She tilted her head a little to one side, not in the coy, fey gesture I'd seen other people use, but as if she wanted to see me with the light a little different. Very serious person, Sunny Rico. Her age was in that, too; even when she smiled, even when she was witty, she was very serious. "Have you ever been back to the World since you first came to B-town?" she asked.

I shook my head.

"I have, a couple of times. Never for very long, or very far in. Every time, the calendar surprised me."

"What do you mean?"

"You know that time in the Elflands runs differently—*lots* differently, sometimes—from the way it does here?"

I nodded again. My friend Strider had told me once of slipping back across the Border after he'd been in town for six months (I didn't ask him why he'd done it, because I think he was taking a risk by telling me as much as he had; Strider's exile, enforced or self-imposed, had a whiff of politics about it). In the Elflands, only two months had passed. Another friend said she'd run away to Bordertown for two weeks, when she was very young, and come dragging home to the Elflands to find it was a little over a year later and her parents had staged her funeral *in absentia* the week before.

"It's also true of the Borderlands and the World. The discrepancy isn't as big, but the longer you're here, the further off you'll find you've gotten from World Standard Time. I'm probably anything from twenty-three to twenty-eight at the moment, depending on when I leave the Borderlands, and you don't know how old you are, either."

"That's silly. You know how long it's been for you, so that's how old you are."

"Maybe. You can count years. You can count days. You can even count hours. But how do you know those hours are as long as the ones where you used to live?"

"They *feel* like it."

"They would, wouldn't they? This is the Borderlands. If everything wasn't different when you got here, why would anyone bother to run away to it?"

"I've forgotten what we were talking about," I said irritably.

"No, you haven't. Go home and think about it. But for God's sake don't take too long."

I stood up and walked past her, down the hallway, through the dining room, to the bright, pleasant parlor. I stopped at the door. "Why did you become a cop?" I asked her, though I hadn't meant to.

"My dad was one," she answered promptly.

"My dad," I said, taking care to get it right, "was a division vice president for a company that designed medical appliances."

"Did he do it well?"

I blinked. "I think so."

"That's the difference, then. Let me know what you decide."

Before I could think of an answer, I was on the other side of the door, and it was closed.


I wandered around town for an hour or two (how long were they? How could I tell?), thinking. To help me think, I bought a fish taco at a stand near Chrystoble and

Delight. The guy who ran it, a tall, thin human with brown hair and dark eyes under tortoise-shell glasses and the kind of long, bony face that a lot of women like, fried the fish while I waited, and gave me my pick of other ingredients. It was, as best I could tell, authentically Mexican, but his accent was authentic Eastern European, and his faded T-shirt was lettered in Cyrillic. The fish was absolutely fresh.

"Where's this from?" I asked, gesturing at the fish.

"From the dock. I buy them there in the morning, and I keep them very cold. It is terrible when they are not fresh."

"What dock?"

He looked over the tops of his glasses at me. "The one on the shore. These are ocean fish. I would not use river fish."

I'd heard rumors about this—that Bordertown was, on some days, in some neighborhoods, when the wind was right, an oceanfront property—but I'd never seen it for myself. I said so.

He shrugged. "Two years ago, I ran away from my uncle's house in Bratsk, in Irkutsk. I struck out across country, thinking that I would join the road far from anyplace where I would be known as my uncle's nephew, and beg a ride west. I did not know where I was going, except that I was going away from Bratsk. I became lost, of course. I was two days in the woods without food, and very cold, when I came out of the trees to find myself on the banks of Lake Baikal. Its closest part is more than four hundred and fifty kilometers east of Bratsk. I could not have walked so far in two days. But there it was, the great lake like oil in the darkness, and on the shore far to my left a city, shining with lights and strange towers like none I had seen in pictures of Moscow or St. Petersburg.

I walked toward it, and at last entered it, hungry and tired, and it was Bordertown.

"In these two years, I have not seen Lake Baikal again. But I think that is because I have not wanted to."

I'd never seen Bordertown's ocean; but then, I'm an inland kind of guy. "Why Mexican food?" I asked at last.

"I like it best."

The only sensible reason, now that I thought about it. I thanked him and finished my taco as I walked.

I had no idea what I wanted anymore. For a moment I wondered what Sunny Rico wanted, what she hoped I'd decide. I would almost have gone back to ask her, except for a nagging feeling that it would be embarrassing, and that it would bother me more to be embarrassed in front of Rico than in front of most other people. And what had she meant about her father, anyway? That he'd been an inept cop? That he'd died at it, maybe? Surely that would warn his offspring away more than anything else.

The problem was, my head was too full. I decided to walk back to Tick-Tick's and see how she was, and run some of this by her.

When I hollered under her window and nothing happened, I didn't know whether to be worried or relieved. She was inside delirious with fever; she felt so much better that she'd gone out. I hollered again.

This time she stuck her head out. She smiled at me, but it was a tired smile. "What, you again?"

"I think so. Which makes two of us."

"C'mon up." She pulled the ring that unlatched the front door.

The picture part of the tapestry that Tick-Tick's neighbor was weaving in the atrium was done. Young Andrew sat sprawling at the base of his tree, his arms and legs in painful-looking attitudes. The bag on his lap had partly spilled into the grass, and the rope weaving was accented with metallic fibers there. The brothers were leaving the clearing at one end—one of them taking a last glance over his shoulder at his handiwork—as the wolves prepared to enter from the other. The border was in progress, but I saw that if Weegee had found his skull, he hadn't installed it.

All the bamboo blinds were let down over the windows on the west side of the Ticker's big room, which made it a little dimmer than I was used to.

"Hope you aren't trying to read in this," I said.

She was stretched out on the couch. "The light hurts my eyes. You can raise them, though, if the gloom weighs on your spirit." She smiled when she said it, but followed it up with a fit of coughing. It was a dry cough, and sounded painful. I filled the kettle and put it on the heat.

"My spirit can take it for the sake of your eyes. How do you feel?"

She didn't answer immediately. I put the first herb tea I could find in the teapot and got the honey out, along with a spoon and a mug. Then I went over to the couch.

Whatever this was, she'd gotten it from Linn, all right. She had that same dimmed and faded look. I put a hand on her forehead, and it was hot under my palm. "I don't know much about diseases of elves," I said apologetically.

"Neither do I, to speak truth," the Ticker said. She spoke softly, maybe to keep the cough at bay. "Though oddly enough, we are healthier in the Borderlands than in the lands that gave us birth. The evil airs that bring disease are ill-suited, perhaps, to this hybrid place."

I went back to the stove, poured water into the teapot, and brought it and all the accessories over. "How much honey do you want in it?"

She shook her head. "I suppose it had better be a lot."

That's what I gave her. We found ourselves dwelling over the commonplaces—"Careful, it's hot," and "Set it down over there," and all the rest of them—and I thought of Rico and Linn, and the giving and taking of orders. And instead of telling her about my visit to Rico, I said, "This isn't a cold, is it?"

She looked up at me, and I could see the fright in her eyes. "I don't know. It might yet be."

"But you don't think so."

"I don't *know*. I've so little experience of sickness—it could be nothing, and I might fancy myself at death's door."

"Linn's in bed with it, and Rico thinks that's odd. *I* think it's odd."

She turned her head away roughly, which set her to coughing until her eyes streamed with tears. I made her drink some tea, and after a bit she could say, in a small voice, "I think it's odd, too."

"What do you want me to do?"

"I think . . ." She closed her eyes, and for a few moments lay still, only the rise and fall of her chest keeping me from panic. At last she said, "I think you should bring Ms. Wu."

Ms. Wu was not, strictly speaking, a doctor, though she knew a good deal of medicine. But she was a powerful magician, certainly the equal of Milo Chevrolet. For all anyone knew, she had been here since the Elflands came back; she might have been created all of a piece with the Borderlands themselves.

"Then you *don't* think it's just a cold."

She caught at my fingers, her hands still warm from cradling her tea. "I'm afraid, Orient," she whispered.

So was Rico. So, for that matter, was I.

# THE TRANSFORMATION
# BLUES

B ORDERTOWN: THE LAND where doctors and high-pow-
ered magicians run Chinese grocery stores. I didn't
actually run all the way to Wu's Worldly Emporium, in
the sense that untrained people use "run." I used the gait
I'd learned as a cross-country runner in high school and
had enough use for over the years that I'd never forgotten it. It ate miles in a hurry, and it tended to drop you
into a light trance, in which you could stand a little back
from your worries—who was behind you, who was
ahead of you, or, in this instance, why you felt the need
to be in such a rush.

So I arrived just a little short of breath, and with the
aura of someone who'd been doing honest work, rather
than being overcome with panic. Elsewhere, the bookstore that Wolfboy and Sparks ran, was right next door. I
had an urge to stick my head in, to tell them that Tick-
Tick was sick—but that would be silly. There was nothing
to worry about. People got sick all the time, and I was

taking care of it by consulting Ms. Wu, so why should I bother Wolfboy and Sparks unnecessarily?

I hadn't been in Ms. Wu's store for a month or two, and when I pushed through the door, I expected a few changes. Like every other retail establishment in B-town, Wu's is at the mercy of the elements, the Border, the independent haulers, and the luck of the draw for its stock. Ms. Wu probably did her own importing, rather than rely on the maverick buyers who set up temporary wholesale dealerships on Mondays in the old Raven Ice Company warehouse down by the river. Still, you never knew when a truck would go unaccountably astray in the Borderlands. It happened often enough that a fair percentage of the Ticker's and my business was in rescuing lost truckers and their cargo from the Nevernever.

I counted on garlic, and jasmine soap, and ginseng tea, and glazed pottery jars of candied ginger; umbrellas, pearls, ebony boxes, bunches of leeks, and sticks of ink. I also counted on Ms. Wu, who looked like Claudette Colbert, smiled like a skinny female Buddha, and laughed more often than anyone else I knew. She would be concerned when I told her about Tick-Tick, but she wouldn't frown; she'd say, "Of course," and turn to the antique apothecary's chest behind the counter and select things from it, put them in her bag and come with me to Tick-Tick's. There she'd make my partner drink weird-smelling things, prescribe an unpleasant change in her diet, tell her to wear nothing but blue until all the symptoms were gone, mess with the *feng shui* of the room, and leave, and everything would be better.

Wu's was much the same as it always was. The change was in Ms. Wu.

She'd never looked middle-aged, though it seemed as if she was; she'd always had one of those terrific 1930s movie heartthrob figures, and her silk-black hair never showed any gray. She dressed with practical elegance, and I'd imagined her coming from a wealthy Hong Kong family, bringing her sense of style and *noblesse oblige* to straitened circumstances on the Border.

Now she sat behind the counter with her head in both hands, her face hidden. Her white blouse sagged, and her trousers were wrinkled and limp. Her hair was dragged back into a twist at the back, and wisps of hair were springing out of it at odd intervals. There was a bell over the door that rang as I came in, but she hadn't looked up.

"Ms. Wu?" I said.

She lifted her head and didn't smile. "Orient." She said it the way one might count off mileposts by the highway, saying them aloud to fix them in place. "Can I help you?"

"I hope so. Tick-Tick's sick with something."

For an instant, her face went slack with despair. Then she shut her eyes and said, "Tell me the symptoms."

I did. She turned to the apothecary's chest in a parody of the scene I'd imagined, sliding out the little drawers and bringing calico-wrapped parcels or crushed leaves in waxed paper bags or tiny brown glass vials out of them. Her hands trembled a little, and the veins stood out in the backs of them.

"What do you think it is?" I asked.

She pushed all the things she'd taken out of the chest into a tight pile on the counter, and stood staring at them. "I think," she began, slowly; then she stopped herself. A much-diluted version of her smile flickered on her face. "I think that not even you would be so silly as to ask the doctor for a diagnosis when her patient is halfway across town. How did you get here?"

"On foot."

"I have a bicycle, so I'm afraid I can't give you a ride back. Tell me the address, and I'll meet you there."

"I could lead you—"

"I'm sure you could, but it would be much slower, really."

I figured out that what she really wanted was to be relieved of me hanging over her shoulder and worrying while she packed her bag. So I did as I was told, and loped off to Tick-Tick's again.

We arrived at our destination at pretty much the same time. Ms. Wu did it on a particularly nice all-terrain bike with fifteen speeds, well-suited to the uncertain topography and pavement of Bordertown. She hoisted her black leather bag out of the wire basket over the back wheel and told me, "Lead the way." I'd remembered, when I'd left to fetch her, to take one of Tick-Tick's keys to the front door, so I did that.

When we came in, the Ticker was sitting propped up against the raised end of the fainting couch with an Arabian Nights-ish shawl spread over her legs, looking tidy and composed. The cough spoiled the effect a little, and the weakness of her voice when she said, "Gracious, that was quick." But it galled her to receive company in a state of disarray, and I knew that, however much effort she'd gone to to make it look as if she wasn't sick, it was necessary to her peace of mind.

Ms. Wu sent me away, which was fine with me. I took a cup of tea out to the front stoop, sat in the ruddy light of the setting sun, and tried to think sensibly about Rico's offer. Unless Tick-Tick recovered immediately, it seemed as if I could ignore it. My first responsibility was to make tea and run errands for my partner, or whatever needed to be done for the duration. What's more, looked at simply as a job, the last thing I wanted to do was police surveillance, or anything like the things I'd already done with Rico. I didn't like the suspense. So I didn't understand why I kept coming back to the question. It was as if I'd flipped a coin on it, come up negative, and found myself wanting to make it best two out of three.

Ms. Wu leaned out of the window above me and called, "Come on up." So I abandoned all the speculation that I'd already decided three times was pointless, anyway.

By the time I reached the second floor, Ms. Wu's bag was packed, and she was towelling her hands at the kitchen sink. She seemed a bit pale and pinched. Tick-Tick looked no better, but no worse. There was a lingering smell of some light, sharp-smelling incense, and red votive candles still burned in holders on each windowsill.

"I would have told Tick-Tick my diagnosis and let her pass it on to you, but this will save her the wear and tear," said Ms. Wu. "Not to mention the annoying questions that she won't be able to answer." Her face was calm, but not smiling; I was nervous enough to think that she might have steeled herself to this. I sat down next to the couch, where I could watch her and the Ticker both.

"Did she treat you bad?" I asked the Ticker.

"Heavens, no," she answered, in the pale version of her usual manner that seemed to be all she had the strength for. "Not even one of her wretched fortune cookies, though if she'd offered me a nice ginger jelly for being a good girl and not crying over the needle, I assure you I wouldn't have minded."

"Oh, hell! I should have remembered to bring you some when I went to fetch her."

"I suppose you were distracted," the Ticker said, pretending to be wounded. I could have enlarged on the pantomime, if she hadn't been folded up just then with a cough that made her clutch at her chest. "My, that hurts," she croaked when she'd finished.

I felt as if someone had taken a pair of tongs out of the freezer and used them on my heart. But all I said was, "Then shut up, for God's sake, and you won't cough so much."

Ms. Wu, who had been pretending not to listen to us, sat down on the other side of the couch. "I've treated fourteen cases of this so far this week," she said. "At least, the symptoms and the onset of them has been the same. After the first six or so, I was driven to do a little research. The early symptoms include a dry mouth and nose, a painful, unproductive cough, a sensation of chill in the extremities, painful joints, headache, and fever. All of my patients have been Truebloods."

The Ticker snorted.

"I beg your pardon?" Ms. Wu asked.

"I have no objection to being called an elf. I don't believe it has any derogatory connotations."

"Others among your people do."

"My people," Tick-Tick said, with fine dignity and a shot of a glance at me, "are widely assorted genetically, and are by no means limited to those who have their origin across the Border."

I remembered my recent objection to her use of "my people" and "your people," and grinned.

"Shut up, round ears," she said, without looking at me.

Ms. Wu's lips twitched, but she only said, "May I go on?"

"Please do," I replied.

"I don't know how familiar you are with the nature of viruses. They're one of the most easily mutated organisms in nature, which is one of the things that makes them so hard to fight, in the World. By the time you've found something that will kill one, it's likely to have turned into something else.

"True—elves living in the Borderlands have had very little to fear from viral infection, for the same reason. The Wall between the Elflands and the Borderlands seems to have a disruptive influence on any virus that passes through it, killing it or mutating it into something harmless. In particular, airborne viruses from the Elflands are unknown in Bordertown."

I thought I recognized a prologue when I heard one. "Until now?"

"Until now. This seems to be a version of a disease known only in the Elflands, and not known well there. There, it's not only rare, but slow to spread. No one I've talked to has figured out yet how it crossed the Border and became viable here. There may be a specific vector, which we can eliminate to slow down the spread of the disease."

"Vector?" I asked.

"I'm sorry. Carrier, more or less. Rats were a vector for the Black Plague, in the Middle Ages."

"Huh. Do rats cross the Border?"

"Only," Tick-Tick supplied, "If they're Trueblood rats."

"So how do you cure it?" I asked, hoping to keep Tick-Tick from making any more outrageous comments.

Ms. Wu pressed the fingertips of her two hands together. "I don't know," she said.

The Ticker and I both stared at her.

"You weren't listening properly," she said in answer to our eyes. "This is, essentially, a new disease. It's related to an old one, but given the difference in contexts, who's to say if the old treatment will be effective? Viruses tend to weaken over time, but that's no help to the population infected with this generation. Besides, when I ask the few people I know who're really well-versed in the medicine of Faerie what the usual treatment is, they get wonderfully vague."

"There are prohibitions," Tick-Tick said.

"On saving lives?"

"I suppose, if it came to that, they might inhibit the saving of lives. But there are many things in the Elflands that can't be spoken of outside them. The prohibitions seem laid almost at random; it's not until you are about to say something that you find yourself unable to do so."

Ms. Wu looked outraged. "Was this a spell? Can it be lifted—or at least an exception made, just once?"

"I was not placed under any enchantment, so far as I know. I think, perhaps, it is in all elves, that we are born with it." Then she gave Ms. Wu a wry little smile. "But if this disease is rare, as you say it is, they may only hesitate to admit that they don't *know* the treatment."

"Well, I admit it in a flash. I've given you something that will reduce the pain and swelling in the joints, and tincture of echinacea for your immune system. Let the candles burn themselves out if you can. If you have to snuff them, do it with your fingers—don't blow them out. I've left willow bark tea; take that in the evening when your fever starts to climb and you'll sleep a little easier. There's a cough syrup for your throat, too. Right now, that's all I can do."

"What . . . what are we expecting?" I asked her.

"I was getting to that. This has the potential to be a very dangerous illness. It is in the Elflands, anyway. I want you to lie there and do absolutely nothing except take medication when you're supposed to. Some of my other thirteen, the earliest, are so sick I had them moved to The Lilacs, where they can be observed around the clock."

"Blessed Mab," Tick-Tick said, on a startled cough. "How many town council members do you know, to have managed such a thing?"

Ms. Wu shrugged elegantly.

"Resources to make a princess blush," the Ticker muttered, and added to me, "Even you would fancy it, my duckling. It's more like a resort hotel than a hospital, and high up on the Hill, far above the fetid airs and cares of town."

"Beggar's snobbery," I told her. "Ms. Wu, what is this virus when it's at home? If that's all we know about it, I'd like to know that much."

"Dangerous. I told you."

"How?"

"Possible impairment of brain function from high fever; damage to the heart, similar to that caused by rheumatic fever; and thinning and breaking down of cell walls in certain kinds of tissue. Do you know more than you did before?"

"My mother was a nurse. Yeah, I do." Something about that description bothered me—besides the obvious fact that whatever the virus did might happen to Tick-Tick. "Are you treating Sunny Rico's partner, Linn?"

"No." Ms. Wu raised her eyebrows. "I've met him, of course, but I don't know either of them very well. Does he have this, too?"

"Yeah. So raise the tally of sick people to fifteen."

"If I've treated fourteen cases personally, there must be a good many more than fifteen," Ms. Wu said softly. "This may be an epidemic. If so, the town faces something of a challenge, since in the past our epidemics have run more to things like mononucleosis."

We were interrupted by a banging at the door in the
street below, and a voice shouting up, "Ms. Wu! Ms.
Wu!"

"How do they know you're here?"

"I left a note at the shop," she answered on her way
to the window. "Yes?" she called down.

"Ms. Wu," I heard the unidentified shouter say, "can
you come? Eglantine is awfully sick."

"I'll be right there." She pulled her head back in the
window and turned to us. Something flashed across her
face that reminded me of the way she'd been in the shop
when I'd gone to fetch her, and I realized that at least
some of her brisk, confident style at the Ticker's couch-
side was an effect achieved with a little effort. "Take your
medicine, and send your partner to fetch me if things
take a turn for the worse," Ms. Wu said to Tick-Tick. "I'll
come back to check on you as soon as I can."

I went to the door to show her out, but she said, "I can
find my way." Up close, I could see how tired she was.

When she was gone, the Ticker stretched and
groaned. "I suppose I'd best explain all my drugs and
doses to you, so you can help me mind 'em," she said,
her voice coarse with the irritation of the cough. "By leaf
and root, this is a tedious business for you, my dear, nursing the invalid. I'm damnably sorry for it."

"Silly. I don't mind." I took the cap off one of the
bottles and sniffed. "Bleah. What does this do?"

"It's meant to soothe my throat."

"Well, it's sure not going to soothe your nose. You
know, if you wanted an excuse to find out how the other
half lives, we could probably trade on Ms. Wu's connections and get you into The Lilacs."

"I have a reasonably clear notion of how the other
half lives, thank you." She gave me a rueful look. "Be-

sides, it is a bastion of Truebloodedness, and they might be rude to you during visiting hours."

"I could stand it."

The Ticker shook her head and gave another little snort. "Truebloods. What, then, are humans? False? Artificial bloods? All blood is true." Her voice was deteriorating into a whisper, which must have been more comfortable. She turned her gaze from me to the shaded windows. "By its nature, all blood is true."

"Except . . ."

Tick-Tick watched me and waited, her eyebrows up.

"I don't know. I was thinking of this drug of Rico's, and the way it changes people."

"Are you saying that people like the girl, Tiamat, are false-begotten, untrue creatures?"

"No, but they're not quite . . . one thing or the other."

"Some say the same of half-elves."

"But that's not true. They're a whole new thing that happens to be part elf, part human."

"What of Wolfboy?"

"He's himself."

"And before he was himself, there was nothing like him. When the Elflands returned, they changed everything. But the Borderlands have never ceased to change, since then. They have produced, and will go on producing, objects and people that are not one thing or another. They have already produced a human with a fey gift, and an elf with a human talent."

I grinned. "Oh, if you're going to make it *personal* . . ."

"You never listen if I don't. The Borderlands are the kingdom of change and transformation. The children of this drug may be more truly the children of the Border than any of us. I told you that there was something in Tiamat that seemed to me more elf than human."

"I'd hate to think that the natural result of being a child of the Border is that you croak early."

"So would I. It would suggest that the Borderlands themselves could not live. And this is my home." She sighed. "I wonder when it became so? It's not mere spite any longer, that makes me say I have no wish to return to the Elflands. This place is strange, uncertain, difficult, and beautiful—and mine. I would not leave it."

"Except for the 'beautiful,' that's a good description of your apartment."

She pulled a pillow out from behind her head and threw it at me, which set her coughing.

"You're not supposed to do anything," I reminded her.

"Then see you don't provoke me. What's for dinner?"

"Takeout from Godmom's."

"Lavish."

"Well, you don't want to eat *my* cooking, do you?"


The Ticker slept on the couch, because it was easier than going up and down the platforms to and from the bed on the highest level. I set up a cot near the workbench because I didn't want to get too comfortable, in case Tick-Tick wanted to wake me up in the middle of the night. Consequently, when she did wake me up in the middle of the night, it didn't take any time at all.

She didn't do it on purpose; she was in the throes of a fever dream, and the tossing and muttering were enough to rouse me. I put the kettle on before I went to her.

Her skin was hot and dry. My hand on her forehead woke her up, and she stared at me blankly for a second.

"Orient? But I thought you—no, I dreamed that, didn't I?"

"I don't know, but probably. It's time for some willow bark."

She coughed. "And the loo."

I helped her to the bathroom door, and helped her back to the couch, and made the tea, and felt reasonably capable. But reasonably capable wasn't quite enough to ensure either the Ticker or me an easy, uninterrupted night. That was why I was only half-asleep at dawn, one arm thrown over my eyes to keep the light out, enduring just a little too much brain activity to make it really worth the effort.

The Ticker sick, and Linn. Rico looking worn to the bone; Ms. Wu looking worn to the bone; and me probably added to the list as soon as I gave up and got out of bed. The girl Tiamat looking the way the girl in the hospital bed probably had before she got quite so far along. So far along what? Was the thing that Tick-Tick hadn't said, but strongly suggested, true: that, up to a point, the drug worked? That'd be one in the eye for the Lords of Elfland. A little tuck and shuffle in the old DNA, and you could make an elf from a human. Except they'd already sort of got that one in the eye, because human-elf crosses produced fertile offspring, which meant that we had to be pretty near neighbors genetically as it was.

So far along. Which was how far? How far was "up to a point"? How long did humans have on that passport to the Elflands, before their visas were cancelled in a big way? And why did the transformation fail?

All to get into the Elflands, when as many kids ran away from it as ran away from the World. Or maybe that wasn't why they did it. Maybe the human kids had come to Bordertown to be somebody or something else, and found out they couldn't change enough to make it happen. They were still themselves, and their selves had never been good enough. Maybe they didn't give a damn about getting across the Border, except to be able to say that they were different, and could do it.

My self had never been good enough; for me, for my mother, for my father, for the people around me who I wanted to be my friends. I'd come to Bordertown, too, with only that, and found it still wanting in this new place. I'd become a River addict, trying to erase the parts of me I couldn't live with. Then I'd found Tick-Tick, who'd been a mirror, a shoulder, and a friend. She'd polished my self on her sleeve and handed it back, so that I could finally tell the real flaws from the tarnish. Without her, my road to the Border would have ended in the river or a box. I wanted to think I'd done a little of the same thing for her, but she'd started stronger, and angrier, and hadn't sunk as low as I'd had before coming back up.

What would I have done, if someone had offered me a synthetic alternative to self-respect? I'd have taken it. I knew it because it was just what I *had* done, and I'd done it with less justification than any poor elf wannabe. They at least had a goal in mind when they took up with their dangerous drug.

Would it make them elves? It wouldn't make them Tick-Tick, with her quirky mix of human and fey idiom, her steady confidence and stubborn principles, her strange notions of how to decorate an apartment. What about the prohibitions that Tick-Tick had tried to explain to Ms. Wu; if elves were born with them, what would happen to an elf who wasn't born, but only grew?

But they weren't becoming elves. They were becoming dead.

I finally acknowledged that I wasn't going to fall

asleep again, and got up. I needed to give Rico her answer; if I wrote a note, I could find somebody to take it by her place, or by Chrystoble Street Station. Depending on what I wrote, it might be safe to leave it at the copshop.

There was graph paper in the drawer of Tick-Tick's workbench, and a fountain pen. I wrote the date at the top of the page and paused over it, thinking about what Rico had told me about time, and wondering what the real date was. No, local time was as real as anybody ever got. I could settle for Bordertown consensus reality.

I stopped again over the salutation. "Rico," by itself, was curt and hostile. "Sunny" was too friendly—I didn't think I'd ever called her that to her face, so why start on paper? "Ms. Rico" made it sound as if I put her in the same category as my high school geography teacher. "Detective Rico" would do—but as soon as I started to write it, it seemed too cold. And should I put "Dear" in front of it? It seemed wildly foolhardy to think of using the word to Sunny Rico.

By this time the ink had dried on the point of the pen, and I had to lick it to make it write again. This was damned silly. It was a note, not the soliloquies from *Hamlet*. It only had to be short and businesslike. I tore the sheet in half, threw away the part I'd muddled over, and wrote on the rest:

> I can't help—Tick-Tick's sick, and I have to take care of her. Hope you find out what you need to know.

Now that I'd written it, it looked thin and withdrawn and kind of mean-spirited. In my head, it had sounded brisk and professional. I wanted, suddenly, to commit to paper all the things I'd been chewing over that morning while I should have been sleeping, to see if they struck any answering chord in her. If I did that, though, the possibility of leaving the note at Chrystoble Street would be right out. I compromised:

> Did I tell you that Tick-Tick thinks the stuff almost sort of works?

That, now that it was on paper, looked downright cryptic. Well, if she wanted to know more, she could stop by. As soon as that occurred to me, it seemed like a very good idea, and I was suddenly pleased with the unintelligibility of the sentence. I signed my name. Then I thought of something else. I considered starting the letter over on a new sheet, but graph paper was expensive, and since the note was already pretty addled-sounding (I'd veered from being pleased with it to despairing over it in mere seconds), I'd settle for:

> P. S. Ask Ms. Wu to have a look at Linn.

After all, if Ms. Wu was tracking epidemics, she ought to be able to authenticate as many cases as possible. And something about this illness had bothered Rico, and nagged at me. Maybe something would come of the exchange of information.

I folded the note up into a packet, rummaged in the drawers for sealing wax and couldn't find any, gave up and used epoxy instead. (There were times, in the Borderlands, when epoxy wouldn't set. But Tick-Tick claimed that this was an improvement on Superglue, which according to her, wouldn't work at all here. I told her that was nonsense. She told me, no, it was magic.) I wrote "Sunny Rico" on the outside of the note, put the cap on the pen, and turned around to find that Tick-Tick was awake.

"Love letter?" she whispered.

I felt my face get warm. "Of course not! Note to Rico."

"Ah." She nodded and widened her eyes at me.

"Is that supposed to mean something?"

"No, no, my dear. But I hope she appreciates the effort involved."

"How long *have* you been awake?"

"Since I heard the desk drawer open."

I thought back over what I'd done since I got the paper and pen out, and what it must have looked like. "I just wanted to make sure it didn't give anything away if the wrong person read it."

"Oh," she said, sounding about the way she had when she'd said, "Ah."

I made a disgusted noise and pushed the chair back from the workbench. "Criminy, she's a *cop.*"

The Ticker nodded. I sat down in the chair next to the couch, to save her voice, if she insisted on having this conversation. "She is indeed a cop. It's that very fact that makes me so concerned for your susceptible heart."

"I. Beg. Your. Pardon."

"Didn't I say, not so long ago, that your preference was for women that any reasonable male would ward off with garlic and crucifixes? I'm afraid that in Sunny Rico, my dear, we see your ideal romantic object."

"Huh-uh. No way. You," I said firmly, leveling an index finger at her, "have a fever."

"Yes, I do, but a fever's always at low ebb in the morning."

"Then I'm counting on you being delirious by noon, because you're already seeing things."

"I always see things. But if you prefer, I won't tell you what they are. After all, I'm at your mercy."

"Good grief," I said, and went to stick my head out into the atrium, to see if anybody else was up yet. Nobody was.

However, it wasn't long before a guy came past in the street below, selling eggs out of his bike basket. I bought some and gave him the note to carry, and went back upstairs to make breakfast. Yes, I can make a perfectly decent breakfast, no matter what sort of comments may have been made to the contrary. But the Ticker hadn't much appetite, and seemed almost too tired to wield her fork if she did have.

"I didn't mean it, about the delirium," I said.

"Faugh. I wouldn't give you the satisfaction. No, I'm only weary. I mean to doze the day away, so if you yearn to run errands, feel free."

I didn't feel free. I didn't want to go very far away, or for very long, because I had the inexplicable twitchy certainty that the worst was still to come. I went out for groceries, and to get some clothes from my place. There was a note stuck under my door, from Yoshi, saying that some girl had come by to see me, and hadn't said if she'd be back.

Some girl? Didn't sound like Rico. Besides, Rico would have left her own note. I went downstairs and banged on Yoshi's door.

He opened it cautiously. "Oh, hi, guy. C'mon in."

I shrugged and stepped into his front room. It was a lot like mine, but with more dirty laundry. "I'm in a hell of a hurry. Tick-Tick's sick, and I'm over at her place taking care of her."

"Jeez, that sounds serious." He knuckled his eye

sockets. Yoshi's natural hours are a lot like mine; he'd probably gotten up fifteen minutes ago.

"It may be. Yosh, what's this about a girl?"

"Oh, yeah. She came by last night."

This would take a while. "What kind of girl?"

He squinted at me. "Funny you should ask. It was kinda hard to tell."

"What?"

"Well, no. I mean, you could tell. She was human, red hair, wore a lot of black. You know, like a lot of people. Only at first I thought she was fat, but she wasn't. And kinda—"

Tiamat. For the love of God, Tiamat had come looking for me. "Tall in places? As if she'd been stretched on the rack? And sullen?"

Yoshi blinked. "Yeah! Only not sullen. I thought she was a little scared, but she might've just been shook 'cause you weren't home."

Shook was right, because it would have taken a lot of shaking to bring Tiamat looking for me. And I couldn't go looking for her, not with the Ticker waiting back at her place. Rico? No. If Tiamat was scared, I wasn't going to help things by sending her a cop. I banged my fist off the doorframe, which made a satisfactory noise, and hurt.

"Hey, guy, do I knock your apartment down?"

"Yoshi—" She might not be at the art supply store anymore. It was the only address I had, though. "Yosh, will you carry a message for me?"

I told him where to find the store on Woodruff. He looked disgruntled. "Why can't you go talk to her yourself?"

"Yosh, I can't. I can't leave the Ticker. If you find her there, tell her where I am. Don't tell anybody else around the place," I added, thinking that Tiamat's friends might not be as ready to talk about it as she was, if she was. "If you don't find her—well, maybe she'll come back here and you can tell her then."

Yoshi was staring at me in a speculative fashion. "Is this, like, really important?"

"It's a lot like really important." I remembered the gun. "But seriously, don't say anything about it to anybody but her. Don't mention my name. And if she's not there, pretend you just came in to look at art supplies."

"You have a really weird love life, guy, you know that?"

"Don't mess around over this. It has nothing to do with my love life."

"Yeah, right," he said.

I wasn't going to convince him. "In that case, did you ever read *Romeo and Juliet?*"

"Sophomore year in high school," he said, confused.

"Remember what happened to the cool best friend, Mercutio?"

"Yeah, he got offed," Yoshi replied, as if he still nursed a sense of outrage over it.

"Good. When you're doing this, think of Mercutio and do otherwise. I gotta go."

"What? Orient, hey—"

But I was on the sidewalk by the time he got to his next question mark.

Tiamat didn't come; Rico didn't come; Ms. Wu didn't come. Nothing came but dinner time, and night, and the predictable rise in Tick-Tick's fever. Her legs and arms hurt her, and her chest muscles from the coughing, and her throat likewise. I wished I had something stronger than willow bark tea to give her for the pain. But I gave her as much of that as was good for her, and an hour or two after midnight she settled into something almost like restful sleep.

I was sitting at the open window looking down into the street, trying to unwind enough to fall asleep myself, when the vehicle nosed in to the curb, drifting smooth as a ghost walking—a ghost that grumbled under its breath in a low-pitched voice. Moonlight slid over the needle-curves of the front fenders, turned the windshield to running silver, and made the driver's rumpled hair colorless, but I knew it was brown. The engine noise died.

My stomach felt as if it were trying to crawl up under my lungs to hide. Tick-Tick's fault for teasing; it was only that I was afraid someone else would think what the Ticker had thought, I told myself. And I couldn't very well deny it if the question didn't come up, because *I* couldn't bring it up. My God, what if—someone else—hadn't noticed anything, and I were to say, "You don't have to worry about me, because *I* don't have a thing for you." I could imagine the look I'd get. I'd have to kill myself out of aggravated embarrassment.

Rico turned her face up to the window, and the moonlight fell full on it. "Orient," she called up softly. "Sorry I'm late."

I hung my head as far out the window as I could, to keep my voice from waking the Ticker. "I'll be right down," I told Rico.

I remembered, for a wonder, to take a set of keys with me when I went; it would look so good to lock myself out of the building.

She was leaning on the car when I came out, lighting a cigarette, and I smelled the smoke of coltsfoot, clover, and bearberry leaf on the cool air. I was about to sit down on the stoop when I realized there was a lit one in her hand already, and she was holding out the freshly-fired one to me. Lordy, I hadn't stopped for a smoke in—days? It seemed like days. I walked over slowly and took the cig, brought it to my mouth and realized with a sudden uncomfortable force that it had just been in hers. She was watching me, so I took the drag and pretended my hands were steady.

"You look like shit," she said.

A list of responses occurred to me, starting with "So do you," which wasn't true, followed by "You don't," which I didn't want to say. I shrugged.

"How's Tick-Tick?"

That was one I could answer. "Lousy. She can't eat, she can't sleep . . . I don't know. Ms. Wu said she'd be back around, but she hasn't come yet. I think I'd better go fetch her. How's Linn?"

Rico's cigarette flared scarlet in the dark. The reflection of it shone in one eye, until a blink seemed to wipe it off. "Lousy. He's up at The Lilacs, which is where you'll find Ms. Wu right now. She's more or less living there."

"Tick-Tick says it's a pretty lah-di-dah place."

"It has been. Right now it's more like a field hospital."

I frowned at her, but she couldn't see it in the dark. "What do you mean?"

"Sorry, I forgot; you wouldn't know. Whatever Linn and Tick-Tick have, it's achieved epidemic status, and The Lilacs is the only medical facility in town that specializes in treating the Trueblood population. They're too crowded and too busy to put on airs, right now." She took another pull at her cigarette, and nothing happened. "Shit," she said, with a little more force than was called for. I fumbled for matches, but didn't have any. Hers were in her jacket pocket; she took them out and struck one. When she cupped it to her cigarette, I saw the reflection off the wet lines on her face.

"My God. What's wrong?" I asked her.

She tossed the match away as if it had betrayed her, which it had. "Ms. Wu lost her first two patients to it today."

I didn't stop thinking—or if I did, it was only for an instant, and after that my head was full of thoughts, running around like people trying to get out of a burning building. This didn't mean Tick-Tick would die. Maybe those two elves were already weak, old or wrung out with wild living, or susceptible to this sort of thing. Tick-Tick wasn't susceptible to anything. She was strong. We'd caught her illness early, earlier than Linn's even, and maybe those two people hadn't realized how sick they were until too late. Just because some people died of a disease didn't mean every person who got it would. People had died of the flu, of pneumonia, of heart attacks, and none of those things killed every person who had them. It would be all right.

But Rico was scared enough to cry. And she'd said "her first two."

"How . . . Does she think she's going to lose more?"

A deep breath from Rico, fairly even. "She thinks so. It's too early, I gather, to get a really clear picture of the progress of the disease. She can't tell yet who to be hopeful about."

I grasped at my last straw. "But she's sure that Linn's got the same thing, and that Tick-Tick has it, too?"

Her head turned a little toward me. "Yeah."

We smoked in silence for about half a minute, before I said, "Should I take her to The Lilacs?"

"You should ask Ms. Wu, but I wouldn't think so. She'll probably rest better here. Keep her isolated, though."

"It's still only elves that get it?"

"So far. Not even any halfies reported, though if I were them, I wouldn't press my luck. Humans don't seem to get it, which means The Lilacs is pulling in human doctors and teaching them fey medicine and therapeutic magic. It's unheard-of, but they have to— three-quarters of the Trueblood staff is either down with it, or showing symptoms, and can't break quarantine."

I closed my eyes. "How many people have got it?"

"I don't know. Nobody knows, in fact—you have to assume there are a lot of unrecognized and unreported cases all over town. It's not as if Bordertown has a public health department. There are leaflets going out to all the neighborhoods, though, describing the symptoms and explaining treatment, and stressing the need for isolation. About all anybody can do."

I finished my smoke and crushed the butt under my sneaker. "How's your case?"

She turned her face in my direction again. "You talked to me yesterday."

"Just thought I'd ask."

"I've been busy." She said it softly. I knew she'd been busy in some of the same ways I had.

"Tiamat—the girl at the art supply store—came looking for me at my apartment last night. I've sent word to tell her where I am. Maybe she'll try again."

Rico shifted abruptly, impatiently. "I can go talk to her."

"You could. But she didn't come looking for you."

"God damn you," Sunny Rico said, still softly. "Don't try to take this all into your own hands."

"She won't come to you, because you're a cop." I felt as if I were accusing her of something, and I think it sounded that way, too.

"There are things I can do that you can't. Because I'm a cop."

With the cigarette gone, I wanted something to do with my hands. I would have put them in my pockets, but my jeans were too tight to make a smooth gesture of it. I took a few steps down the sidewalk because I needed a couple more cubic feet of air. She stood stiffly, one hip against the car, as if she wanted to follow me and wouldn't. I sat on the curb next to the Triumph's right front headlight and laced my fingers together on my knees.

"I don't want to take this all on," I said slowly. "I don't want to take any of it on. I thought I did, for a while. Now all I want is for my life to go back to the way it was last week."

"It never does," she said. "I've wanted something like that at least once a day for the last few years." She came over and settled herself on the front fender, one booted foot on the chromed tubing of the bumper. She took her cigarette case out of her jacket pocket again and handed me one. "But I understand. If that's what you want, I'll leave you alone." The match scraped, and flared, and was held a cigarette's length from my face.

The timing, I realized with an uncomfortable rush of anger mixed with something else, wasn't accidental, and the heat in my face wasn't all from the match. I held her eyes for a second, to show her I'd caught the trick, and drew the flame into my cigarette.

"Do you want me to leave you alone?" she pressed.

"What, couldn't you tell?"

"You have a better poker face than I gave you credit for," she said lightly. "I'm sorry, it's a habit. Some people bite their nails; I manipulate as a reflex."

I watched the ash grow on the end of my smoke. "What about Tiamat?"

"I hope you'll pass on anything I need to know, but you don't have to. Hell, if you really want out of it entirely, you could leave town."

I looked up at her, outlined in moonlight. "I can't leave town."

"Because of Tick-Tick? She could go into the hospital. Or you could hire a nurse to stay with her; there are good ones around."

"No. I couldn't—I couldn't go, and not know what was happening. She might not mind, but I would."

"And you objected because *I* insisted on taking responsibility." There was ever-so-slight mockery in her voice.

I took a mouthful of smoke, and was glad the cigarette hadn't gone out. The last thing I needed was another revealing match. "We go way back."

"That's a mixed commodity in this town, have you noticed?" she said, and the mockery had been replaced by a sort of mild speculation. "Friendships of long standing are valuable. But a long friendship, here, is four or five years. And nothing goes back to before, either to the World or to the Elflands. Before we came to town. We all pretend that when we hit the Borderlands, our pasts were cut off like six inches of out-of-fashion hair."

"That's part of the point of coming."

"Of course. But it's still just pretend."

It doesn't take nearly long enough to smoke a cigarette. I flicked the remains of mine into the middle of the street and stood up. "If the results are the same, what does it matter?"

"Are the results the same? You don't like hospitals.

You're not sure you like yourself. Is that because of things that have happened to you since you got here?''

I was angry. It seemed to me she was picking at a scab, and I wasn't even certain whether it was mine or hers. And when had I given her permission to tell me about myself? "I don't know. What do you think? You're the one with the father who was a bad cop.''

That stopped her; or at least, she sat still, and that might have been the cause. If she made a sound, I couldn't hear her. I couldn't, in fact, hear anything much around us, and I wondered that I hadn't noticed earlier what a quiet night it seemed to be.

"How are you using 'bad cop'?'' she asked, in a voice that seemed merely curious. "One that's not skillful? Or 'bad,' as in 'a bad apple?' Rotten?''

I said, carefully, "I don't know. I'm just quoting you.''

She sighed. "One can lead to the other, it turns out. I grew up thinking my dad was a good cop. It was the religion of my youth, in fact. I had a pretty fuzzy notion of Jesus, but I was certain my father was a good cop, and that everyone admired him. His precinct buddies would come over to play cards, or for backyard picnics, and they'd take me on their knees and say, 'Bet you're proud of your daddy.' And they were right. I was so proud of him that I hardly had to think about it. That was one of the pillars that held my life up—that my daddy was a good cop, and I was proud of him.''

"What happened?'' I asked.

"About what you'd expect, given an introduction like that.'' Her cigarette followed roughly the same arc as mine had, into the street. "He wasn't good, at least when the going got tough. I think first he was unskillful. Then he tried to make up for it by being crooked. It turned out a lot of those guys who'd held me on their knees were

taking a little something and looking the other way—
from party houses, stolen car parts rings, coke dealers.

"But I didn't know about it for a long time. My mom
knew before I did. He knew that she knew, and they'd
fight, and after a while he started to hit her. That was
when I realized there was something wrong. And . . . one
night, when he was on duty, I got her to tell me what it
was."

I thought I knew how that must have felt. I remembered what it had felt like when one morning my mom
had come home at the end of her shift, and lost her tem-
per over something, and said to me—no, never mind
what she said to me. But I knew the feeling, as if your
insides were an elevator in a tall building, and someone
had just set off the fire alarm. Straight to the basement,
do not pass Go. "Did you . . . confront him with it?"

"Oh, yeah. Perfect timing, too. That night he and his
partner had had to chase a vehicle, and he'd banged his
head on the rear-view mirror in the squad car when it
jumped the curb. So he came home with a bandage on—
like yours only smaller, actually. I was very brave and
called him a crook anyway."

"What did he say?"

"He said I didn't understand."

"Did he—did he straighten out eventually?"

"I don't know." I saw her shrug at least one shoulder.
"We screamed at each other 'til the neighbors phoned in
a noise complaint, and then I ran away from home." Her
head lifted, turned a little to one side. She added, sounding almost amused, "It wasn't like I could call the police."

"Yeah," I said after a moment. So was she a cop to
prove to herself it could be done right? To even the over-
all score for her father? I remembered her reaction when
she'd realized that one of her fellow officers had to be

part of the group that put, and kept, the passport on the streets. "And you still can't."

Some quick motion of her head showed me that she understood the reference. "No. There's just me."

Maybe she thought, after that account of her history, that I'd answer with something melodramatic, like, "And me." An appeal to the swashbuckler after all. What I said was, "I'd better go see if Tick-Tick's still asleep."

She stood up and stretched her spine, both hands on the small of her back. "Give her my best."

"Sure."

I stayed where I was, expecting her to get into the car and drive away. Instead she reached out two fingers and pinched a lock of my hair that had fallen down in my eyes. "You need a haircut," she said, and deftly flipped the lock back off my forehead, never touching the skin. "G'night."

*Then* she got in the car and started the engine. The Triumph pulled away primly, as if out of respect for the night and the sleeping locals.

A haircut. A *haircut*, for crying out loud.

At least maybe nothing would happen to make me have to admit to Tick-Tick that she'd been right, that I did have a thing for Sunny Rico. If I was very lucky, maybe nobody would mention it to Sunny Rico, either.

My scalp tingled, in the front, right along the hairline. I scorned to rub it.

Tick-Tick rallied in the morning, as she had the day before, but she didn't seem quite as rallied as she was then. Since neither her household nor mine could boast a fever thermometer, I could only judge from the feel of her forehead what her temperature was, but it felt high. I could tell from her face that she was in pain. She turned down food again; she drank some orange juice, and I wanted her to drink more, but she said it hurt her throat.

I had the windows open, so I heard the banging on the front door. I hopped up three platforms and stuck my head out to see, wondering why, if the Ticker had gone to the trouble of installing a remote mechanical latch for the front door, she hadn't rigged up a doorbell, too. Probably wasn't enough of a challenge.

It was Tiamat. When I whistled she looked up, and I saw the evidence of tears on her white, pouched face.

"Oh, Jesus, you *are* here," she said.

"I'll be right down." I could have let her in, but I didn't think she'd be a useful distraction for Tick-Tick. And I remembered the way she'd looked at the Ticker, and spoken to her, as if being born on the other side of the Border had made her the author of Tiamat's miseries.

As Rico had reminded me the night before, it hadn't been so awfully long since the last time I'd seen her, and consequently, the last time I'd seen Tiamat, too. She didn't seem taller, or thinner, or paler, and her hair was still red—though that, I realized, seeing it in sunlight, wasn't the color it usually was, anyway. But her skin seemed dry and dull, and her eyes were bloodshot, as well as red from crying.

"I wasn't going to come," she said, as soon as I came out the door. "Everything was okay then, when I talked to you."

"I know. Have a seat," I told her, in as soothing a voice as I could manage. Hers was hoarse and inclined to crack, suggesting that she was prepared to have hysterics if the occasion called for it. My nerves weren't exactly titanium-wrapped, what with one thing and another. I settled down on the stoop and stretched my legs out in front of me, and pretended I was relaxed.

Tiamat didn't sit down. Instead she shifted from one foot to another on the sidewalk in front of me, and fixed me with a desperate glare. "I don't know what you can do about it, anyway. Except you seemed to know all about this before anybody else did. Jesus, you've got to be able to help me."

"I'll try. Are you sure you don't want to sit down?" Maybe she could be helped—maybe she wasn't so far along that the effects of the passport couldn't be reversed, or at least, stabilized.

She looked down, rummaged in the inside of her denim jacket, and came out with a folded sheet of neon-yellow paper, rather dog-eared and stained. "I wasn't worried until I saw these. I thought everything was going like it was supposed to. But then I read—" She stopped and swallowed. "I read these. And I knew that it wasn't okay. That I have it."

I took the paper from her. As I unfolded it, I asked, "Have what?"

Tiamat drew a sharp breath, as if she meant to use it in snapping at me. But a cough interrupted. When she was done, she said, "The—the disease. Like that." She nodded at the paper.

Rico had mentioned, last night, that flyers had been posted all over town. This was one of them. I tried to read the warnings, the description of symptoms, the recommendations, but they kept going in and out of focus. This was a much more comprehensive list of symptoms and consequences than Ms. Wu had recited for the Ticker and me, I could tell that much. Of course, now that Ms. Wu had seen the end of the disease as well as the beginning, she had a better idea what it could do.

"I have it, don't I?" Tiamat asked, her voice bobbing and cracking.

In my mind I held up her white, frightened face to Tick-Tick's; then to the face of the girl in the Bolt Street Clinic. I had been so stupid. I had asked the wrong question. I'd wanted to find the drug that had killed her, but of course, she hadn't been killed by a drug. She'd been killed by a virus. The evolving half-humans, with their underdeveloped, un-fey immune systems, were the vector that Ms. Wu had speculated on.

"Yes," I said. "You have it."

I'd asked the wrong question. I could ask the right one now, and find out where the passport was. Did I want to do that? I had no obligation to, I realized. It was my choice, and Rico would know I'd made it only if I chose to tell her.

The girl who waited, still barely hopeful, on the sidewalk in front of me had nothing to do with that choice. She was an imperative, the responsibility of life for life.

I stood up. "Come on," I said to Tiamat, "we have to get you to a hospital."

And as I dusted the grit off the back of my jeans, I asked the question. Thataway, Thataway, Thataway. It was all over town.

# ✳ 10 ✳

# GHOST OF A CHANCE

N UMBER SIX," SUNNY said when I came back to the car. She could have sounded accusing, or bitter, or even mocking, maybe. What she did sound like was the way I felt—a little numb, a little spacey, a lot tired. We'd been chasing after my sunburst of Thataways. It wasn't a speedy process, no matter how careful we were about the geography. Each location had to be triangulated; each had to be carefully surveyed to see if it was full of dangerous wicked people and their hirelings trying to subvert the human youth of Bordertown (this part was exclusively Sunny's—I was ordered to stay with the car). And since none of the six locations we'd checked so far had been the hoped-for issuing office of the passport, the next part was mine, as a relatively well-known and trusted face around town. I got to play public health officer, going into each place and finding out which resident or residents had gotten their passports, explaining to them about the virus, and making them swear to report to the

closest of the free clinics for monitoring. As some of the
residents were inclined to be resentful and belligerent,
this wasn't much like selling candy bars door to door. It
was sunset. I wanted some dinner, and I wanted to go
visit Tick-Tick at the care hostel. I told Sunny so.

"Which first, dinner or Tick-Tick?"

"Tick-Tick," I said, realizing that it ought to be dinner.
The last thing an invalid needs is a visit from her partner
when he's low on calories and running on half a brain.
She'd be patient, but I ought not to make her work so
hard. And it wasn't as if she were alone, since Wolfboy
had volunteered to sit with her. Nobody knew if Wolfboy, himself something of an avatar of Borderland transformation, could get the bug. But when asked, he'd
raised one jutting hairy eyebrow, considered it, and given
a bark (literally) of laughter that I thought was meant to
be ironic. He'd written on his notepad, *Doesn't jive with my
secret origin. Only vulnerable to silver bullets and the color yellow.*

"Yellow?" I'd said.

He'd written, *Clashes with my eyes.*

Sunny drove with her usual terrifying panache,
which didn't have any apparent effect on her conversation. "How was that last one?"

"Not so bad. Except—" I sighed, which she wouldn't
hear anyway, in the open car at this speed. "I don't
know. I just get around to deciding that I won't mind
anything as long as somebody doesn't threaten me with a
baseball bat again, when I walk into a little bare squat
with cardboard over the windows and find nobody there
except one undernourished thirteen-year-old girl with a
pain in her chest and half her fingers longer than the
other half, who only wants everything to be beautiful."

We went about a block and a half before she said,

"You know, you're pretty articulate when you're re-volted. That's what this one was?"

"That's what this one was."

"Well, try to think positive thoughts. We're here."

We hadn't been when she started the sentence, but at that speed, she wasn't a liar by the time she got to the last word.

It was very little like a hospital: an enormous brick pointy-Victorian mansion that at one time had served as a convent. It was still a little of that, since it was being run by the Daughters of Brede, an all-female Celtic Pagan nursing order. They took their work seriously, and had been one of the first places to volunteer their services when the epidemic became public. I'd roused Tick-Tick up and moved her there—with her consent, of course—as soon as I'd come back from getting Tiamat down to Bolt Street, and sending someone off with a message for Ms. Wu at The Lilacs with the particulars as I knew them and a recommendation to find Rico and pump her for the rest. Which she must have done, since in fairly short order Sunny found me. No, she didn't draft me. She didn't know yet that there was something to draft me for. I volunteered.

The Daughter on visitors' duty looked like she'd just walked out of an old Marlboro cigarette ad, tall and bony and tan with cropped gingery hair and a network of crow's feet at the corners of her blue eyes. She smiled at me, which I decided she wouldn't have been able to do if Tick-Tick were failing.

"The Trueblood girl in room 24, right?" she asked me. I nodded. "I'll check. I think second floor meds were half an hour ago, so it should be fine." She went to a cord hanging behind the visitors' desk and tugged on it several times in an irregular rhythm. After a moment or two, there was a short spate of clacking from a box mounted on the wall next to the cord, and I noticed that a similar cord, coming from the box and disappearing up through the ceiling, was moving.

The Daughter came back to the front of the desk. "You can go up." She saw the direction of my gaze, and added, "Morse code, levers, and string. Real hospitals have radio things, they tell me, but this works fine for us."

The Ticker would like it, I thought. When she got well, I'd show her the setup on our way out. She'd probably make me learn Morse code.

Sunny and I went upstairs, past a brown-skinned woman in jeans and a gray cotton sweater who balanced a tray of bottles and jars against one shoulder. She didn't seem to hurry, but she got down the stairs pretty quickly for all that, and without so much as the clink of glass on glass from the tray. Not much like what *I* thought of as a hospital, anyway. There were more members of the staff working upstairs, in their assorted clothes and their quiet, competent style.

"I'll wait for you," Sunny said outside the door of 24.

"You can come in if you want."

"I know. I'll wait."

Wolfboy must have overheard us. He came out of the Ticker's room and showed a few of his teeth in a smile, then gave a casual index-finger-to-the-eyebrow salute to Sunny.

"How is she?" I asked him.

He made a gesture with his hands and shoulders that was expressive of not much of anything. Since it obviously didn't satisfy me, he sighed and took out the notebook. *Not any better,* he wrote.

"Are they treating her okay?"

*Like a goddess.* He paused, then wrote, *I have to go back to the store tonight. Think that'll be okay?*

I knew what he meant. There was nothing either of us could do, by being there, to make her well, but if we went away, it felt as if we weren't trying. Still, Wolfboy had a business to run and a relationship to keep up. "Go ahead. I'll tell her you'll be back in the morning."

As soon as I saw her, I knew Tick-Tick was worse. I'd been warned that she would get worse before she got better, but that didn't really make it easier to look at and smile. Her face seemed sunken and worn away, her eyes and hair dull. She wasn't coughing, but I knew she was being medicated for that, and that it was only a symptom.

"Am I interrupting anything?" I asked from the doorway.

She scrunched the corners of her mouth, and beckoned me in. When I got within whispering distance, she said, "Are you having fun questing?"

I thought about lying, and rejected it. "No. It's godawful. Are you getting well?"

"I believe I am, my dear. I know I *look* devilish, but it's always worst in the evening. And if I don't recover, I'll will you the bike, and we'll both feel like characters out of a Richard Thompson song."

"That's not funny," I told her, a little more sharply than I'd meant to.

"It will be, eventually."

There wasn't anything much to say, but I didn't want to go yet, and I thought she didn't want me to leave. Finally she said, "Is Rico bullying you cruelly?"

"No. She's out in the hall, by the way."

"Does that mean you only said 'no' because she might be listening?"

I shook my head. "This isn't much easier for her than it is for me. For about the same reasons."

"How is Linn?" she asked, because she understood what I'd meant.

"Pretty crummy, from the sound of it. I haven't seen him."

"Will he die?"

There; she'd said the damn word. "I don't know. Nobody's figured out yet how to tell in advance who gets the lucky numbers." My voice sounded harsh in my ears.

She nodded once, her head settling deeper into the pillow. "The influenza epidemic of 1918."

"The who?"

The Ticker smiled, which made her look tired. "It's a piece of the World's history. Ask one of the Daughters. They're the ones who explained it to me—one of them. I can't keep them all straight." She frowned and closed her eyes.

I frowned, too, because not keeping people straight was such an odd thing to hear about Tick-Tick. "I guess I should go. Gotta get some food, and go back to the bloodhound job. Wolfboy's gone to take care of business, but he'll be back tomorrow."

Her eyes flew open, silver and red-rimmed. "Must you go?" Then she made a scornful noise. "Yes, of course you must. Ignore me, my chick, I am in a weakened state. And it's time for my nap. Orient—" Her hands were outside the blankets; she turned one palm up, and I put my hand in it. Her fingers were hot and dry. "You'll take care?"

I returned the pressure of her grip. "Much as I can."

She studied me gravely. "I am satisfied with that."

Neither of us said good-bye, in so many words, probably because it seemed like bad luck.

Sunny was down the hall, looking out a window. If she'd been eavesdropping, she'd had the grace to move well out of earshot before I came out. One of the Daughters, a small woman with straight brown hair braided halfway down her back, came out of the next room wheeling a cart full of clean sheets. "Excuse me," I said to her. "Do you think you could answer a history question for me?"

She widened her eyes at me. "I guess I could try."

"What was the influenza epidemic of 1918?"

She looked startled for a moment. Then her expression sharpened and settled. "That's right, you're the friend of the girl in 24. Some people can only be brave if they're ignorant about what's happening to them. She's not one of 'em. Made me explain to her everything we knew about this damn bug."

"How does 1918 come into it?"

"Well, not for scale, at least. Not yet, anyway. But that time, there was no way to tell who would get it, and once they'd got it, there wasn't any sense in who got a light dose and who died of it. Whole families would come down with the influenza, including babies, and the only ones who'd die would be the parents, who ought to have been strong enough to hold out. This thing is like that. Years from now we're still going to be studying to figure out the population at risk."

"Does that mean that people have recovered from it?" I asked.

Sunny had come up behind the Daughter. Her face was composed, but she seemed a little white around the mouth, and I knew she was waiting for the answer as much as I was.

"Too soon to be sure. If we can get the fever to break, there's a good chance of the person pulling through.

We've had a couple of patients already who've gotten over the hump. I think your friend's temp is just about to peak. If we can get her through tonight okay, she may be in the clear."

"If we can get rid of this gene-transforming stuff," I said, "then everybody will be in the clear."

The Daughter looked at me oddly. "The genie ain't going back in the bottle."

No, of course it wasn't. The mutation, if that was what it was, had happened; the virus had crossed the Border, and was doing a fine job of ditching its half-evolved hosts and fastening on the real elves. I'd been careening along with the blinders on, half-convinced that if I did my job, everything would be fixed. But the passport and the virus had never been the same thing, and only one of them was my job. Sunny was watching me, and from the way she was doing it, she might have known what I was thinking.

But all she said was, "Come on. It's dinner time."

"Taco Hell?" I asked when we got to the car, which twilight was making sleek again.

"I don't think I can face any restaurant south of Ho tonight. Do you mind?"

"I'm easy." I blushed when I heard what I'd said, but Sunny didn't seem to notice.

It wasn't that I'd forgotten I had an embarrassing fascination with Sunny Rico; but since that morning it had been pushed a little to one side by the press of Tick-Tick's health, Tiamat's news, and the hunt for the passport and its victims. I'd been riding around in a little sports car with nothing but the sliver of air between the bucket seats to separate me from her, and hadn't been bothered. Suddenly I was reminded, and if I could have perched on the edge of the upholstery and still fastened the safety harness around me, I probably would have. It was a lot shorter drive than it seemed.

We ended up in what I recognized as her neighborhood. I took a mental sighting on her apartment building, in fact, and found it in the middle of the next block. For a moment, I thought we were going there, and suffered a ridiculous little inner twitch. But Sunny led me instead to a brown brick building on the corner where yellow light slipped out around the curtains in a first-floor window, and where a completely unintelligible sign (well, to me, anyway) suggested that it might be a place of business.

It was a restaurant of some Central European flavor—or maybe all of them. The oil lamps gave it a nice homey glow and a not-so-nice suffocating heat. If I'd been in charge, I'd have pulled the curtains and opened the windows, and atmosphere be damned. But the people in charge didn't seem bothered, and that was the only thing I could have complained about. The cash register stood next to a big glass case full of breads and pastries, most of which seemed to have something to do with walnuts, apples, poppyseeds, or all of the above.

"Is this a reminder to save room for dessert, or do they expect you to just go ahead and eat it first?" I muttered to Sunny, as we passed it on the way to a table in the back.

"They expect you to not have room for dessert, and to get it to take home and eat three weeks later when you're hungry again." She handed me a typed menu on which I recognized maybe a dozen words. "Get the *gulyás.* Unless you want vegetarian, in which case get the eggplant, peppers, and noodle stuff."

I would have balked at this high-handed style, but I didn't know anything about any of this food. I decided I'd have a better dinner if I was humble.

We were served by a round, stern, red-faced man

with hair that nature had made black and white over the course of time. "Gulyás" turned out to be what it was pronounced as; in other words, goulash. Around here, that translated as a really good beef stew made with paprika and served over homemade noodles. It wasn't anything like my mother's goulash, thank God.

Sunny's table manners were excellent, even when she ate fast and didn't seem to be paying attention to what was on the plate.

"If you eat like that at Taco Hell, Mingus gives you the bum's rush," I said.

She looked up blankly. "What?"

"This is very good food."

"Oh. Yeah. I come here a lot."

"I figured that. It being right down the street from your apartment."

"That's right, you've been there."

I was a little disappointed that she could have forgotten. I wasn't likely to. "Slow down. Anything I've found once, I can find again, and nobody can know that we're out combing the town for this stuff. You have time to eat your dinner." I shrugged. "Besides, I'm having dessert."

She stared at her plate and took a deep breath, very slow in, very slow out. Her hands lay clasped at the edge of the table. Then she looked up at me, not quite smiling. "But if I eat slow I'll have to talk between bites. And the only things I can think of to talk about are bad for my appetite."

"No small talk? Here, have some bread. It's great."

"I know that, remember? Small talk is for wimps. Where I come from, we talk big manly talk."

"Heard any good music lately?"

Sunny smiled and shood her head. "I never hear any music. I have a job."

"Yeah, well, so do I. I find having a life helps me to tell when I'm working." Involuntarily, I thought about the last couple of days, when I'd been working and when I hadn't, and how hard it was, in that case, to tell. In other words, I found myself standing at the edge of a conversational pit. *All right,* I thought, *to hell with small talk.* "Would you have extradited me?"

She met my eyes, and looked away, and met them again. "I don't know."

"It would have been the good cop thing to do, wouldn't it?"

"No. Good cops don't use threats to force people to help them."

"They did on all the cop shows *I* ever watched."

"Then you're probably qualified to join the force." She smiled, a little lopsided. "That's the Police Academy around here, you know. Cop shows and mystery novels, and even some firsthand experience of being busted, out in the World. The police here do what they do because they watched a whole season of "Steeltown Beat," and think that's how being a cop works. Or because they watched it and think that being a cop should be anything *but* that. We're all making it up as we go along. Maybe we should go back to the old Renaissance model of rich people's neighborhood bodyguards."

"Then who looks out for the poor people?"

"Who looks out for 'em now?" she said with a snort.

"People like you."

"Who says we have to be cops to do it?"

That stopped me for a second. Then I answered, "You did."

Sunny raised her eyebrows. "I did?"

I knew I'd asked the question once before, but I

couldn't think of another way to put it. "Why did you become a cop?"

She stared, and for a moment I thought she was angry. Then she threw her head back and laughed. I suppose that didn't preclude her being angry. "To look out for the poor people? Oh, maybe. And maybe it was the only thing I thought I knew how to do."

"What did you do when you first came to town?" I knew that she'd been a friend of Dancer's, that they'd been in a gang together, that Dancer had, after a while, started Danceland and stopped being in a gang. I didn't know any more than that.

"What I did wasn't much like doing anything at all. Do you think you can spend your life riding motorcycles around town, dressing up tough, crashing parties, picking fights with strangers on the basis of who they hang out with, and eating whatever you can mooch or browbeat out of someone? What did you do, when you first got here?"

"You forgot the drugs," I said.

"You're right, I did. Or was that your answer?"

"Sort of."

"And?"

"I spent a while . . . I was hired by an aspiring gangster type to find things for him. He gave me room and board and all the drugs I could ingest, as long as I wasn't passed out when he had a job he wanted me to do. I kind of got a taste for River water."

"You weren't a Wharf Rat?"

"Uh-uh. Much more genteel. Same addiction, though. Things would have turned out pretty bad, except that Tick-Tick met me and took a liking to me, for Mab only knows what reason. She put me on my feet and kicked me in the butt, and here I am today."

For a miracle, she let me get away with the flippant version. With her fork she drew lines in the last of the sauce on her plate. "You can't just hang out. You can't just mooch, and panhandle, and suck all the . . . the sustenance out of life. Bordertown is a scary place, an angry place, and sometimes you'll see it reach out and crush somebody. But for every one of those there's dozens of people . . .

"I used to have a recurring dream, that I woke up and the city was gone, and all the people who lived in it were walking around in the big empty field that was left, trying to figure out where they were supposed to go now. And in the dream it was because we'd used the city up. Just used it up, like a loaf of bread, and there wasn't even a wrapper left."

I'd finished my dinner. It looked as if she'd finished as much of hers as she was going to. I hoped I hadn't really raised subjects that had killed her appetite.

"We should go," she said, dragging herself back from whatever abstraction she'd fallen into.

"This is embarrassing, but I don't have room for dessert."

"I told you, you get it to go, and eat it three weeks from now."

At the cash register, I went for my pocket, but she shook her head and informed me that it was on the city.

"Won't it disappear?" I asked.

"What?"

"The city. Like your dream."

"I think you've put enough in today that taking a little out isn't going to hurt. Don't you get expenses?"

So I let her pay the check, and we stepped out into the night. The temperature had dropped with the sun—had dropped radically, in fact, as sometimes happens in summer. The hood of the Triumph was pebbled with dew, and the sidewalk edges were dark with it. I could smell the moisture in the air, it was so thick.

"Look," Sunny said softly, and pointed to the tree-planted median strip down the middle of the street. A sheet of thin mist lay about six inches above the grass down the length of the block, broken by tree trunks and concrete benches and lines of shrubbery. "Ground fog. The parks are going to look like a Dracula movie." She tossed the waxed paper bag that contained half of a rolled pastry thing full of walnuts into the space behind the driver's seat, and swung her legs over the driver's side door.

"Do you ever open the doors on this car?" I asked.

"My God, they come up to my knees. Why should I?"

They were a little higher than that, but it was still a good point. I climbed over my side and buckled myself in. The seat was cold and damp from the dew.

"Where to?" she said, as the car growled to life.

I got my new mental fix. "Thataway."

"We're outta here."

I don't know why that style of leaving the curb is described as being like a bat out of hell. I've never seen a bat that could lay rubber.

We were a little under a dozen blocks away when sparks spat out from under the dashboard, once, twice. "Oh, hell," said Sunny, "not the wiring harness again. It must be the damp. Can you see anything?"

There's not much space inside a Triumph Spitfire; the ideal position for looking under the dash is with the door open and your knees on the pavement. But by unfastening the safety harness and turning half around, I got my head upside down at the right level without actually having to put it in Sunny's lap.

The other thing about that car, and that vintage, is that it's a pretty straightforward machine. Everything built in the last few decades of the twentieth century has wiring like rainbow linguine under the dash, for the computerized fuel injection, the electronic ignition, all the power extras. Sunny's Spitfire had ignition, dash lights, and the headlight switch—not even a radio. So it wasn't hard to spot the taped-up bundle fastened to the underside of the dashboard with a wad of sticky stuff, and the gleam of fresh-cut wire ends.

I stayed exactly where I was, with my head upside down, and said, "It's a bomb."

I had the sick, empty feeling at the base of my spine that comes from being able to count the fillings in Death's molars. My face was twelve inches away from the thing, which would probably go off in a second. Nobody would be able to identify me even if they *could* find my head.

Sunny's foot had come down on the brake and her right hand had gone for the ignition, in reflex. She stopped herself before she touched the key and slapped her hand back on the wheel. "Can you see the wire that's sparking?"

I cleared my throat. "Yeah."

"What color is it?"

"Red."

She sucked air in through her teeth. We were only doing about 30 mph now, so I could hear it. "Should have gone off when I started the car. Maybe it was the damp that screwed it up."

We were down by the river now. I could smell the sweet-sick odor of the water of the Big Bloody, running red and strange out of the Elflands. The Triumph was still slowing down.

"Jump," said Sunny.

"What?"

"Jump. If I go any slower, I'm afraid she'll stop."

"I'm not go—"

"God damn it, asshole, *get out of my car.*"

I think I must have vaulted clean over the door, because I don't remember touching it. I did remember to roll when I hit the pavement, and only scraped the palms of my hands and my elbows and my knees, a little.

There was a concrete slope, a ramp, down from the street and into the river. Maybe it had been a boat ramp once, before Faerie came back and the river ran red. Maybe it was the driveway to an underground garage, flooded by a change in the river's course. Whatever it was, Sunny was aiming the Spitfire down it. I understood now why she was afraid of letting the speed drop too low.

It was her turn to jump—wasn't it? I was chanting it in my head, *Jump, jump, jump,* like a crowd watching somebody on a building ledge. The Spitfire's engine revved, and the back bumper tilted up as the front end lunged down the slope.

She jumped and landed hard, harder than I had, and almost rolled off the edge of the ramp into the river. But she was up in a flash, on her feet, and running toward me. The river was making gulping sounds over the car, as if it were chugging a pitcher of beer. Based on the way the Spitfire went down, I have no reason to believe that British-made convertibles float.

At first I thought nothing was going to happen. The only movement was Sunny, running, and the water swirling as it closed over the car. Then the surface of the river bulged up, shining; the ground heaved under me; Sunny sprawled on the pavement; there was the roaring, rushing sound of the explosion, and the racket of breaking glass. The river came down like a cloudburst all over us, stinking of madness and fish. A few of those came down, too, dead before they hit.

The quiet afterward might have been only in contrast to the noise, or I might have temporarily been a little deaf. I ran to Sunny, slipped on a dynamited fish, and sat down hard in the road next to her.

She pushed herself up on her arms and shook her head vigorously, and made a sound that I'd rather not try to spell. "You okay?" she asked, squinting up at me.

Reaction was setting in; some things in this world you can always count on. "Wonderful," I said.

She pulled herself upright, and sat cross-legged in the street, looking at the river.

"People are going to show up pretty soon," I suggested. "Maybe we should leave." Then I realized that I wasn't certain what cops do in cases like this. Maybe they were supposed to stick around when their car blew up and took out half the windows in the neighborhood.

"Do you know how many of those were left in the world?" Sunny said, still looking at the river.

I figured out that she meant the car. "More than there are now."

"It's not funny. I slaved over that car. I *loved* that car. Like *family*. When I find the bastard who did this, I swear—" I watched the way she closed her lips tight over the rest of the sentence and realized that this, too, was partly reaction. "Which way do we go now?"

I pointed. "We're in trouble if it's very far."

"Then we'll be in trouble. So what. Oh, *damn* them all, and all their nearest kin!"

Sunny's attachment to the Spitfire reminded me of Tick-Tick, which reminded me of something else. "We have wheels. Come on."

The Ticker's bike was parked in the garage on the

other side of the alley in back of her building, shining, tuned, and looking downright eager in the lamplight.

"You can drive it?" Sunny asked.

"D'you think the two of us would have gone out into the Nevernever alone if only one of us knew how to drive the bike to get us back? I even stay in practice. Tick-Tick drives because it's her bike, and because the traditional place for the navigator is in the sidecar." I'd brought the keys down from the apartment, and I jingled them now. Sunny hung back as I put my leg over and felt for the ignition in the dark. For just a moment, I thought about explosions; but the Ticker's lock had been secure on the door, and her spell still in place on it.

"She'll be back," I whispered to the bike, laying my hand on the gas tank. "She'll be back soon." I turned the key and the engine caught without a hitch, just as one would expect of a piece of Tick-Tick's hardware.

Sunny held the door wide, and when I'd rolled out into the alley, she locked it behind me. Then she climbed into the sidecar. It was an awkward movement, not like the way she'd gotten into the Triumph.

"Take it away," she said, fastening the second helmet under her chin.

Driving didn't feel strange, but not having to give directions did. Except for that, we followed the same drill we had all day. I found our spot, and waited on the bike while Sunny did her reconnaissance. I had a twitchy certainty in the pit of my stomach that this was the one, this was the place the passport came from. From that I passed on to realizing that I had no idea what Sunny planned to do about it. Whatever it was, she wasn't crazy enough to do it by herself. Was she? On the other hand, they had just blown up her car.

So when Sunny came up beside me out of the dark

and shook her head, telling me that no, this wasn't The Place, my feelings were mixed, to say the least. I stalked in without a thought for baseball bats or anything else, and told the six complete strangers living there, all of them larger than me, that I knew they didn't have two brain cells to rub together among the lot of them, but if they wanted to hold on to any of the rest of their pitiful personal attributes, they'd flush the goddamn passport down the nearest toilet and get their butts down to the free clinic for a virus check. Unless they didn't want to, in which case, I sure wasn't going to cry at their funerals. They stood, slack-jawed and empty-handed, while I delivered my advice, and not one of them moved to stop me when I left. I suppose my being damp, filthy, and stinking reinforced my image a little. In retrospect, I recognized one of Tiamat's friends from their fight with Tick-Tick and me, but I couldn't remember which one she'd been.

I slammed back out of the house and threw myself on the bike. Sunny was already in the sidecar.

"Now where?" she asked, in a rather small voice.

"Thataway," I growled, and pulled into the street.


The little hand-lettered sign on the door said it was a cooking school. We looked at each other.

"It's always the last place you look," Sunny said, peeling the helmet off.

I made a quick inward check, and found another location in the queue. "This isn't the last place."

"Last one *I'm* going to tonight."

"What if this isn't where Mister Big hangs out?"

Sunny raised her eyebrows at me. "I wonder? I've been assuming that the brains of this outfit will have enough of them to stay as far away from the product as he can. No, I'm not expecting to net the big fish here. But I think we may find some evidence to connect him to the stuff."

"Don't talk about fish," I said. "You sound as if you know this is the place."

She gave me another significant look. "A cooking school?"

"Not all bad guys have a sense of humor."

She slithered out of the sidecar. "I'm going to have a look."

"Wait! If this *is* the place, what are we going to do? Is this a go-in-with-guns-blazing kind of gig?"

"You know, I can see white all the way around your eyes. Since I have exactly one gun, which works exactly some of the time, I don't think that would be the best plan, no."

"Then what *is* the plan?"

"I'll tell you as soon as I make one," she said, and walked off into the dark.

I sat on the bike in the lee of the building across the street and reminded myself of all the reasons I was there. They were good and sufficient, but they didn't take up much time. I thought about Tick-Tick. Her bike had started on the first try, which seemed to me like an omen. If anything was in tune with her health, it was this engine. Tomorrow morning I would go to visit her and be told that her fever had broken, just at the moment I'd cranked her bike, and that she was on the mend. And what the *hell* was keeping Sunny?

I could have recited poetry to myself to make the minutes pass, but I've never been able to memorize any. What if I heard gunshots? What if I didn't hear anything at all? Why didn't this job come with instructions?

Across the street, in the shadow of the cooking school wall, I saw Sunny in silhouette. She jerked her head at me in a come-along gesture.

For a moment I didn't think about what the gesture meant. But it wasn't "no." This was The Place. The bad guy—or guys—had a sense of humor after all.

There was a multi-paned window along the side, the kind that pushes out at the bottom to open. It was a warm night; the window was open. The glass was frosted, but if you stood to one side you could look through the opening and see part of the little room beyond. That's what Sunny and I did.

The last time I'd seen that particular kind of mess was when I'd helped Wolfboy move out of his apartment. It had that characteristic look of a place half dismantled, half thrown away, half packed. There were a couple of cardboard boxes on a counter with things wrapped in newspaper sticking out of them, and a wooden fruit crate on the floor leaking excelsior at the seams. Beside it was a spray of broken glass and a puddle of liquid. Several bags of trash were propped by a door, and a broken chair teetered on top of them. A filing cabinet drawer hung open, with a file folder sticking out; more file folders were scattered on the cabinet's top.

My first thought was that they knew we were on to them, and were trying to clear the place out before we got there. A little reflection told me that was impossible, and that there was a much better reason why they'd be packing up and skipping town. It was the virus, of course. They would have figured out before we did what the vector was. They might even have decided to quit making the stuff in the interest of public welfare. No, based on what was going on in there, it didn't seem like they'd decided to quit.

All the people in the part of the room I could see were elves. Three of them sat at a long table, each one doing a different job: measuring sky-blue fluid into little glass tubes, sealing the tubes with metal foil, writing something on the seal and poking each tube into—the end of a candle? It certainly looked like a carton of household-grade candles, each one with the blunt end hollowed out to fit the tubes. Sneaky. Pop the thing in a wall sconce, light it—nobody but me would be likely to find someone's stash in the bottom of a half-burned candle.

As I've said, it's hard for humans to figure out an elf's age with any accuracy, but I like to think I'm pretty good at it, and my guess was, the three at the table were hardly old enough to be out after dark. Runaways from over the Border, working for food and a place to sleep, most likely. Not mastermind material.

The one who stood on the other side of the room was older than the kids, with a narrow, clever face and his silvery hair worn in Romantic-poet curls over his forehead. He was scowling.

He snapped at someone in the part of the room we couldn't see, "I'm not a tradesman. The cost of materials is no concern of mine. If you can't afford them, I shall find another patron."

The person he talked to said something in a low voice. The angry elf replied, "That has nothing to do with me. You are a shopkeeper and the child of shopkeepers; you think only of profit, and not of honor nor of knowledge, which may win you honor. It is these peddler's instincts that have drawn strife down upon your head. Had you but supported my work openly, as would any knight of the true lands, no ill fortune could have attended the enterprise."

I still didn't hear what his companion said, but I heard

the voice more clearly. It seemed familiar. I stole a glance at Sunny, and found her hard-eyed and tense.

Whatever the speech was, it made the curly-haired elf sulk. "I could have done it. That we fell short at first was only to be expected. With money and time I could have refined the process; relieved of secrecy, I could have matched each dose to its taker, like a glove made to fit a hand. By queen's blood, I could have raised even you!"

"That's enough!" growled the other voice. Definitely familiar. Whoever he was, he had to be pushed before he'd project well enough to be heard out a window. I couldn't make out a word of what he said after his outburst.

The older elf turned to the table and snarled something in the language of the Elflands, and the kids, looking frightened and resentful, filed out of view, past the speaker we couldn't see. They must have left the room; a door slammed, and the older elf winced. Then he snatched the box of candles off the table in a careless, haughty gesture, and carried them off what I thought of as the stage, toward the other person. A few more indecipherable sentences, and we heard the door slam again.

Sunny grabbed my arm and yanked me toward the back of the building. We were trying to be discreet and quiet, so we made it to the rear corner just in time to see the back door open. It and the steps down from it were lit by a torch in a bracket. Torchlight was enough to keep someone from falling down the stairs, and enough to make it easy to recognize the man on the steps. Toby Saquash, who'd had third shift desk duty at Chrystoble Street Station the morning I found Walt Felkin.

Sunny didn't look surprised; she must have had all the reaction she was going to when she recognized his voice. Saquash put the box of candles in a hardshell case over the rear fender of a dark-colored Yamaha Virago and mounted up. When he started the engine, Sunny said next to my ear, "Would you be able to find him?"

I nodded. I'd *liked* Toby Saquash. How could somebody I liked have been responsible for the passport, for the virus, for bombs, and death by falling, and my partner weak and sick in the care hostel? "You're not going to let him take that batch out of here, are you?"

"Calm down. He won't distribute it in a hurry—he can't. He knows as well as I do that when these things get rushed, people make mistakes, and that's when they get caught. Besides, we spent the whole day playing jacks with his customer base."

The Virago bounced away down the alley, taillight dark. "Now what?" I whispered.

"We find out how many people are in the building."

As far as we could tell from looking in and listening at windows, we'd already seen all the occupants. Sunny tried the front door, and nodded when it wouldn't budge.

She knelt down beside the lock. "Keep a lookout," she ordered. I did, but the street was deserted, so I saw most of what she was doing. She took a piece of thread out of her pocket, and a box of matches, and pulled a hair out of the back of her head, where it grew longer. She wet the thread on her tongue, twisted it together with the hair, and wrapped both around the lock plate. Then she struck a match and poked the paper end into the keyhole. The words she murmured weren't in the language of the Elflands, or in any language I'd learned in the World. They might have been Latin. She said the last one with extra force, though still softly, and as she did, the flame disappeared down the matchstick into the lock and went out.

"Didn't work?" I asked.

"Nope, worked just fine. Look." Around the lock plate there was a line of faint iridescence where the hair and the thread had been.

"It's unlocked?"

"No, it's locked to anybody but me or my designated surrogate. Doesn't matter which side of the door you're on, or whether you have the key." She stood up and dusted off the knees of her jeans. "There are a few advantages to police work in this town. Come on, we're going in the back."

She put her hand inside her jacket when we moved into the torchlight, and brought it back out holding her gun. On this door, when Sunny tried the knob, it turned. "Heavens, not very wary, are they? Stay behind me," she said, and opened the door.

The hall was dark, but wavering light leaked out of a room on the right. Voices did, too, the musical rise and fall of the language of Faerie. I expected Sunny to do the kick-open-the-door-and-yell-Freeze routine that I'd seen in movies. What she did was slide through the opening and level her pistol in a long sweep that covered the whole of the little space. It was the three elf kids in what was obviously their dormitory. The light came from one fat candle stuck by its own wax to the top of a battered footlocker. One of the kids sat on the lower mattress of a bunk bed; another sat on the floor at her feet, his back against the bed frame; and the third sat on the cot against the opposite wall, which wasn't far away. The three of them were smoking one herbal cigarette, passing it around like a joint, and I wondered if they were on short rations, or if it was just their last one.

Sunny warned them not to move. She didn't say it loudly, but she'd mastered the voice of authority that made volume optional. She'd also mastered a darned

good accent in their language. I suspected that was Linn's
doing. She said some other things, too quickly and too
well for me to translate exactly, but I think they were the
rest of the warning that goes with "Freeze," the stuff
about keeping your hands in sight, and why you should
pay attention to the person ordering you to do all this,
besides the fact that she's the one with the gun.

The kids really were straight out of the Elflands. They
hadn't had the time, or maybe the inspiration, to do
funny things with their hair and clothes yet, though the
girl on the bunk had cut hers off untidily to about chin
length. It shone like mother-of-pearl, white with a hint
of rainbow shadows, in the trembling light. She wore an
embroidered knee-length gown with scalloped hanging
sleeves lined in red, and red hose. Her bare arms were
white as a marble statue's, but still child-skinny. Her
companion on the floor wore a boy's long jacket, indigo
blue, with deep cuffs and lapels of pale gray that showed
the grubbiness of constant wear. The shirt underneath
still had fragments of lace so fine they looked like scraps
of mist. The one on the cot, now that I could see him
better and at full length, I decided had run away from
home during the elven equivalent of his senior prom. His
doublet hadn't been made to stand up to daily use, but in
its heyday it had been green and silver tissue, and his
narrow black pants were velvet, trimmed with silver
knotwork, now torn in places. His feet were bare, as
white and childlike and vulnerable as the girl's arms.

I'd stopped paying attention to the flow of Sunny's
words, but the silence brought me back. The youngest
boy, after a startled, wild-colt look at Sunny when she
came in, had kept his eyes on the floor, but the girl had
watched Sunny throughout the speech. Now she said
something quickly, apparently to the room at large. The

other two looked at her. Then the girl on the bunk gave a cool little shrug and stood up. She moved with breathtaking grace, like water flowing, as if she and the air had some kind of agreement. The little boy beside her scrambled up, too. The boy—the young man, or whatever they call them in Faerie when they've stopped being children but haven't quite made it to adulthood—in green and silver sat for a moment longer, trying to keep his emotions off his face. But he, too, rose at last, slowly, and stood at parade rest with his chin high.

To me, Sunny said, "Let 'em out the back door, and make sure they leave. I don't want them hanging around to give any warnings or get in the way. Oh, and here." She rummaged in her jacket pocket with her gun-free hand, and produced three of the seven-sided gold coins that Tick-Tick said were called lion's teeth in the Elflands. "Give them to the girl. The little prince there," she said, nodding at the one in green and silver, "won't have the common sense to accept."

"You'll be okay here?"

"I won't stir without you," Sunny answered drily.

On the back steps, I gave the girl the remains of my last pack of cigarettes, and the coins. The torchlight gave the three of them a particularly supernatural glimmering look, glossing their skin and touching their ruined clothes discreetly, and I thought about how my ancestors, centuries ago, had written about visitations from *their* ancestors. Faerie rades, changelings, dancing under the hill.

The girl looked at the coins in her palm. The kid in his ball dress said something sharply to her, but I shushed him just as sharply, thinking of Sunny inside, and what might happen to her, or me, if somebody decided to check out the argument on the back porch. The girl wasn't any better at keeping her feelings off her face than her well-dressed compatriot. I saw her pride put up a fight and take a serious blow as she closed her fingers over the money. I felt as if I'd hit her, instead of making it possible for her to get along on her own. But learning to distinguish false pride from true is a survival skill, and if the first lesson had hurt—well, if she hadn't wanted to grow up the hard way, she shouldn't have run away to Bordertown.

She went down the steps and into the alley, where the light barely fell on her, and jerked her head to order the others to follow. It was the first ungraceful motion I'd seen her make. The younger boy came promptly, and she started away, an irregular brightness in the night. The older one paused, and looked at the door and me one last time; then he, too, disappeared into the dark. I hoped that when the girl gave him his share of the gold, he'd have the brains not to refuse it.

Sunny may have thought I was silly to worry about her, but she'd kept her word anyway; she was still in the little dormitory. "Okay, extra careful," she said. "Don't assume there's only one person left in the building, and don't assume that just because he seems like a self-absorbed wanker he can't do you damage."

There was, as it turned out, only one person left in the building. And he might have been able to damage us, in some other place, at some other point in his life, under some other set of rules. Just then he was sitting at the table where the kids had been packing contraband, holding up his head with both hands, staring at the tabletop.

This time Sunny did the rap in a language I could follow. "Police. Don't make any sudden moves, and keep your hands where I can see them. I accuse you of taking life and of conspiring to take others, and declare that your freedom is forfeit until such time as this accusation may be tested in fair trial. If you attempt to flee this test now or in future, it is my sworn duty to stop you, even unto the resort of causing your death. And I have to admit, that would give me a lot of satisfaction right now."

Not the same one she would have used on the kids; and I was pretty sure that the last sentence was not standard.

Our quarry looked up as she began to speak, his eyes wide, and as she went on his face, his whole body, sagged. It was one defeat too many to be called a setback. "So!" he said when Sunny finished. "My dear companion sold me out to his fellow officers, did he?"

Sunny shook her head. "He's next."

Bitter satisfaction flew across his face. "That's more than I had hoped, that the others might be held to some account."

"Why shouldn't they?" Sunny said, seeming about as casual as the context allowed for.

"Oh, they meant the blame and all the payment to be mine. Small minds are the same in any land. I did the best work I could with what they gave me, and they never gave me what I asked. But here is all come to ruin through their smallness, and it's 'Hai, Malicorne, you evil dog, you have set the Gatherer upon your own race!' They will lie, they will lie, but it was none of my doing. None. Upon the Crown and upon the Hill, I meant no harm."

It's not true that elves can't cry. That's a piece of slander left over from what the World used to believe about witches. It's true that they don't do it easily, however. This one certainly didn't. Grief and fear swallowed up his fey prettiness; his white skin blotched pink as the tears ran past his nose and down his chin. He gave a gulping sob and his long fingers scrabbled at the tabletop. Then he pushed himself roughly out of his chair and turned his back on us, his shoulders hunched.

"As I remember it," Sunny said, "the old command is *'Do* no harm.' It doesn't say anything about 'mean.'" Watching her, I thought it was better that the elf had turned his back. She didn't show any signs of being in a forgiving mood.

And if Sunny didn't forgive him, it suddenly occured to me to wonder, what were we going to do with the bastard? We couldn't take him to the copshop in the side-car with Sunny in his lap, for God's sake. I wasn't even sure we could take him to a cop shop at all, given there was a cop involved; how chummy were the various stations around town?

"The harm was none of my doing. How can you presume to judge me, who are not of my kind? I would have given you the means to raise yourselves, but you are too weak, too weak."

"I don't presume to judge you," Sunny said. "I only presume to bring you in. The judging part is somebody else's job. But I wouldn't advise you to give me too much crap about it, because my best friend has the virus and is looking pretty bad, and I'd hate to find I was unduly influenced by that."

He looked over his shoulder at her, open-mouthed. "Your best friend is . . ."

"Some of us are more broad-minded than others. Now, you have a couple of choices to make. I can tie you up and leave you here, so I can find you in a hurry. Or you can tell me where you live, and swear on the stars of the four quarters and the moon in their net to go home and stay there until I come and get you, and not speak to anybody in the meantime."

I stared at her, shocked; but then, so did the elf. "May that oath burn your lips! No human should speak of such."

"I warn you, I meant it when I said don't give me trouble. You'd rather be tied up?"

He thrust his fingers into his poet's curls and yanked on them. "I don't—"

"Remember," Sunny told him, sounding a little less implacable, "I'm willing to believe that whatever else may have happened, you aren't an oathbreaker. If you prove that I wasn't wrong, it'll weigh in on your side with the people who hear your case." She looked toward the dark window, which meant that I had a better view of her face than he did. I thought she might be speculating on something—it was a gambler's look. "And I'd need to know that you wouldn't try to escape across the Border."

There was a moment's silence. Then he said, in a small voice, "I cannot . . . go again into the true lands."

Sunny nodded briskly. "I'll hear your oath, then."

She coached it out of him. I could tell that this was something she'd done a lot of, by the watertight nature of the results. If he abided by it, he'd be as safely locked away as if she'd sent him to San Quentin. If he abided by it.

I waited until he'd hurried off down the street, and Sunny was doing the hair, thread, and match trick with the back door lock. Then I said, "I can't believe you did that."

"Did what?" she asked, once the recitation was done and the match had gone out.

"You let the son of a bitch go. Why do you think he's going to do what he promised? What's going to keep him from running away, going to ground someplace, and starting work on the next batch?"

Sunny smiled up at me, the torchlight gleaming sharply off her teeth. "What, can't you find him again?"

I shut my mouth so hard it was lucky I didn't bite my tongue.

"Besides, I think he will keep his promise. You heard what he said about Faerie. I think his bridges are burned in a big way there. And if he's grateful for a little mercy, we might be able to get some help out of him."

"Testimony."

"That, too. I was thinking of the kids that are half-changed, and the virus. If he's actually the originator of the passport, he may know enough of his stuff to repair some of the damage."

She stood up, and the torchlight fell full on her face. She was tired, and angry, and nothing like any movie cop I'd ever seen. I was fascinated by the texture of the skin on her forehead, the tight lines of her lips. She met my stare and frowned.

"Vengeance is somebody else's," she said. "Don't ask me whose. But it's not in my job description, no matter how much you or I wish it was."

"That's not what I was thinking," I said.

Lightning was shuttling between clouds, where the sky showed between gaps in the buildings. "I need to take the bike back to the garage," I said, as she settled into the sidecar. "Do you want me to drop you at home?"

"Are you staying at Tick-Tick's apartment?"

"No, I'll walk back to my place."

"I'll stick with you, then, and walk you home."

I looked at the sky. "You'll get rained on."

Sunny shrugged. "Now that I've lost my wheels, I better get used to walking in the rain."

I pulled my helmet on, to avoid saying anything else,

and to dodge her eyes. As we pulled away from the not-a-cooking-school, I thought about how it might work. If I had the nerve. I wouldn't have the nerve. Stopping on the sidewalk in front of my building, inviting her to come up for a beer—did I have any beer? Damn it, no, I didn't, and I couldn't invite her up for one and stop at Yoshi's on the way to bum some more beer. Well, tea. I could offer her tea. I wondered if the apartment was marginally clean. I should have said I was staying at the Ticker's, where there was something in the icebox.

Someone sprang up off the stoop of the Ticker's building as we drew near in the street. I almost recognized her. I stoppped the bike and tugged off my helmet, and it came to me. Small, with a long brown braid—she was the one who knew history at the Daughters of Brede. The temperature around me seemed to have dropped ten degrees.

"Orient? You're Orient, right?"

I nodded. Sunny had her helmet off, too, and was watching me. I didn't look at her.

"Can you go to the care hostel right away?"

That was all she said. I could have asked why, but that would only have been stalling. Sunny pulled the helmet back on, and I put the bike in gear.

# PARADISE LOST

AT THE DOOR to room 24, I looked at the bed with Tick-Tick in it and had two thoughts at once: The Daughters were wrong—she was sleeping; and I was too late—she was dead. I was wrong on both counts.

A Daughter I hadn't seen before was in the room. She wasn't bustling around, or measuring things, or taking a pulse. She was just sitting, keeping watch, keeping the Ticker company. Now she stood up and touched Tick-Tick on the shoulder, and said, "Your friend is here. Is there anything you want?"

The Ticker's eyes were closed, but she smiled. "Not now."

The Daughter nodded as she passed me, and left the room.

I sat in the chair she'd vacated, which was in hand-holding distance. I didn't take advantage of that.

"How goes the quest?" the Ticker whispered.

"We're winning, I think. We found the source, any-way."

She opened her eyes a little, just enough to squint at me, and I remembered her complaining that the light hurt them. The light in the room was already low, but I leaned over and blew out the lamp nearest the bed. "Too late," she said, with a dry, windy chuckle. "I got a look at you. Was this source in a midden?"

I'd forgotten the state of my grooming. "It's sort of a long story. But we had to borrow your bike. Sunny's car got blown up."

I regretted it the instant it was out of my mouth. Pain moved her features. She shook her head a little on the pillow. "A Triumph Spitfire. The dearest things—part of their value is that they cannot last." Then her eyes squinted open again, and she grinned. "Blessed Mab, what an awful thing to say at such a time."

I clenched my hands on the chair arms. "Sunny wouldn't mind."

"Sunny be damned. You know what I meant."

"Stop it."

She closed her eyes and frowned. "If you mean to be mealy-mouthed, go away and send the nurse back in. I did not wish for your company so that I could share in a lie."

"The middle of the night is always the worst time for sick people. You'll be pretty damned embarrassed about this in the morning."

"You are wasting time, and I at least have very little of it. Stop playing the fool."

The Daughters of Brede was hardly like a hospital at all: no bright, hard lights, no hushed terrors, no smell of pain and death, none of the things that Bolt Street Clinic couldn't help but remind me of. But pain and death could still enter here, and the people who had to sit helpless and watch them come felt just the same, wherever they did it.

"Orient?" she said. "I didn't mean to scold."

I took her hand. I'd known I would, eventually, and I'd known that when I did, it would be to acknowledge the thing I didn't want to know, to let in the word I'd tried not to hear. I swallowed and said, "Never mind."

" 'All that has been mine is yours to keep, to guard, or give away.' " She drew an uneven breath. "There. That's binding, you know."

"I know."

"All those tools you haven't the faintest notion how to use." She grinned again.

"And your apartment for mountain goats."

"And my curious furniture."

"I like your furniture."

Her grip tightened on my fingers. "I meant what I said, my dear. This is my home. These are my people. You are more to me than any brother of my blood. I have no regrets."

*I do,* I wanted to cry out, *I have enough for both of us. Don't leave me.* "I'll remember," I said.

"It's well," Tick-Tick announced. "I am satisfied."

Sunny was prying my hand away, gently, one finger at a time. It prickled as the circulation came back. The room was colder than it had been when I'd come in, and a little brighter, too. Sunny had turned the wick up on the remaining lamp. "Stand up," she said, and I realized I'd been sitting for a very long time. She half-lifted me out of the chair. "Come on," she ordered, and I followed where she pulled me. After a little walking she made me sit down again, and put something in my hands and told me to drink it.

Coffee—very good coffee. Cops always know where to find it when the rest of the town is short. There were no beds in this room, only chairs and a couch and a square table with folding chairs pulled up to it. There were scattered playing cards on the table, and two coffee cups. It looked like a nurses' break room, and looked, too, as if Sunny might have chased a few of them out of it.

A seedybox was playing softly in the corner, "Bonnie Barbry-O" by . . . what was the name of that band? Bards of a Feather. Clever name. I carried my coffee cup over to the window. Such a good version, pretty and mournful, and that low bass harmony on the refrain like something out of a South African men's chorus, singing, "Bid a fond farewell—"

It was raining. What a melodramatic piece of work. It wasn't any better than Tick-Tick's comment on the passing of precious things—

Oh, hell, out of coffee—

"You should try to stop crying. You'll dehydrate," Sunny said from somewhere behind me.

"I'm not crying."

"Oh," she said.

She took the coffee cup out of my hands and replaced it with a full one. Then she managed to catch it again before I dropped it. God forbid, I thought, gripping a fistful of the window drapes in each hand, God forbid that we should waste precious things.

When I could think again, I found that Sunny had made the effort mostly unnecessary. She only wanted to know if I was fit to drive, or if she ought to. I weighed the alternatives carefully: driving the Ticker's bike (I'd promised it she'd be back soon; her voice saying "All that has been mine . . .'') versus sitting in the sidecar and the person driving not being her. "I'll drive," I said.

By the time we got out to the curb in the rain, I remembered to ask, "Where are we going?"

"My place," she said. "It's closer."

"I—I'd kind of like to be by myself."

"No, you wouldn't. Trust me."

I tried to marshall a couple of civil arguments, or even an uncivil one. She interrupted with, "Do you have a shower?"

I thought of the barrel in the backyard, in the rain. "Not . . . really."

"I do. Drive, or give me the keys."

I drove. It wasn't raining hard enough to substitute for the shower, but it made my clothes damp enough to bring back the awful river smell in them, and chilled me pretty thoroughly in the bike-made breeze. A passable set of distractions. Would it be very long before I could quit worrying about where my next distraction was coming from?

Sunny's street was quiet, and almost all the windows were dark. "It's late," I said.

"It's that. So try not to throw any pots and pans down the stairs."

There was a candle in a holder, on a little table inside the front door. Sunny lit it and led the way up, and I put all my effort into not missing a step in the wobbling light. On the third floor landing, Sunny turned to me. "Wait here."

I remembered that she was on the fourth floor. "Why?"

"Because. Not scared of the dark, are you?"

The light disappeared with her, up the next flight and around the corner. I heard her stop at her front door.

There was a long silence before the jingle of keys reached me, and the sound of the door opening. It was a well-made building, so I couldn't hear anything after that.

It seemed like several minutes before her head appeared around the turn in the stairs. "Coast is clear," she said softly. "Come on up."

The lamps were all lit in her apartment, and the white walls had warmed to a kind of buff color in the glow. "Coast is clear of what?" I asked.

She tipped her head to one side and gave me a look that suggested she was being patient and I should appreciate it. "Of anything that might have been left by the person who made my car blow up."

I stared. "I forgot." Ye Gods, how could I? I'd had one surprise at Walt Felkin's front door; wasn't that enough to make me permanently wary? Well, I had a lot on my mind—which reminded me of what and how much, and I turned away and sat down in a chair in the living room, blind for an instant with the return of feeling.

Sunny stood for a moment in the open front door. Then she shut and locked it, and said, "Company gets the first shower. There's towels in there already, and I'll hang a robe on the hook, since you won't want to put those clothes back on. Don't dawdle, okay? I want one, too."

"You can go first."

"I prefer second."

She went off toward the back of the apartment. I stayed where I was for long enough to be sure that she was in the kitchen, before I went down the hall and discovered that one of the doors that had been closed on my first visit was the bathroom.

It reminded me of her kitchen, clean, plain, with white towels and a rag rug on the floor, and soap that smelled nice, but only like soap. (What was it? Flowers and strong perfumes for the bath?) The robe on the door hook was navy blue cotton flannel. Had the Triumph been Sunny Rico's only indulgence? She mostly lived as if she didn't want to leave fingerprints.

The water was very hot, and there seemed to be a lot of it. I cried in the shower, because I knew Tick-Tick would have asked how they heated water for the building. It was harder to stop, knowing that no one could see or hear me do it. Was that why Sunny had assured me I didn't want to be alone? I dried off, and combed my hair, and noticed that I'd be the better for a shave. One of these days. The robe fit. I carried my towel and my dirty clothes into the kitchen.

Sunny was standing at the counter looking at nothing. I thought she jumped a little when I came in, as if she knew someone was there but didn't expect it to be me.

"If I wash these, is there some place I can leave them to dry?" I asked her, holding up the clothes.

She let her breath out. "There's a line on the balcony out back. You can hang the towel out, too. Don't worry about washing it."

Sunny closed herself in the bathroom, and I did a hasty job on my jeans and T-shirt in the kitchen sink. It had quit raining by the time I stepped out on the balcony, and I set to work pinning things on the clothes line. The ordinariness of it was comforting. Everything had just changed—except that clothes still got dirty, and I could still make them clean again the same way I had before everything changed.

*Don't think about it,* I insisted.

Sunny had made coffee while I showered. I poured myself a cup, and was carrying it down the hall to the living room when the bathroom door opened.

Steam puffed out, and light into the unlit hall.

Sunny's robe was white terrycloth, as ascetic as the one I was borrowing. She stood in the doorway, her bare pink feet over the sill, the light outlining her head with the wet hair combed down sleek as otter pelt. Her eyelashes were dark with moisture, and her eyes looked larger than usual. She was so close I could feel the damp heat from her skin, and see the beads of water gathered on her breastbone between the lapels of the robe. She was a little shorter than me. I was surprised; maybe I'd been thinking of myself as a version of me at sixteen, when all cops were taller than me. Maybe she was taller when she wasn't wearing a robe, when she wasn't warm and damp and smelling of shampoo.

I should have said something casual, but I couldn't talk at all. I forced my feet to carry me toward the living room and an armchair as far from the hall as I could get.

If I'd expected anything, I'd have thought she would go into her bedroom for clean clothes. Instead, she came into the living room, too. She didn't seem to be able to hear my heart beating, which was a relief. "Think you can settle for the couch?" she asked.

I swallowed, which didn't help, so I just nodded.

"Are you hungry at all?"

I shook my head.

"Well, that's good, because dessert was in the back of the car." When I didn't respond to that, she asked, "Did you lose your voice?"

Surprise made me cough. "No. No, I'm fine." I was too restless to stay where I was; I stood up and went to the front window, and parted the curtain enough to see the street. It was still there. The bike and sidecar waited by the curb, and everything gleamed with the polish of rain.

"Are you tired?" Sunny asked.

I ought to have been. I probably was, if only I could figure out how to tell. "No," I said, looking out at the street.

"Me, neither," she said, and sighed. "I keep wondering if I should have heard something from The Lilacs."

I couldn't think of an answer to that.

After a moment Sunny said, "I could leave you alone, if you wanted. Maybe I was wrong—maybe you would have preferred to be by yourself."

"No, you were right." I looked over my shoulder at her and found her closer behind me than I'd expected. She looked disarmed, and it had less to do with the robe and the wet hair than it did with the absence of something in the set of her mouth and the way her eyes tracked, an armored attitude that she'd had as recently as when she went to take her shower.

I had my back to the window, though I couldn't remember turning around. I was also forgetting to breathe, and compensating for it by taking in little gasps of air. Sunny put her hands on my shoulders. I could feel the heat of them through the robe. Her eyes tracked over my face, her expression grave, as if she was looking for something. I didn't know if I wanted her to find it or not. My hands reached out, almost by themselves, and curved around her waist. I waited a moment to see if she'd hit me.

Her fingers slid up from my shoulders to my neck and moved lightly through my damp hair. I gave up waiting, pulled her to me, and kissed her.

She wasn't waiting for me, and she wasn't embarrassed about it, either. She pushed the robe down over my shoulders to my elbows and searched across my skin with her fingertips as if they were eyes. She followed them with her lips, until I stopped her by putting my arm around her and drawing her near again. I ran my hand slowly down her neck, over her collarbone, into the space defined by the opening of her robe, and finally under the cloth to the slope of her breast, soft over the firmness of her pectoral muscle. My fingers brushed the nipple, and she drew a hard breath and opened her mouth on mine.

It was an urgent matter, that lovemaking, without time for subtleties, for talking, for sweetness. It didn't celebrate anything, or symbolize anything. It was two creatures who needed an extreme of comfort from each other, without delay, and got it. Afterward we lay in a tangle of skin and robes on the living room floor, and still we didn't say anything.

One of the oil lamps began to smoke furiously. Sunny untwined herself from me and from her robe and blew it out. As she moved to the other side of the room and the other lamp, I watched her, watched the long muscles show themselves and disappear in her thighs, watched the curve of her buttocks rise and fall just a little out of synch with the rhythm of her steps, watched the light slide off her shoulder blades and define the vertical path of her spine. Then she put the other lamp out, and I could barely see her at all, until my eyes adjusted to the dark. When they did I saw her standing above me, reaching out her hand. I took it, rose, and let her lead me into the bedroom.

We both had to hunt down that state of exhaustion that would let us sleep. But eventually I found myself lying on my back looking at the bedroom ceiling through half-closed eyes, aware, but not desperately so, of the strong, supple body stretched out and touching mine, thinking about rolling over toward her and wondering if I would fall asleep before I got it done. Something about the light on the other side of the bedroom blinds suggested that dawn was close.

I turned my head and saw Sunny, her head raised a little by the pillow and one hand, watching me, her expression detached and a little speculative. I remembered, all in a rush, where I'd seen the expression before: when she'd collected me from the Hard Luck, when she'd asked about Richard Weineman, when she'd wanted to know the story of my last great disaster out in the World, the last major roadmark on my trip to Bordertown. And I wouldn't tell her. I wouldn't even tell Tick-Tick, that hungover morning over waffles and strawberries, which was—oh, God, only days ago. Only days. And I'd said to the Ticker that if I told anybody about it, I'd tell her. Already, in a few days, it was too late.

I rolled over abruptly, but in the opposite direction from the one I'd thought about a minute before. Sunny said, "It's all right. Go to sleep."

I didn't think I could anymore. But as I waited for sleep, I heard myself say, "I didn't even think I was on my way here. I was just getting away. I didn't know I was getting away to Bordertown. I was hitchhiking—I got one of those rides that your parents tell you about to try to scare you off hitching. God, if anybody ever got one, of course I would."

She didn't say anything at first; then she said, "You don't have to tell me this."

"I know I don't have to," I said, and sucked in my breath against the pain. "That's why I can." *If I had to, I'd fight it like death itself. But with you, I don't have to.* That was what I was echoing: Tick-Tick's words.

I pressed on. "I'd taken some recreational drug, I don't remember what. I was almost always on something back then. I thought I could turn off the finding ability with it, if I just found the right thing to take. And this guy stopped for me in his big damned boat of a car, and he had some hash, and some pills of some kind, and the next thing I knew it was night, and he'd pulled off the highway down a dirt road by a creek.

"I can't remember it all. I know I woke up and looked out the car window, and saw him setting up a camp under the trees. I got the door open and tried to walk away, back up the dirt road, but walking was . . . I couldn't coordinate. And the driver spotted me, ran up and grabbed me by the collar and threw me out of the road, into the grass. I kept trying to get up and he kept hitting me. Then I was further off the road, where he was pitching camp, and he had something in his hand, and I was so scared. I felt something under me, in the grass. I picked it up and swung it at him. I didn't know until it hit him that it was his camp hatchet."

I stopped for breath, and Sunny didn't say anything. Maybe she'd fallen asleep. Maybe I was reciting this for my own benefit, and in the morning I'd discover that I'd gotten it off my chest without ever spilling the secret. "The next thing I remember was trying to get his car, his huge damned Chrysler with its damned stick shift, turned around at the end of the dirt road without getting stuck in a ditch, and the headlights lighting up the long grass and nothing past it. I just knew it would be like in a horror movie, that he'd come lurching up out of that grass with his hatchet still stuck in him, and break the windshield and kill me."

"Instead, you got the car turned around and came here," she said behind me. I rolled over and stared at her. She was propped up on her elbows, gazing at the brightening window. "And as soon as you got here, it never happened. You came to the Borderlands, and your past was cut off like six inches of hair. It never happened at all."

We lay there like that for what might have been a long time. Then she said, "Go to sleep," and I curled up and obeyed orders.

I woke up several hours later with sun knocking on the blinds. I was alone in bed. I remembered whose bed it was pretty quickly, and I remembered at about the same moment that there wasn't any Tick-Tick anymore.

The first fact warred with the second, and won. I couldn't lie there staring at somebody else's ceiling all day, the way I could have if it had been *my* ceiling. But I thought about the logistics of it, and felt a whole new reluctance to get up. My clothes were on the back porch, and my borrowed robe was in the living room. I hadn't realized before just how much ambiguity there was in going naked in the house of a woman you'd just had sex with for the first time, who you might be in love with but who you were pretty sure was not in love with you.

I worked up enough courage to slink out into the hall. There were noises coming from the kitchen, but I made it to the living room and got the robe on without seeing her. The white one was still on the floor.

I headed for the kitchen, trying to make a little noise myself. "Good morning," said Sunny. "There's coffee left over." She was dressed: gray pants, a green Boiled in Lead T-shirt, and her shoulder holster. Fully armored.

"You've had less sleep than me." Now *that* was clever. What the hell had I been trying to say?

She shrugged. "Messenger came this morning." She poured a cup and handed it to me.

"Where from?" I asked, before it occurred to me that if she wanted me to know, she'd tell me. "Never mind."

She seemed to think about it for a second before she

said, "Ms. Wu sent a note. She thinks Linn's come through the worst of it."

I looked into my coffee cup and throttled my most primitive worst instinct, and said, "I'm glad." She had seen my friend die, and knew that hers might, as well— might already have died, and the word not reached her yet. Tick-Tick's death and the threat of Linn's had been in the mix last night, in the place where my grip on Sunny met her grip on me. Now she could stop being afraid, and I could try not to think, *Why does her friend get to live, when mine died?*

"I know," she said, in the matter-of-fact voice she'd been using all morning, and I got the feeling she wasn't answering what I'd said out loud.

I fetched my clothes in off the line and put them on in the bathroom. The jeans were still damp around the waistband, but they'd warm up, if they didn't actually dry.

"Breakfast?" Sunny asked when I came out.

I tried to imagine sitting across the table from her, the effort involved in not crying and not saying any of the wrong things. "I don't think so. What do you need me to do today?"

She took a gray linen jacket off the back of a chair and shrugged it on. It lay nicely over the holster. "Nothing yet, though if anything goes wrong, that'll change. Today's work is tricky business, and some of it I have to do alone. I need to get a lid on this before Toby finds the lab has been sealed, or has the chance to talk to his boy biochemist and maybe convince him to break his oath and blab. I have to get authorization to lock up a cop. Once I get it, I have to move like hell to get to him before somebody tells him about it. In the meantime, I want to look like business as usual, and you're," she said apologetically, "unusual."

"You have to get permission to jail a cop?"

"Yeah." She smiled that smile that wasn't amused, and added, "It's a wonderful world. That's because none of the stations are in very good communication with any of the rest of the stations, and they say if we mess with each other without some higher office giving the go-ahead, we'll screw up ongoing investigations. That's what they say."

"Might be true."

"Sure. And maybe you *can* keep water from boiling by watching it." She checked the back door lock, and asked, "Where can I find you if I need you?"

"My apartment, on Sentiment."

"I know where it is."

Yes, she knew. "Can I drop you someplace?"

She shook her head. "I've got a neighbor who used to rent me his bike every time I had to pull the engine on the Triumph. I'll check with him."

She let me out the front, and I walked down the stairs alone. So what were the most stressful experiences in most people's lives? Death, love, job changes, and moving? Well, the job was kind of built in, but maybe I could find a new apartment and complete the set. I told myself that Tick-Tick's bike was happy to see me; at least it started right up. My God, the first time it didn't was going to be a landmark bad day.

When I got to my block I stopped at the market, which had been a bar when the World had just been the world, and Bordertown just another city. Now the shelves behind the bar in front of the mirror were the candy counter. Oswald Assai was the only member of the family in the place, though there was a hired kid stocking shelves. Ozzie greeted me noisily, and asked me how I was, and I wished I'd gone for groceries in some part of town where I didn't know anybody.

"I'm fine, Ozzie. Is there any beer in?"

"Yeah, Fern Hobarth brought in some brown ale yesterday. You want that?"

"Sure. Six—no, make it twelve." After all, I'd probably be getting condolence callers. Oh, God, what a horrible, horrible thought.

I shopped without an appetite, which always makes for an interesting icebox. Ozzie helped me carry the stuff to the sidecar. I was afraid he'd bring that up, what was I doing with the Ticker's bike, or was she here? But I complimented him on his hair, and the subject didn't come up.

It was my apartment. It was just my apartment, and nothing had changed, and maybe if I went up to the roof to work on my tan, maybe everything would start over and I could make it come out different this time. I put the food away and started to clean house.

The laundry and the bedclothes went first, and the rugs and towels. I separated them into loads on the picnic table in the back yard, and started the first one thrashing in the gas-powered washer on the porch. Then I took the cotton mattress out and beat it, and left it to air in the sun, put another load in and hung the first one to dry. I went back upstairs and took a broom to the cobwebs in the corners, moved all the furniture (there wasn't really very much) into the hall and swept the floor. Downstairs again, to tend the next load of laundry and get the bucket and the scrub mop.

I washed the windows, which I could almost sort of remember how to do. I was surprised at how well the wood floor boards responded to the mop; I'd have sworn they'd never been that color while I lived there.

By then I needed another shower, but there was no point in having one before I finished. I was careful not to think of how nice it would be to use Sunny's shower again, where the water was actually hot. I changed into cutoffs and dropped last night's shirt and jeans off the upstairs porch railing onto the last load of laundry. There went another piece of history; there went another inch of hair.

I came back down the hall to find that someone had threaded his way through my furniture and was knocking on my front door. It was a tall, thin person with long white hair, and for a second in the dim hallway I didn't recognize him. But he turned when I came near, and I saw Captain Hawthorn's long face and severe features. My heart gave an ugly kick, but he smiled when he saw me, that annoying warm paternal smile, and I relaxed.

"Captain Hawthorn. Hullo." He put out his hand, so I gave him mine. I was suddenly afraid that this might be a sympathy visit—but no, it was the wrong smile. "Come on in—oh, I guess you'd better bring a chair."

He laughed and picked up the big armchair, which didn't seem to give him any trouble. "Where do you want it?"

"Anyplace is fine. Can I get you a beer?" I hoped he'd say no and go away. Whatever I was doing, I didn't feel as if I could stop in the middle of it.

"Thank you, I'd like that." He sat down, and I pried the cap off a bottle and handed it to him.

"What can I do for you?"

He drank some beer, and sighed. "That's a good one," he declared, nodding at the bottle. "I've come to ask a favor, if I might."

"Ask away."

"I need to find Detective Rico."

Ah, well done. He hadn't asked the question, which would have forced me to do the same and live with having the answer, whether I felt like giving it to him or not. I walked across my nice clean floor to the front window. There was a motorcycle down below, a dashing number, with a raked front fork and sweep bars. Hawthorn's? It seemed out of character—he didn't seem like a bike guy at all—but I supposed he had to drive something, or walk. "Nice wheels," I said.

"Thank you." He seemed about to add something to that; then he changed course and said, "About Detective Rico . . . ?"

"I'd be glad to take you to her," I told him, "but I don't think I ought to."

"I beg your pardon?"

This was going to be difficult. "She's busy."

"Young man, I am also busy." Hawthorn seemed about equal parts offended and amused. "I wouldn't like to violate your professional ethics . . ."

"I'm sorry. It's not that. It's just—something she told me makes me think that she shouldn't be interrupted right now."

He folded his lips together tightly and sighed. "It's a matter of great importance."

"You could leave her a message—"

"And I'd prefer to be as discreet as possible."

If this had to do with getting Saquash locked up, Sunny might very well break my neck when she found out I hadn't helped. On the other hand, if my making it possible for Hawthorn to find Sunny was involved in tipping Saquash off, Sunny would break my neck for absolute sure. "I really can't do it," I said finally.

He shook his head and stood up. "Excellent principles, if a little misguided in their application," he sighed. "I will not hold that against you."

"You can finish your beer before you go," I offered, as an apology.

"I'd best take it with me, if you've no objection."

"On a *bike?*" I asked.

He laughed. The cap was still on the counter; he picked it up, fitted it over the mouth of the bottle, wrapped his thumb and index finger around its edge, and squeezed. "Thank you for the beer. I hope we'll meet again soon."

"My pleasure," I called after him, slightly stunned. Now *that* was grip strength. He gave a jaunty wave as he headed down the stairs. A moment later I heard his bike pull away.

I shook my head and began to retrieve my furniture from the hall. I had the kitchen table in the door before I realized what I'd seen.

Had he done that on purpose? Had he *expected* me to put two and two together? Or did he think I wouldn't remember that he'd handed me a sealed beer bottle that night at Chrystoble Street copshop, the night I was drugged?

I dropped into the chair, because it's better to sit still when your brain is doing highway speeds. Two cops. Saquash doing the legwork, and Hawthorn . . . oh, what odds wouldn't I give that Hawthorn was the big guy? *If* the pyramid even stopped with Hawthorn, which I didn't want to think about. Sunny would find out, once she started investigating. Why hadn't Sunny realized it might go beyond Saquash? I hadn't, because I hadn't had any practice at this kind of thinking, but shouldn't Sunny have been more wary?

Why was he looking for Sunny? Ye Gods—because of the sealed lab. There was no reason to expect Saquash to come back after picking up his parcel, but Hawthorn could have. Hawthorn would know the lab end of the business had been smoked.

And he came to me—maybe to find Sunny, but probably to find out what I knew, too. He would want to know if Sunny was after him. Well, she wasn't yet. I'd have to find her after all . . . except that the same problems arose in finding Sunny that I'd explained to Hawthorn, or rather, hadn't been able to explain. I understood just enough of what she was supposed to be doing to know that I didn't dare interrupt her at it.

I had to find Hawthorn instead. If I could follow him, keep him from destroying evidence, warn Sunny if it came to that—well, I had to try. I stuffed my keys in my pocket, loped downstairs, got a clean T-shirt off the line and put it on, and went out to the street for the Ticker's bike.

I hopped on and almost turned the key without looking. I called myself some rude names for being a slow learner. I slid off the seat carefully and looked the bike over, including in and under the sidecar. It was clean.

I settled back down behind the handlebars and thought about that. It would have been easy to get me out of the way by wiring the bike. Even easier to bump me off in my apartment just now. But he'd checked me out and decided I didn't know he was in it, so it wasn't necessary to kill me. It was almost comforting to know that we were dealing with someone who was at least that fastidious about his trail of bodies. I fastened my helmet, started the engine, and got a Thataway for Captain Hawthorn.

Up the hill and Up the Hill was where it led me, to the

costly confines of Dragonstooth Hill, where if people aren't well fed it's by choice. Bordertown is taller there, and not just because of the slope of the land. Wealthy elves live in pastel glass spires that sometimes top a hundred feet, that look as if you could bring one down with a single well-placed brick. Except all the bricks are in the humans' buildings, and so is the pink granite and the pale gold sandstone, shaped into neo-castles and pocket skyscrapers that their owners are terribly proud of whenever the elevators work. Little parkways twine between the feet of buildings, dotted with fountains and sculptures and gardens with roses imported from the Elflands at Great Cost. It's the kind of neighborhood where you'd never expect to find a hair in the sink, except when people in paint-stained cutoffs and faded T-shirts ride up from the great downbelow. Then passersby look at you as if you've come to take the caps off all the toothpaste tubes in town.

I homed in on one building, and circled it to be sure. The answer to my question about Hawthorn was, Right here and straight up. I hoped the elevators were working.

I didn't know what building it was, but it seemed to be a public one. People stared at me, but no one told me I had to leave. I walked purposefully toward the back of the center lobby, found a small, badly-lit corridor, and followed it to the service elevator. It was on some kind of chain-lift system and made an ungodly noise, but it got me to the top floor, which felt like the one I wanted.

Now all I had to do was tramp up and down the halls looking conspicuous until I found a door to lurk outside. If I ever did this detective thing again, I was going to pack a disguise kit.

One dubious "Can I help you?" spoken in a penetrating voice, and I would have been pinned like a butterfly in a box. But I was lucky; all the doors in the hallway were closed, and nobody seemed to be going in and out of them. And the door I was looking for, the Thataway door, was right in front of me.

There was no name on it, only a symbol, a ring enclosing three clusters of leaves. It was flanked by two huge planters, big enough to hold a young tree each, which is pretty much what they held. It was a good thick wooden door, with no transom and no inset window. It did have a mail slot, though. I knelt on the floor, lifted the flap slowly, and put my eye to the opening. Nothing; the slot sloped down on the other side, and blocked my view. But the sound wasn't bad.

A female voice I didn't recognize was saying, ''. . . here? You're mad. Take your little murders back down into the slums. You said that's where they'd stay.''

''This is different.'' Hawthorn. The pull that had led me disintegrated.

''But on my doorstep? By the Crown, you promised me—''

''Why not? What better way to control all the evidence? Do as I say and you're in no danger.''

''No. You've made a mull of the business. Our agreement—''

''You would find it . . . disagreeable . . . if I were to be taken, and made to testify.''

There was a moment of silence on the other side of the door.

''I certainly would,'' said the one I didn't recognize, and for the first time in my eavesdropping, I thought that, given a choice between being caught by Hawthorn and being caught by the woman he was talking to, I might as well flip a coin.

They'd been sitting down, which was all that saved

me from having to make the flip; I heard the chairs scrape as they stood up. I let the mail flap down as slowly as I could force myself to do it, with all of my nerve endings screaming at me to run. If it made a noise, I hoped it was small enough to be covered by the sounds in the room. I scrambled behind one of the planters and made myself very small as the door opened and Hawthorn came out. The door shut behind him. He pushed through another door to the right of the service elevator, and after a moment, so did I. The sign on that one said "Roof."

The stairs came up in a greenhouse. I realized that they came straight up into the greenhouse without any more enclosures or doors just in time to be able to keep my head down below the floor level. I could hear Hawthorn moving around, rustling, banging things, sliding things. I stretched my neck and stole a look between the stair railings.

I couldn't see a thing. It was a beautiful greenhouse, with full-sized trees and ornamental shrubs and basins and beds of flowers, and my line of sight was full of leaves. I crawled up the stairs on my belly, to the end of the railing, and all I got was a view of a different bunch of leaves. I could hear Hawthorn, though, off to my left. There was a row of tall, narrow evergreens growing along one glass wall; if I could get to those without being seen, and get behind them, I could straighten up and have a look.

As I slithered across the floor, deaf to anything but the hammering of my own heart, I wondered if Hawthorn had a gun with him. Though with a grip strong enough to cap beer bottles, he didn't really need one to take care of me. I could smell the evergreens. Then I was between them, my back against the glass, and I could breathe al-

most normally again. I stood up and peered out through
the boughs.

He was wiring up a bomb. It looked pretty much like
the one I'd seen under Sunny's dashboard, though ad-
mittedly I hadn't been able to see that one very well. He
wrapped a couple of connections and proceeded to tape
the whole thing to the underside of a little rustic bench
beside a potted azalea. I watched him work and found
myself agreeing with the unseen woman downstairs:
Hawthorn had to be nuts. Did he think he could blow up
something on the Hill and not start up a hue and cry?
And on his own doorstep?

No—that was exactly why it would work. Nobody
would believe that the woman downstairs had anything
to do with an explosion that had happened near enough
to take the plaster off her ceiling. And when the hue and
cry started, Hawthorn would throw Saquash to the
hounds—ideally, dead, so he couldn't deny anything.
Case closed, heat off, back to business as usual.

But that wouldn't work, because Sunny had found
out about Saquash, and would get a statement out of him
damn soon, if she hadn't already—

Wake up, Orient. Who did you think the bomb was
for?

Hawthorn's head came up sharply. "Who's there?"

I could have sworn I hadn't made a sound. Could he
have heard Sunny, arriving earlier than he'd expected?
No, he wouldn't have spoken aloud if he'd thought that.

"Don't make me hunt you out. Show yourself."

Every minute was worth something. He could
damned well come and find me.

The suspense made my stomach churn. I watched
him come toward the greenhouse wall, steadily nearer,

and when he began to penetrate the evergreens I gave up and stepped out of them, about three plants down.

He didn't cry out, "You!" and fling out a hand dramatically. So much for old movies, or wherever it was he learned his affable stage persona. That's all it was; no one would have seen anything paternal in him now. He stood within reaching distance of me, but he didn't reach. He just looked, his head a little to one side, his eyes narrowed.

"I would have taken an oath," he said at last, "that you didn't suspect me."

I swallowed with a dry mouth. Wolfboy had taken me to every *film noir* picture that had ever hit town. I proceeded to mine that resource with both hands. "I never would have, except that everyone else seemed to."

His expression didn't change. "Indeed?"

"Sunny's got half a file drawer's worth of stuff on you. And if you go down to the lobby, you'd better leave the elevator with your hands up, or they might get the wrong idea. The nice lady down on the top floor sold you out."

He let me think it was going to work, I know he did. Then he smiled. "Pull the other one," he said. "It's got bells on."

I met his large, warm silver eyes and kept my mouth shut.

"I would like to hear how you came to suspect," he added. "Surely it can do no harm now."

I drew a long breath and let it out. "The beer bottle," I told him.

I saw his face change as he worked that out. He shook his head. "The snare of vanity."

"Where did you learn to blow things up?"

His eyes narrowed a little more, and he smiled. "From

Walt Felkin, actually. He rigged the abandoned apartment. And he advised me on the plans for his own house, though of course he had no notion that that was what it was."

"You blew Walt up with his own explosives?"

"No, just his expertise. The materials were police confiscated property."

Among Walt's last words had been "backstabbin' sonofabitch." They seemed pretty accurate. "This is—this is the part of the movie where the villain tells the hero everything, because he's going to kill him anyway. Except that I can't think of any more questions."

"You aren't the hero," Hawthorn said, rather kindly. "You're a pawn. And I really tried not to have to kill you. Go sit down on that bench."

I looked at it and shook my head. He grabbed my arm and pulled me toward him, then twisted my elbow up behind me. The grip strength wasn't just for beer caps. I didn't have any choice but to walk to the bench and sit on it. "You might not have wanted to kill me, but you came pretty close a couple of times."

"And in every case, there was no reason why I should have expected you to be there. You're a fairly well-known person in Soho. Your death would have been noticed. I thought we should avoid being noticed for as long as possible." He knelt down by the bench, and I leaped up to make a dash for it. He shot out a hand, caught my wrist, and yanked me back down, damn near breaking my arm in the process. Then he unrolled a long, thin wire from under the seat. "In a minute, I will be going downstairs. You'll be staying here to wait for Rico."

From the direction of my evergreens, behind me, Sunny said, "Oh, why don't we all stay?"

I wanted to turn and look at her, but I was looking at

Hawthorn instead, the expression on his face, and the motion of his hands toward the package taped under the bench. I kicked him in the face.

It would have worked better if I'd been wearing something heavier than sneakers, but he still fell back. I sprang off the bench. Sunny fired her pistol and I was instantly deaf as a blue-eyed cat, but I saw a leaf fly up from a bush next to Hawthorn's neck, and a pane of glass in the greenhouse wall shatter.

"The bench is wired!" I shouted to her.

She'd stepped forward to keep Hawthorn in her sights. She was a storybook cop brought to life: the gun braced with both hands, her stance wide, the jacket falling open over her holster, her mouth a straight, uncompromising line under her sunglasses. She scared me to death, but I knew she wouldn't scare Hawthorn.

My ears were working again; I heard Hawthorn scream something. I looked toward the sound.

The plants were moving. The azalea stretched out branches into the path, the potted trees writhed their limbs and bent their trunks, and the evergreens leaned and twisted in toward the center of the greenhouse, toward me. I heard Hawthorn's running steps, but I couldn't see him.

Sunny was beside me, the pistol aimed along what had been the path, before the plants had crawled into it. "It's an illusion!" she yelled, and pulled the trigger. Nothing happened. "God damn it," she growled, "why do I carry this thing? Come on!" And she leaped straight through a thrashing vine and disappeared.

By the time I reached the top of the stairs, the greenery was all back where it belonged, and Sunny was careening through the door at the bottom. I followed.

The door I'd listened through was standing open; so

was the door inside that, that connected the front reception room to the beautiful dark-panelled office beyond it. An elf in a pink silk suit, her fine straight white hair cut to sweep her shoulders, stood in front of the rosewood desk. Her eyes were beautiful, and round with horror. She had a silver letter opener in her hand. Hawthorn lay on the rug at her feet with his throat cut, and a little above the hem of the pink skirt there was a thin arc of dark red.

The elf looked up as we came in, her face full of terrified appeal. "He—he tried to—I had to defend myself."

I don't think we stood frozen for more than a second. It seemed longer because I was busy. He couldn't be dead, not so quick as that. It must be another illusion. But no, Hawthorn was Thataway, on the floor, which meant this was real, didn't it? Could an illusion trick that sense, too? The elf's voice was the one I'd listened to through the door, talking to Hawthorn, the one who had agreed, in that cold, steady way, that she wouldn't want him to testify.

"The hell you did," I heard myself saying, and I walked forward.

I thought, as I did, about the way any trick seems to work once in the Borderlands, and how so few of them work twice. But I closed my hand over Hawthorn's still-warm wrist, and had just enough time to realize that this was one of the second kind, before I went down into the dark under a large dose of his life and death.

I came to with my face in the carpet, and there was a bit of time when I couldn't remember why. Then I groaned and rolled over, and interrupted, I'm told, a speech in which the elf assured Sunny that the trauma had probably killed me.

I suppose, if I'd taken the time to think about it, that I had trusted Sunny to know what I was doing, and to make it work. I hadn't been wrong. By the time I was conscious and noticing my surroundings again, Sunny had explained to the elf how well my adventure with Bonnie Prince Charlie's corpse turned out, and did she prefer to wait until tomorrow morning, or would she like to just confess now and save everyone a lot of trouble? All that at gunpoint, of course.

"This is nonsense," said the elf woman. "Think what you're doing, my dear. The word of one rather scruffy young human person against mine, and the influence of my house? Blessed Isle, everyone knows that kind of magic never lights on humans."

"Well, it's lit once before, Secretary, and in front of witnesses. Cut your losses, and maybe the judges will be nice to you."

The elf woman's jaw clenched. "Whatever I say, they will be *nice*. My house will see to it, as it will see to breaking you for your presumption."

"Honey, right now your house couldn't break eggs in this town, and you know it."

This was all going over my head. I had dragged myself to my feet with the aid of the edge of the desk, and was standing with both hands braced on the glossy expanse of rosewood, waiting for the bees to get out from behind my eyes. Things swam slowly into focus on the desktop: a silver fountain pen, a black leather blotter holder, a black leather box embossed with silver, open, with sheets of stationery in it. Thick white sheets with hair-thin red and blue fibers in the weave. Paper that remembered its maker.

The woman in the pink silk suit had yanked Hawthorn out of our hands—*my* hands. Hawthorn had walked through Soho and seen us, the people who lived there, and knew that some of the ones he saw would die because of what he was doing. He had looked us all in the eye and set death loose among us.

This woman might never have seen Soho, but that didn't make it better. She'd never had to decide to kill; only to do business. Death was an operating expense. Even Hawthorn's death. His blood was, literally, on her hands, and all that was to her was the cost of solving a problem. The collapse of the passport ring was only an affront to her professional pride. The mutation of the virus was nothing to her at all.

I crossed the room unsteadily to stand in front of the elf woman.

The skin between her nose and her upper lip twitched, as if she had controlled a sneer. "Stand off from me," she ordered. "I don't like the way you smell." But her eyes cut away from me and back, and away, as if trying to run.

"Orient," Sunny said sharply, "if you do anything I will throw you down the stairs."

"Why?"

"Because it's my job."

"To protect her from me? My God, then who the hell is left to protect *me* from *her*?" I swung around to glare at Sunny. She'd never lowered the pistol, and her eyes hadn't left her prisoner for more than an instant. I said, "If there were any fairness in the world, she'd be dead. Instead everybody else is, the world is unfair, and it's your job to enforce it?"

If she hadn't been tanned, Sunny's face would have been almost as white as the elf woman's. "Vengeance is not mine, remember? My job isn't punishment. It's not even dealing out justice. I don't get to decide right and wrong. *I only get to bring them in.*"

My breath rasped over a burning lump in my throat.

"You don't want to be a good cop," I said. "You want to be a Knight of the God-damned Round Table. There's a limit."

"There is a limit," she said, in a fierce, quiet voice. "I know exactly what it is, and you don't. Now shut up and go downstairs. You'll find Cascade and Wally and Kathy Hong in the lobby guarding the doors. Send them up."

I had to go, or I would have choked on the coal in my throat. If she forgave me for those last words, it would be more than I deserved.

Cascade was the green-haired halfie cop from Chrystoble Street, and Wally was her human partner. Kathy Hong I remembered from the remains of the derelict apartment building. I sent them up, so they could read the elf her rights, or whatever the real-world equivalent was in Bordertown. I was so tired I could have dropped down and slept on the floor. I wanted to go away, but it would have seemed like breaking something. And I wanted to go back upstairs, but I knew I had no place there. I sat downstairs in the lobby and told myself it was so I wouldn't have to look at Hawthorn lying there being dead.

Eventually I felt a touch on my shoulder, and raised my head off my knees. It was Sunny.

"Can I go home now?" I asked. "All my furniture is out in the hall."

She raised her eyebrows. She'd taken the sunglasses off, and she looked almost as dazed as I felt. "That's not delirium talking, is it?"

"No."

"Well, you can't go home, because if I'm going to have to sit up watching you sleep again, I'd just as soon do it in the comfort of my own place."

"That's right. Oh, boy. I get to find out what having your throat cut is like."

"If you're lucky, I'll time it right, and it won't come to that."

"Did you know Hawthorn was in this?"

"Not until he sent me a message asking me to meet him here. I thought there might be somebody besides Toby—I couldn't see Toby *running* the thing—but I didn't know who until then. As soon as I got his note, I realized he was it, and the note was his one stupid mistake. So I came early and brought some friends."

"You trusted them—Cascade and Whatshisname, Wally, and Hong?"

"I had the least reason to *mis*trust them, anyway. Why were you here?"

"Because I didn't know you already suspected Hawthorn."

She snorted, and rubbed her eyes. "Well. I'm glad you did it."

"Ye Gods, why?"

"You don't think you helped?"

"No. No, I think—" The hot thing materialized in my throat again. "I'm sorry for what I did and said up there. I didn't mean it."

Sunny shook her head. "I know how much of it you meant. It's all right."

I looked up at her.

"Honest," she said. So I believed her.

I stood up and sagged a little, and she caught my elbow.

"You want me to drive?"

"Ah. Yeah, I think you'd better." I handed her the keys. "Who was the elf woman?"

She was helping me into the sidecar before she answered. "First Secretary of the House of the Weeping Birch. A commercial family with interests on both sides of the Border, and a reputation for being . . . intent on growth. Maybe at the expense of a few other things. It looks like Weeping Birch was Hawthorn's backer. The next challenge is to prove they knew what they were backing."

"I heard them talking, when I first showed up. It sounded as if *she* knew."

I put my helmet on, sank back into my accustomed place, and pretty much passed out for the rest of the ride. I was too tired to feel more than an aching nostalgia about the change of drivers. I wasn't worried; I knew it'd hurt like hell again later.

I slept on Sunny's couch that night, in my clothes. Neither of us said anything about alternatives to the arrangement, either past or potential. I had a dream that Hawthorn's last moments were a sad, sordid betrayal scene, and woke to the knowledge that, of course, it was true. Also incriminating, but by then that was almost beside the point. Sunny roused me up just before I could absolutely swear that the little silver knife had been the murder weapon. The omission wouldn't bother anybody, and it certainly didn't bother me. Eventually, I would describe the dream to a roomful of solemn people, some of whom were taking notes. It's in the court records, if anyone wants the details. I don't have any taste for repeating them here.

# ✳ 12 ✳

# GETTING ON WITH IT

I MOVED MY furniture back in, every piece of it in a different place from the one it had been in before . . . before. Then I rendered the whole effort pointless by spending most of my time at Tick-Tick's. I was housecleaning there, too, boxing up the things I didn't plan to keep, sorting the things I did, and in between, stopping in the middle of whatever I was doing and staring at nothing until something brought me back to the present. By the second day of housecleaning, people began to figure out where to find me; then the interruption of the trancelike state would often be a friend dropping by with a little food, an offer of help, and a couple of words that, if they didn't make anything better, at least gave me an excuse for talking out loud. Yoshi showed up, around mid-morning of that second day after Hawthorn's death, with a cheesecake.

"Where'd you get this?" I asked.

He looked mildly affronted. "I made it."

"Yosh, you amaze me."

"Hey, the way I figure it, you gotta eat. So you gotta learn to read a recipe. It's like being able to tune your bike." He flushed and shot a quick glance at me, to see if that had been an unfortunate thing to say.

I asked quickly, "You mean you do stuff besides cheesecake?"

"Oh, yeah. But hey, I didn't take home ec. or anything. I taught myself how."

I nodded. "More manly that way."

"Like you'd know, guy. Hey, that woman, the cop, what's her name? Rico. She was by your place a couple times."

Ah. "Did you tell her I was mostly over here?"

Yoshi looked down at his feet for just long enough to suggest that there was a story in that, and that he wasn't going to tell it to me. "Well, the second time I did. Like, once I figured that you'd want me to, I told her. I mean, you *did* want me to, right?"

"I did. You're a standup kinda guy, Yosh." Well, maybe I could ask Rico—Sunny—what they'd said to each other. If she dropped in.

Wolfboy and Sparks came up a few hours after that, to consult me about the last arrangements for the funeral, which was the next day. I didn't know Sparks very well, and I'd been afraid I'd be uncomfortable putting matters partly in her hands, maybe having to accept the wrong sort of sympathy from her and be polite about it, for Wolfboy's sake. But she seemed to be transformed by the occasion from sweet, self-conscious, and slightly vague to capable, sensible, and slightly brisk. When I hinted at that (a lot more tactfully than I've described it here), she nodded. "I turn into my mom, my granny, and

all my aunts. What they don't know about laying people
out's not worth knowing."

We settled what needed settling, and I asked, "How's
the store?"

Sparks looked at Wolfboy as he limbered up his pen,
and I was impressed. I'd known a lot of relationships
where one partner answered all the questions addressed
to the other one, and those had been pairs of people who
could both speak.

*Slow,* Wolfboy wrote. *Didn't realize how many of the cus-
tomers were elves.*

I frowned, and he pulled the notebook back toward
him. *You've been away. The virus is spreading, and the ones
who don't have it are staying out of public places so they won't
get it.*

"I guess I have been away. And I didn't even go anywhere."

*Knew that,* he wrote. *You'd have sent me a postcard.*

"Trust me," I told him, "the view really sucked."

He made a "whuff" sound that was as good as anybody else's "I hear ya." No, better, because I knew he
really did.

"Plan on dinner at the store tomorrow," Sparks said.
"Bean soup, big salad, hard-boiled eggs."

I met her eyes, startled. She nodded just a little. You
ate hard-boiled eggs after the funeral, during *shivah,* to
remind you that life was always renewed. I felt the tears
start, the ones that could still too often be surprised out of
me. But I got them blinked away this time. "I'll come," I
told her.

She and Wolfboy said their goodbyes. As they stepped
out into the hall I saw them reach for each other's hands.

Several fits of abstraction later, I heard knuckles on
the doorframe and looked up to find Sunny standing

there. I wished suddenly that I'd closed the front door downstairs, just so I'd have had a little warning.

"Is this a bad time?" she asked.

I thought of a possible response, rejected it, and then said it anyway. "Depends on what you want to do with it."

"Just wanted to pass on news. It can wait."

My God, did she *want* me to send her away? "No, now's okay. Have a seat. Oh, wait a minute." I cleared the debris off the nearest likely chair, which was the one with the dairy-cow cushions.

"Thanks."

"Yoshi said you'd been by my place."

"Oh, your housemate." The corners of her mouth twitched upward. "I hope he never takes to a life of crime."

"What'd he do?"

"Nothing terrible. I just had to convince him I wasn't there in the line of duty before he'd say anything to me but, 'I don't know where he is, and I'm not telling.' "

"Sheesh. I'd think Yoshi is exactly the kind of criminal a cop would want."

"Nah. I'd feel sorry for him, and let him go. Oh, and when I told him that not only was I not on duty, but I was a friend of yours, he said, 'No way!' I'm surprised he's still speaking to you."

"I'm surprised he dares, the lunk." I owed the lunk another favor. A little of the awkwardness had fallen away during that conversation. "So what's the news?"

"They're letting Linn go home this afternoon."

"Already?"

"He's still pretty limp, but they need the bed. The number of cases is still on the rise."

"Have they figured out any kind of treatment yet?"

"Nice lead-in for my next piece of news. Hawthorn's lab boy, Malicorne, is on limited release, provided that he works with the people who are trying to develop a vaccine. Which means he's going to spend his days shoulder to shoulder among the test tubes with Milo Chevrolet, which will either broaden his outlook or drive him to suicide. Milo says if Malicorne gives him any trouble, he'll tie him up and make him watch Rocky and Bullwinkle episodes until he can say, 'That trick never works.' "

"Are they having any luck, though? With the vaccine?"

It was a moment before she said, "It may be a long time."

That was almost a comfort, really; nothing could have saved Tick-Tick, not even finding the lab sooner. "What about Saquash?"

She ran her hands through the cropped part of her hair. "Nothing's decided yet. The judges' council has heard the accusation, and commissioned the gathering of evidence. I gave them copies of Linn's and my files yesterday, and you'll probably be called to tell your part of the story. Justice takes a little time."

"If . . . what'll happen to him?"

"If they decide he's guilty? Depends. But they may ask for banishment."

I turned away to the kitchen window, and pretended to be tidying the counter.

"Does that seem too light? Toby's been here for almost ten years. His life is made here. And in all those years he never went back."

"No," I said, looking at the skyline. "Not too light. Maybe too heavy." If he was banished, how could he make it up to the city? How could he put back what he had taken out? One of the things he'd taken out was

Tick-Tick, and somebody had to make good on that loss, didn't he?

"Oh, and Weeping Birch's charter is suspended, pending the resolution of Toby's case. If they have any excuse to, the city will vote to revoke. They've been wanting a reason for months." I heard her get out of the chair, and after a moment she was standing next to me. I smelled her shampoo, which only smelled like shampoo, and not like rosemary or mangoes or cloves. "So there. Is that enough vengeance for you?"

I shook my head. "You were right. Vengeance isn't mine, either. Justice is, maybe, because I live here, and I wouldn't want to if there wasn't justice. But that's not the same as vengeance."

Sunny brought her index finger down lightly on my shoulder. "I dub thee Sir Gareth."

"Sunny—" Oh, Lord, had I ever called her by her first name to her face before? I could feel my ears turning red. I shot a sideways glance at her. "The night Tick-Tick died—when we—"

"It never happened," she said, with a little crooked smile.

I turned around, braced both hands behind me on the counter, swallowed hard, and said, "Yes, it did."

She regarded me gravely, her hands deep in the pockets of the gray linen jacket. "But if that's so, what if it never happens again?"

*Ouch? I think so. I think that's what that is.* "Then I guess it doesn't. So I should stop holding my breath, huh?"

She looked past me to the window, with the not-seeing-much expression I was coming to know. "That night, neither of us had much chance to consider it beforehand. It was something that happened to us more than something we did. I don't know about you, but I'd like to do a little thinking now."

I felt as if something was slipping away from me, very gently. "No problem."

Sunny chuckled, a real, full-throated, genuinely amused one. I stared at her. " 'Ye lie, ye lie, ye false'—I don't remember the rest of the verse. I tell you what: In six weeks I'll come around and take you out to dinner, and we can talk about it then. How's that?"

I swallowed again, and wondered if it could be good for one's insides to be made to feel like a volleyball in motion. "Deal."

She went to the door and glanced back over her shoulder at me. "Now I'll go tell Yoshi you're in jail."

"Bad cop," I croaked. "Go lie down by your squad car."

She narrowed her eyes. "Get a haircut."

By the time she got downstairs into the street, I had my voice back. I sprinted up three platforms to the front window and yelled, "I'm growing it out!"


Late that afternoon, Tick-Tick's brother arrived on her doorstep.

The first news I had of it was a voice with an Elflands accent down in the street calling, "Excuse me? Hello, the—the building. Is someone there?"

Damn, had everybody else in the place gone out? And one of them must have closed the front door. I bounded to the window again and stuck my head out.

He looked like her. It almost undid me. I would never have mistaken him for her, but you could see her in the straight, rather high-bridged nose, the long eyes, the undercut lower lip.

He called up, "Is this where—" He dropped his chin to his chest for just an instant, then tipped his head back again to look at me. "Is this where the one who called herself Tick-Tick lived?"

"You're her brother."

He seemed surprised. "Yes. I was—I am."

"Come on up," I told him, and pulled the ring that unlatched the door.

"This way," I called over the balcony railing when he came into the atrium, and after that let him find his own way up. He stood in the doorway half timid, half arrogant, and each one made the other harder to deal with, I bet.

"Come in. My name is Orient." This one wouldn't want to shake hands.

"Do . . . don't humans usually have two names?"

I couldn't keep from smiling a little. "Sometimes."

"Oh! Oh, of course. You are the one who was her partner."

That surprised me. "I didn't think she kept in touch."

"In touch? Oh. No. That is, there are those who do—who write to their families, who visit—and I asked that they convey word of her, when they could." He scowled at me suddenly. "I did not have her spied upon. Some families do, whose children have fled."

"No, I don't think she would have let that happen." Once I saw him up close, I was willing to guess that he was older than Tick-Tick. He wore an expensive-looking wide-skirted coat in a sober shade of dark green, and a silk cravat, and had a heavy gold ring with what was probably the family crest embossed on it on his left hand. He looked like a fine upstanding pillar of the Faerie community. He also looked completely out of his element and aware of it, about evenly concerned for my good will and his dignity.

I slung another assortment of stuff off the dairy-cow print chair and said, "Make yourself comfortable. And I didn't catch your name."

"I—my name of custom is Vissa. You may use that."

"Thank you." I did know my manners, and that included Faerie manners, so I offered him food and drink before asking him what I could do for him.

He refused the refreshments and said, "I have come to take my sister home."

I'd thought it might be something like that. I filled the kettle and lit the fire under it, which would have been an embarrassing gesture if the gas hadn't decided to flow today. Out of the corner of my eye I saw him watching the procedure. Not scornful, not amazed, just interested. "What happens to the bodies of dead people is always a big topic with humans. Some of us figure the occupant has moved out, and they're compost. Some of us think there's still a connection between the dead person and the body, and that what happens to the latter affects the former. And some of us think it doesn't matter one way or the other, but that the people who are still living should be content with the arrangement, whatever happens to the remains." I couldn't think of Tick-Tick as "remains" yet, but it had been two days. Sometimes a strange artificial distance would set in, as if she'd gone on an extended jaunt into the Nevernever and I didn't expect her back for a month. I think it was what Ms. Wu had called denial, and I was pretty sure it wouldn't last.

"And where," asked Vissa, his chin up, "do you stand, on the matter of the bodies of the dead?"

Haughty—but not as haughty as he might have been, I realized. I knew some nose-in-the-clouds feel-mypedigree Truebloods who would have asked what the opinions of humankind had to do with the funeral customs of real people. "I'm not sure," I told him, rummaging in the cupboard for the new tin of Earl Grey. "This is—" my voice cracked; I took a deep breath and backed up. "This is the first time I've had to think about it, really. But my first impulse is to respect her wishes."

He made a harsh noise which wasn't quite a snort, and said, "And have you some way to ask her what they are? I have none."

"No. But I—she was my best friend for four years. And from that, I'd say that if you want her at home, you should leave her here. Because that's what she thought of Bordertown as."

He shook his head, a quick impatient gesture that was a little like one of hers. I couldn't call back the picture of her doing it, though. Such a short time, and already she was sneaking away. This was proving to be one of the few sensitive discussions I'd ever had that I would have preferred to be able to conduct on the telephone.

"I will believe that this was her home, as any place may be that shows the exile a kind face, that offers food, shelter, work to do, and a circle of friends. But the place of one's birth and raising may show one whatever face it may and still be at the center of the heart. Its loss leaves a hollow place, like a nutshell without the meat. She would not have spoken of it, for one does not speak of what one thinks cannot be mended. But I cannot believe she did not feel the loss."

I thought about the place of my birth and raising. Maybe it was an attachment that only occurred in the landed gentry. "Are you sure you're not judging the way she felt by the way *you* do? I'm sorry to keep on about this, but I was here, and I can't remember her ever suffering from anything that looked like homesickness."

I had the impression that he thought I was just being dense, that I was missing his point. He turned his hands palm up and spread them wide, as if opening a box, as he said, "Her spirit should be sent forth from the home of her kin. How else can it be? Generations of our family have been sung to their rest there. We held that land as ours before any human nation that still stands was formed."

"Yes," I said, "but she *left.*"

He stared at me with a bleak, arrested look that reminded me of the way I'd felt when, the day before, I'd called out to ask her if she had any twine and she hadn't answered.

I set the tea to steeping, and put out the good cups and saucers. By the time I brought everything to the table he had his face under control again. He would have been within his rights to remind me that he hadn't wanted anything, thank you, but he didn't do that. I poured, and he lifted his cup and drank as if his mind wasn't on it. I sipped at mine and kept my mouth shut. I'd just played what I considered an ace, and it was up to him to respond.

Finally he set the cup down with a little click. "I am sorry if it gives you pain," he said, in his measured, rather formal way, "but I must carry her body back. That is all."

Not an ace, after all. But he'd sure looked as if it was. "Why?"

"It is the duty I owe to the memory of . . . of the ones who have gone before us. To our family."

I had less sympathy with that argument than some people would, but it seemed to weigh a lot with him. "You have a duty to her, too, don't you? To her memory.

Because if you came here at all, you must not have dis-
owned her."

China rang softly as his hand bumped the saucer. He
jumped a little and put both hands in his lap. "It cannot
be discussed. Please, please, do not press me, but be assured that it is of the greatest importance to me."

It was unsatisfying; it was unsatisfactory; it did, in
fact, give me pain; but I didn't know what else to say.
Tick-Tick's last four years meant more to me than anything that could happen to what was left of her now.
Vissa hadn't had those four years. Maybe he needed her
funeral more than I did. I didn't look forward to explaining to anyone who showed up for it tomorrow why there
wasn't going to be a ceremony after all, but I could do it.

And what if he was right? She had been my best
friend, but there had been things we didn't talk about,
boundaries we didn't cross, questions we didn't ask. If I
knew more about her than I had actually been told by
her, I didn't mention it, and she did the same. It had
something to do with pride, with recognizing its require-
ments in each other and respecting them. I'd shared the
last four years of her life, but he'd shared the ones before
that. He might know things I had been too respectful to
ask.

"It must be important to you," I said at last, "or you
wouldn't have come. All right. You can take her body
back." I rose and walked up those three platforms to the
front windows. Why my crazy partner had wanted it to
be so much work to look out at the street was beyond me.
I supposed a few other things might have been beyond
me, as well. I braced my hands on the window frame
and looked, at the empty street sunk in twilight, at the
trumpet-fanfare sunset in orange and rose and azure, at
the rooftops, at nothing.

A little noise behind me made me turn. I'd left the cupboard door open when I got out the tea things. Vissa stood in front of it, cradling something in his arms, his head bent. It was a moment before I could tell that what he held was a bottle with a brittle brown label. The liqueur, the one Tick-Tick had said was from over the Border, that she'd poured on strawberries and set fire to. Vissa clutched it as if it were a child, and on his face I could see tears standing.

"What is it?" I asked, coming toward him.

He whispered, "This . . . is from our vines, our cellars. The work of our family, for centuries, is in this liquor."

My heart gave a little sinking lurch. She'd talked defiance toward her family while she poured it, but still, she owned some, and that seemed to mean something to her brother. He was right, and I didn't know as much about her as I'd thought.

Then he raised his head. It was the wrong kind of sadness. It was as if she had died long ago, and still hadn't quite died until now. "I was mistaken," he said slowly. "I should not have come. Ah, blessed Mab, she *did* leave, and a curse on us that we hardly knew it!"

"I don't understand," I told him.

"No. This," he nodded at the bottle, "is an unintended message, and only I have the reading of it."

"Well, can you tell me what it is?"

He smiled, just barely. "She did not decant it."

I stared, and at last, in desperation, added, "Huh?"

"To use this from the bottle is—oh, our father would have raged to see it done so! It is against all custom, all— you may trust me, it is not thought of, and in my house, had the thought been made a deed, what would have come of it would make you think no storm terrible, no raised hand to be dreaded. But if anyone would scorn the custom, it would be she.

"That was ever her way. I was the elder; I would bid her show respect for her father and mother, for our line, for tradition. I bid her do as I did, for I showed respect always. But what I showed always was not. . . . She told me that I feared more than I honored. She never feared. Our father hated her skill at devising and constructing, and forbade her to use it. She would flout him, and he would play the tyrant, and she would defy him even to laughter." He dashed the tears away with one hand and lifted his chin. "I thought I would find that, in her heart, her home and mine had been ever the same. I thought, when she left, that she had left only him, and not the land, not the past, not—" He brought himself up short. "But if that was so, you see, she would have decanted the liquor."

He set it back in the cupboard, like someone setting a memory away.

For a moment, we stayed like that, hanging between old beliefs and new ones. I said, "The funeral's tomorrow. Would you like to come?"

His brows drew together. Then his face cleared and became almost serene. "Yes, that would please me, if it can be done."

We finished the contents of the teapot, and eventually switched to beer. There wasn't any trouble finding something to talk about: we talked about her. He told me about her as a child, about the tree fort that she'd designed and bullied her brother and his friends into assembling, with an elevator made of a wooden platform, a rope, and two pulleys, complete with a friction brake which, he assured me, laughing, worked most of the time. She'd gotten hold of some eyeglass lenses from out in the World and tried to build a telescope.

Children and even much older kids brought her broken things to fix, and she'd do it in secret, in trade for whatever bits of mechanical or electrical things they could find for her. The electrical things were almost impossible to get, but they were her favorites. One night, when the whole house was asleep, she'd crept to her brother's room and woken him, and insisted he come to hers. Then she made him climb into the wardrobe with her, to show him what she'd hidden there in the dark: an electric clock working off an improvised battery, its lighted face glowing greenish-silver like the moon behind a cloud, its second hand making its steady way around the dial, its motor running with a faint, buzzing whisper.

She'd been clever as an adolescent, too, he told me, as well as wild and lonely. There were fewer stories that he could tell me from that time, though; an adolescent lives in a larger part of the world than a child, and the prohibitions that keep elves from talking freely about the land they come from applied more often. But from what he said, added to what Tick-Tick herself had let fall now and then, I thought her reasons for running away hadn't been very different from mine.

In turn, I told him about her adventures in Bordertown, trying to give him some of the aspects of his sister that he'd missed out on. Sometimes he shook his head; sometimes he frowned; but more often he smiled, and I wished, for his sake and hers, that he'd set family tradition aside and shown up on the doorstep a year earlier.

"I did not—stand by her," Vissa said once, when it was very late and the beer was getting low. "I might have defended her against my father's anger, against the little cruelties of others. If I had, perhaps . . ."

I could fill in the end of the sentence as well as he could. Even though one of the endings was, ". . . she would be alive now," I couldn't wish him a different past. If it had been different, she might not have been herself, Tick-Tick, and I might never have known her. But I reached out my hand and laid it lightly over his, and said one of those inadequate things about it being all right.

He turned his palm up and clasped my fingers, hard. "No, it is not. But it is done, and now we must seek our happiness in what we have made, and set aside these phantom joys."

Back in the World, I had never really sat *shivah,* when for seven days after the funeral the family gathers to remember and talk about the dead. By the time I was old enough to pay attention, my branch of the family was estranged from the rest, and that we didn't participate had less to do with lack of respect for the dead than lack of willingness to speak to the living. But Vissa and I remembered Tick-Tick to each other until the sky began to pale, and I understood the custom at last.


I'm sure there are funeral traditions in the Elflands, and heaven knows, there are thousands in the World. But the Borderlands haven't been around long enough for what could be called traditions. Weddings, funerals, births, namings, whatever: either you bring old practices with you and use those, or you take a handful of what you remember, another of what you've heard of, a dash of invention, stir until blended, and call it custom. When this works, it does so because the participants come prepared to take their part in an act of creation.

Tick-Tick's funeral was one of the second sort. There was some of the Elflands in it, and some American plains nomad, some ancient Roman, some traditional Japanese—the sort of result you'd expect from putting the ceremony in the charge of two people who ran a bookstore. It was held in a meadow on the southern edge of the city, under a bright blue cloudless sky and the occasional outraged diving attacks of red-winged blackbirds, like little fighter planes. A space had been cleared away in the middle for the scaffold. Its uprights were sections of young pine trunks, the scaly bark intact; the bier they supported was made of laced pine boughs. There were dried herbs and fragrant plants heaped on it, sage, artemisia, sweet woodruff, rosemary; and on that mattress lay the body, cocooned in scarlet silk and strewn with yellow summer flowers. The fire was laid and ready to light under the scaffold: apple wood, cherry, rowan, and oak. A lot of the people who came wore white, though not by any apparent prearrangement.

No, not everyone in town showed up. Not even all the people who had known Tick-Tick showed up; some of those were down with the virus, others were afraid of catching it and were staying home, and a few, I was afraid, had died as she had. But the staff of the Hard Luck had closed the place and come, as had Mingus from Taco Hell. Most of the people who worked at Snappin' Wizard's and Magic Freddy's had come, as had Sunny, and Wolfboy and Sparks, of course, Ms. Wu, Milo Chevrolet, Yoshi, Camphire, Weegee, Kathy Hong and Cascade from Chrystoble Street copshop, Dancer and Val from Danceland, a contingent of the all-elven Bloods, at least as many members of the all-human Pack (after all, you couldn't afford much anti-elf prejudice if you wanted to get your motorcycle repaired by the best mechanic in town), a lot of the Horn Dance folks, and a whole great crowd of people whose faces I did and did not recognize, whose names I did and didn't remember, to whom she had meant something. You don't take a head count at a funeral. Let it suffice to say that there were a lot of people there.

Some of them had brought offerings, of objects they'd made, poems they'd written, things they'd grown, or food or drink or perfume or incense. A band, composed of a fiddle player, a drummer, a guitarist, and a woman with Uilleann pipes, played while the offerings were left, on the bier or beside it, as the givers saw fit.

A few people brought things to read aloud. The last was Sparks, who raised her unassuming little voice with surprising strength to recite one of Shakespeare's sonnets, in an artless, easy way that made my throat ache.

> Thy gift, thy tables, are within my brain
> Full charactered with lasting memory,
> Which shall above that idle rank remain
> Beyond all date, even to eternity;
> Or, at the least, so long as brain and heart
> Have faculty by nature to subsist,
> Till each to rased oblivion yield his part
> Of thee, thy record never can be missed.
> That poor retention could not so much hold,
> Nor need I tallies thy dear love to score.
> Therefore to give them from me was I bold,
> To trust those tables that receive thee more.
>   To keep an adjunct to remember thee
>   Were to import forgetfulness in me.

Silence fell, just for a moment. Then a sweet voice, Camphire's, began a song in the language of the Elflands, and one by one the people there who knew it joined in. I've never been good at translating words of songs on the fly, but the tune was beautiful, and not at all sad.

Vissa had been beside me the whole time. I'd wondered what he was making of the business, whether he thought it was appropriate, or shocking, or tasteful, or gauche. I didn't worry about it, but I did wonder. But when Camphire began her song he moved suddenly at the edge of my vision, and I heard him draw an unsteady breath. Halfway into the second verse he added his voice to the rest, and it trembled with tears. Eventually the fiddle player caught it up, and the guitarist. Wolfboy beckoned me up to the scaffold, lit the torch, and handed it to me. For just a moment I thought about the symbolism of it; then I turned back to Vissa and held out the torch. He accepted it. Still crying, still singing, he sent his sister's spirit forth.

Other people would stay to make sure the pyre burned down safely; that wasn't my job. Sunny started to give me a brisk handshake when she left, but it transformed itself halfway through into a fierce hug, and she walked away quickly across the grass. I sent Vissa back across the Border with assurances that he would be welcome in Bordertown whenever he liked. I didn't think he'd avail himself of the opportunity, but that was up to him. Eventually I went home, not to Tick-Tick's apartment (it wasn't hers anymore; I would have to get used to that) but to mine (my old one; I had two now, and I would have to decide between them soon). I had an hour to kill before dinner.

On the one hand, nothing had changed. Over there on the other, everything had.

I could go back to the World. There wasn't a very good reason to, but I could. I could probably even face my mother and father, now that I knew who and what I was, and didn't have to believe in what *they* thought I was. I could survive out there now. But what could I do? What did I have to give back, that the World would accept?

If I stayed, it would be like having lost the use of one eye, at least for a while. And it would hurt. At least, in the World, there were no reminders of Tick-Tick. That was as much a disadvantage as a recommendation, though.

I could become a cop. Could I go to Sunny and say, "Dinner in six weeks aside, would you teach me the trade?" Or maybe I only wanted to ask her to make me part of something. I had been part of something, before the other part died. I would hate being a cop, but at least I would share it with someone, and that person would appreciate what I was and what I could do.

I wanted to *do* something, to renounce or embrace something, to make a sacrifice, to make a gesture. It was a dangerous moment. Heaven knows what I might have done if there hadn't been a knock at the door.

I opened it to a halfie boy with light blue hair and mismatched eyes. I remembered him, a little, from the funeral, and from months before in the street in front of Tick-Tick's, with a bicycle.

"Sorry to bother you," he blurted out, "today, you know. I mean—" He gave up and changed direction. "My little sister's missing," he said in a rush. "My stupid wiener brother was supposed to look after her, but he went out back to roll dice with his friends and Lumi wandered off. I'm scared—"

I stopped him with one finger, held up. He looked at me past it the way I used to see people look at Tick-Tick when they'd described the sound the engine made before it died. Maybe they'd always looked at me that way, the people who'd asked me to find something. A little awe, a little doubt, and a whole lot of hope.

"We have to find her in half an hour," I told him, checking my pocket for my keys. "I have a date with some hard-boiled eggs."

He looked baffled; then he realized that I'd said I'd do it.

"Thataway," I announced, and led the way.

# ABOUT THE AUTHOR

## OUR STORY SO FAR

Emma Bull (P. J. F.) was born in 1954 in Torrance, California. Many other significant events occurred worldwide in the same year, but she can never remember any of them when she sits down to write an About the Author. She first visited the Twin Cities in 1976. When, bleary-eyed in the very small hours of the morning, she looked out the window of the car she was riding in and saw the large green sign announcing that the Cretin Avenue exit was a mile away, she knew she'd found a home.

She likes road trips ("Look! It's Carhenge!"), coffee, didgeridoos, fabric stores, the Aubrey-Maturin books by Patrick O'Brian, the films of John Woo, her husband Will Shetterly, and her idiot cats Chaos and Brain Damage. She doesn't like liver, heights, waiting in line, or any sentence in which "impact" is used as a verb.

The soundtrack for this book includes, but is not limited to, most of Richard Thompson's work with special emphasis on *Rumor and Sigh*; *Homeward Way* by Bards of a Feather; *No Regrets* by Danny Carnahan and Robin Petrie; *Orb* by Boiled in Lead; and *El Rayo X* by David Lindley. All wholesome ingredients guaranteed to build strong inner ear bones. By now the author is probably listening to the new Flash Girls tape/CD release, *The Return of Pansy Smith and Violet Jones*. This is narcissistic, since the author is half of the band. If you would like information on the Flash Girls (or Cats Laughing, which the author is one-fifth of) and their recordings, please send a self-addressed stamped envelope to SteelDragon Press, Box 7253, Minneapolis, MN 55407.